HUMANITY

Also by AG Claymore:

Humanity Ascendant

Human

Humans

Humanity

Ragnarok

Rebels and Patriots

Rebels and Patriots

Beyond the Rim

The Gray matter

The Black Ships

The Black Ships

The Dark Defiance

The Orphan Alliance

Counterweight

Asymmetry

Firebringer

Terra Cryptica

Prometheus Bound

Humanity

Published by A.G. Claymore
Edited by B.H. MacFadyen
Copyright 2020 A.G. Claymore

ISBN: 9798728560685

Get Free e-Novellas

free **stories**

When you sign up for my new-release mail list!

Foothold

Standing Judgement
ComiCon, San Diego

"And next up, we have Gleb from the... planet of Kish?" The announcer chuckled. "Way to stay in character, bro!"

Aberdeen gave him a shove. "Get up there!"

He moved to the edge of the stage as the announcer resumed.

"Gleb is wearing an EVA combat suit made from... self-replicating nanites..."

The buzz in the crowd changed slightly and a few laughs rang out. Gleb frowned. He'd already figured out that this was just a costume contest. He was going along with it for now so he'd be better able to integrate himself with Aberdeen and her friends.

He was reasonably certain, if this was the Irth of the old stories, that he'd found the world that Scylla had been created for. He needed time to find out why the Chironans were bringing Humans here.

To sort this out, he needed time and he needed help. That was why he'd agreed to this farcical contest, though he couldn't see what was so funny about nanites.

"So," the announcer drawled, "either his daddy's some ultra-rich tech-oligarch or he just doesn't want to give away his secrets. You

1

guys be the judge. From here…" He turned to watch as Gleb walked onto the stage behind him. "I'm guessing a combo of worbla, EVA foam and fabrics. Gotta say folks – from this close, the detail is incredible!"

Gleb heard a smattering of polite applause as he moved to the middle of the stage. He'd watched them put up an image on a large screen behind him for the other contestants but he hadn't given it much thought until now.

He accessed his heads-up-display. The crowd let out a collective sigh of appreciation as the data panels projected in front of his face. He picked a record from the battle he'd just escaped and told his CPU to hammer it into a format the convention's projector could use.

Using something these Humans called Bluetooth, sensor data captured by the Stilletto flashed up on the screen behind him.

He'd been able to push the fight out of his mind in the strangeness of his new surroundings. His mind was programmed to be borderline sociopathic but even *he* couldn't ignore the facts.

Someone had figured out how to target the Human ships. He'd seen a lot of good people die before he left. Gleb had no idea whether any of his friends still lived. His fists clenched in anger.

His suit, sensing his agitation, triggered a close-up command.

The nanites flew into place with brutal speed, blocking out the HUD from external view. One moment his face was visible and the next, an armored shield had replaced it. Some of the nanites arranged to give the impression of a painted white skull and his sensors lit up with an angry, orange glow.

The crowd went wild.

The shout brought him back to the present. He opened his helmet again and waved to the crowd, steadfastly determined not to resort to the standard 'hero' poses of earlier competitors. He shut down his HUD and left the stage, sending a kill command for the replay on the room's large screen.

"All right, folks," the announcer shouted. "Give it up for Gleb and his nanites!"

Gleb walked over to Aberdeen and her two friends. "How was that?"

Kace grinned at him. "Dude you totally killed it!"

Killed it? Gleb turned in alarm, looking for whatever he'd killed. *Slang? Gods, I hope it was...*

"OK, folks, let's hear it for Aberdeen, Kace, and Dexter; the Three Amigos!"

Aberdeen started to put her helmet on but stopped, leaving it perched on top of her head. "Gleb... You gotta come back out with us! You can be a rebel or something. We'll surround you and try to shoot you but end up hitting each other!"

"I don't doubt it," Gleb told her. "Surrounding me would be a tactical error..."

"No, dumbass," Kace cut in. "The joke is we're Stormtroopers..."

"So we can't aim for shit," Aberdeen finished.

"This is known," Dexter intoned solemnly.

"Stick to the franchise," Aberdeen scolded. She grabbed Gleb by the shoulder and aimed him toward the stage.

The polite smattering of applause grew when he stepped back into the spotlight behind Dexter and Kace but it doubled when Aberdeen appeared.

"All made from vacu-formed plastic," the announcer said. "Entirely scratch built by the Amigos. And it looks like they've cornered a victim! Watch out, Gleb of... Kiss? I dunno, I don't have my notes. Maybe he's in a scifi tribute band or something..."

"Hands up, rebel scum," Aberdeen shouted.

Gleb complied but then remembered they were supposed to be shooting at him so he lowered his hands and advanced on her menacingly.

The three 'stormtroopers' jerked their weapons as though they had some kind of recoil, which seemed odd if they relied on directed energy. All three then dropped to the stage as though shot.

The crowd loved it. The three Irthlings got up and bowed.

"Give it up for the Three Amigos and their rebel scum!" the announcer boomed.

They left the stage, pleased with the response from the crowd. As they walked off, Gleb noticed a woman waiting for her turn, wearing what looked like a collection of vines – very skimpy vines.

"Let's hear it for Ivy!" the announcer shouted.

Ivy must have been known to many in the crowd. The cheering was deafening, so loud that Gleb couldn't even hear what the costume was made of. He shrugged and looked back to Aberdeen who was rolling her eyes at her two friends.

Their eyes were glued to Ivy's backside as she sashayed onto the stage. They watched, spellbound, as she aimed a beckoning gesture toward random locations in the crowd.

Aberdeen realized Gleb was looking at her and she gave a small twitch of surprise. "Tired of looking at Ivy?" she asked him, raising an eyebrow.

He shrugged. Nudity was no big deal for him, after all. "Not much of a costume," he replied, his HUD bringing up an image of the character she was probably trying to emulate. "I'd say she started out with an idea but only made the absolute minimum. Lazy, if you ask me."

"Riiight…" Aberdeen nodded sarcastically at him. "She was so lazy that she didn't bother to cover anything more than her nipples and a couple square-centimeters of her crotch."

She shook her head. "Just lazy. Sounds legit."

"Sounds like we have a winner!" the announcer shouted into his microphone. "'Cause I think we'd get torn limb from limb if we decided otherwise!"

"There you go," Aberdeen said in resignation. "We designed and built our own vacuum forming table but she wins with a couple ounces of molded latex and some spirit-gum. Skin wins."

"Apparently," Gleb agreed. "'Cause I'm wearing, in relative terms, a marvel of advanced technology…" He gestured to his suit. "… I mean, hello, functioning EVA suit here, and I only come in third."

"You came third?"

"Yeah. Kind of hard to hear over the crowd, but I came third because skin wins." He pointed to her belly button. "Your skin seems to have won you second place."

He could feel the conflicting emotions from her. There was a tinge of guilt for employing the same sexual strategy that Ivy was using, even if it was less extreme. That feeling was balanced by the pleasure at being able to help someone… Kace?

"You guys came here for more than just bragging rights, didn't you?" he asked.

She squinted at him in surprise. "Yeah. The cash prize will help Kace pay for his mom's surgery." She shook her head. "Hell… if I'd known how effective a little skin was, I'd have skipped the armor and just showed up in a bit of body paint. A little humiliation is a small price if it helps save Mary."

She walked on the stage with Kace and Dexter, leaving Gleb in a state of shock. His suit had provided the context of the word 'mom' for him.

These Humans were naturally born…

Loose Ends

Jay's old apartment, Kurnugia

"Open it!" Eth pressed his pistol against the landlord's neck.

The landlord was nervous. Who wouldn't be nervous with a pistol ready to blow a hole in his neck? But he remained resolute. Sure, his life was in danger but this was Kurnugia. Danger was a part of the scenery and there was an angle for profit here.

"The Alcmeonid has a reputation for discretion, my good sir!" he said calmly. "I can hardly start betraying the trust of my clients every time a gun is aimed at my person. There are standards to be maintained."

"Ah!" Eth exclaimed in mock surprise, knowing a bribe was being asked for. "Integrity! You see it so seldom in these troubled times. It's a thing of beauty, don't you think, Eve?"

"Oh, it's beautiful alright," she crooned in a tone that made the landlord shiver. "His integrity would look even nicer splattered all over that wall…"

Eth pushed that image into the landlord's mind, made it clear how much he 'wanted' to pull the trigger.

"Alright!" the fellow squeaked. "I'll open it!"

His eye twitched a couple of times and the door slid open.

Eth shoved him over to Eve, not needing to tell her to hang onto him. The landlord would seize any opportunity to turn a profit out of this. If he couldn't make a few credits from the contents of Jay's apartment, he still knew there would be someone interested in the fact that two Humans were searching the place.

Eth stepped to the door and looked in from an angle, trying to see any booby traps that may have been placed to kill intruders. Then he chuckled, shaking his head at his own stupidity. He moved back to look straight into the small room and then simply removed himself from the hall and placed himself in the middle of Jay's living/sleeping room.

The landlord gasped. "Gods! It's true! You guys are *maegi*!"

Eth ignored him. He looked around the room. *Where would Jay have hidden anything?* He thought. When they'd caught him stealing equipment in the fleet, he'd been using a ventilation outlet to hide his extra credit chips.

Eth had sent him to Kurnugia so he could actually *be* a criminal, fit in with the locals. He'd managed to become a good source of intel for his fellow Humans.

Unfortunately, he'd become a source for others as well…

Eth looked around the room. The fresh air vent was on the wall above the entry door. He shook his head. The fresh air vent was a hand's breadth away from the exhaust vent which was probably why this room stank so much.

It was unlikely that Jay would have used the return vent as a hiding place. On the off-chance that it actually worked, there'd be the risk of items being blown out of reach. The circular vent-grilles simply sat in rounded channels without fasteners.

Eth focused, pulling heat from the carboncrete walls, and he waved a hand for dramatic effect. The fresh air grille rolled out of its channel and dropped to the floor.

I'm getting good at this, Eth thought, reveling in the landlord's wordless grunt of fear.

There was a corner of something visible inside the vent, a data-chip from the look of it. He pulled more heat from the surrounding wall, vapor condensing into frost on the surface. He converted it into a small nudge of kinetic energy and the chip flew out of the opening.

He caught it, managing to make it look natural, though he was probably more surprised at that than the landlord. *Doubt there's anything of use on this.*

He looked around the room but it was a perfunctory search. Their main reason for coming here was to remove any trace that connected to them. Jay had been executed. Death by small furry creature… He wasn't really expecting to find anything of value in Jay's lodgings.

Best to just burn it down.

Then he noticed the button wired to the wall on the left side of the door. From it, wires led off in several directions and each seemed to terminate at a small container mounted just above a power converter. Clearly, Jay wanted to make sure nobody would be able to use the contents of this room to trace him.

At least the traitorous little hump got something right, Eth thought. He walked to the door and slapped his palm on the button. At least eight small fires started as he stepped back out into the hall and closed the door.

The building was built to code, mostly, and there was more chance of Eth winning a beauty contest than there was of this fire spreading from Jay's place. "Time to go," he told Eve.

They released the landlord when they reached the lobby and he scurried off, most likely to place a few frantic calls.

Or maybe they weren't necessary…

A small group of thugs was waiting in the courtyard out front. Eth strolled out to stand in their midst. "Only seven guys?" he asked, looking over his shoulder at Eve. "Disappointing, don't you think?"

"Just give us whatever you found up there," one of the thugs said, "and maybe we'll let you go." His three eyes narrowed into an evil squint. "But her, we'll keep around…"

"Disappointing?" Eve snorted. "Seven low-level 'lifters' that can't put together a single sentence without their gonads taking over their brains? Downright insulting."

"I don't have all day!" the alien snarled.

"You don't realize how true that is," Eth agreed. He leaned in a little closer. "You should go," he told him quietly. "You've pissed her off. You should forget how tough you are and just run for all you're worth, maybe even squeal like a frightened child."

Eth wasn't bothering with the fear projection. That was partly why Three-Eye wasn't taking this seriously enough. After all they'd been through, Eth didn't feel particularly charitable toward the various assholes coming out of the woodwork, looking to take a piece out of his people.

Three-eye pulled a long knife from a sheath behind his back. "I'm done playing around!" he warned his would-be victims.

"Yeah," Eve said, suddenly behind him. "You are."

The other six assailants twitched, almost in unison, when they realized she'd shifted her position. All of them started reaching for their weapons out of pure reflex but they mostly stopped before completing the action.

Eth shifted behind the one who was still making an attempt to get his gun into action. He drew his knife and shoved it into the back of his opponent's skull, angling it to the side as he pulled it back out.

Eth's victim fell to the pavement at more-or-less the same time as Three-Eye. The remaining five stared in horrified fascination as Thee-Eye fell forward, Eve's blade sliding out from the base of his skull as he dropped.

The spell was broken when he hit the pavement. Two of the assailants made a move for Eve and one went after Eth. The other two, sensibly, took his earlier advice and ran for their lives.

Eth faced the rushing alien, knife at the ready, then he shifted himself to kneel behind his opponent. He slashed downward, just as the startled creature was starting to turn, and severed a tendon at the back of his ankle.

Eth came to his feet, giving the downed alien a kick to the back of his head to discourage further mischief. Eve had already dispatched one of her attackers and she simply spun to the left and hammered the heel of her right palm into the nostril on the left side of the last attacker's face.

He… it… whatever… sank to its knees, maddened by the sudden pain in its sinuses.

"Sometimes the old fashioned ways are a little more satisfying," she said. She stepped over to the sidewalk at the outer edge of the small courtyard. "No sign of his friends. I bet they…"

Eth twitched at the sudden flood of emotion from Eve. He stared at her in surprise as she turned back to face him, eyes wide in shock and fear.

She tried to reach up to her chest but her hand only made it halfway before she sank to her knees, a second shot just missing her head and burying itself in the corner of the apartment block.

Her confusion and fear were already fading into incoherence. For all the power their new abilities gave them, Humans were still as vulnerable as anyone to pure physical damage and she had taken a sniper round to the heart.

Eth stood there, his shock and sadness being shouldered aside by pure rage. He was in no mood to make rage play nice with his other feelings. He was playing favorites and he didn't care who knew.

Actually, he cared very *much* who knew.

"Fornicating bastard!" Lev's voice sounded shaky and it wasn't because of the speakers in Eth's suit collar. "Shooter on five. I swear I was just looking there…"

Lev had been left in an abandoned commercial unit just up the block as one of their lookouts. He'd been keeping an eye on five of the nine probable sniper nests in the area.

Should've had more lookouts, Eth thought in a fit of remorse before rage pushed its way back to the front. "Lev, keep eyes on. I'm going after him."

He took a deep breath and reached out for Lev's perceptions. He could see the balcony they'd designated as probable number five. The back of someone's head was just coming into view as the sniper stood.

Eth shifted into place on the balcony, shivering with the cold of his hasty, emotion-laced pursuit. The shooter was stepping through a door leading from the balcony to the living unit beyond and Eth reached out for his heat, pinching off his motor control for a brief moment as well.

The shooter went down in a sprawl, his pulse rifle tumbling out of his bag in three hastily disassembled parts. The electrical nodes were still arcing between the components.

Someone had warned this assassin to flee as quickly as possible after the deed was done.

"You should have just left the rifle and run," Eth snarled. He reached into the deepest part of the sniper's psyche, the maximum-security place where dark thoughts get shanked by the *really* dark ones.

He pulled up the most hideous possible torments, ones that Nergal, the lord of the underworld himself, might speak of in hushed whispers. He shuddered in a mix of anger, disgust and delicious vengeance and he shoved those thoughts into the mind of the sniper.

The half-frozen creature let out a strangled scream, throwing himself over onto his backside and trying to push himself away from Eth. He shook his head from side to side, not so much a gesture of negation but, rather, an involuntary and futile desire to avert his gaze from images that were projected directly into his mind.

Eth shivered violently, pulling heat from his victim, and tried something new.

Most sentient species in the Holy Quailu Empire could process information faster than the biology of their senses could collect it. This sniper was a Seleucid. His people had minds that operated at speeds that were orders of magnitude higher than the speed of their sensory input.

Seleucids had created half the technical advancements in the HQE over the millennia and most had come from dreams. Freed from the constraints of optic nerves and inner ear structures, their minds could come up with incredible leaps of discovery.

Humans were no slouches either and Eth had been designed for a command role. His mind was a match for the Seleucid in terms of speed and he was the one setting the pace. In what would have looked like mere moments to an outside observer, he put the sniper through a subjective eternity of hideous torment.

The Seleucid lost his sanity in a matter of heartbeats. He'd seen creatures of indescribable, indefinable horror. He'd watched as they defiled everything he held dear, time after time, and he tried to claw his own eyes out.

The assassin had made the attempt in his own mind and Eth had allowed that to translate to the physical realm. Because the two efforts were linked, the Seleucid's fast mind was forced to tear his inner eyes out at the glacial pace of his outer, physical body.

He screamed, a raw animal noise translated from his pain and terror. It was utterly bereft of any sentient filtering. There was nothing left of the person who'd pulled the trigger.

"Boss?" Lev's voice pulled Eth out of the wasteland that had been an assassin.

He stood there for a moment, confused and angry. After all the time he'd spent in the accelerated time-scape of the Seleucid's mind, he'd forgotten where he was.

It came back to him like a distant memory.

"Meet me at the shuttle," he ordered his spotter. He looked down at the moaning thing on the ground. "We're done here."

Counterscam

Hold Your Ground Coffee, San Diego

"Here's to new friends, moderate winnings and free coffee!" Aberdeen held up her mug. "Thanks for the joe, Gleb!"

Gleb returned the gesture, raising his mug before taking a drink. *What's the deal with this planet?* He set the mug down on the table, glancing at his three new friends. *The Chironans had Humans at Kwharaz Station. They were for 'Project Irth'. Did they set this place up? Stock it with apparently wild Humans?*

A warbling tone cut into his thoughts.

Aberdeen's right eye took on a slight sparkle and she sighed. "Another scam call," she groused. She blinked twice. "Hello."

She tilted her head, a grin spreading across her features. "Very well. Please hold for Aberdeen…" She blinked again.

"Let me guess," Dexter said, his mug halfway to his mouth. "The IRS wants you to send them some gift-card codes?"

"Yeah, 'cause apparently I'm a complete moron," she confirmed. "And for your information, Mr. Skeptic, it's not just the IRS. It's the 'Department of the Enforcement' of the IRS." She chuckled.

"Why keep him on hold?" Kace growled. "I'd just curse him out and hang up."

"Where's your sense of civic duty?" she shot back. "The longer you keep them on the line, the less time they can spend calling someone like your uncle Barry."

"Yeah, well, he's not about to fall for that a second time…"

"Everybody's got an Uncle Barry," she reasoned, holding up a palm. "Yes, hello. Is this Aberdeen? No? Well, when do you expect her back?" Her eyebrows furrowed.

"Don't you play games with *me*! There's no Aberdeen here. *I'm* calling *you* from the IRS Department of the Enforcement Internal

Affairs and Occasional Indiscretions Division and I demand to speak with Aberdeen immediately!"

She slammed a fist down on the table, startling a customer at the order counter. "Sir... Sir! I will not be put off by your shenanigans! I have been assigned this file by the highest authority. I will find out who's been taking the director's hummus from the breakroom refrigerator. Believe me, heads will roll..."

She tapped her right ear. "Hello?" She shrugged and reached for her mug. "I guess he changed his mind about the gift cards."

The CPU in Gleb's suit was feeding him a flood of context. The IRS was the tax organ of the local political entity. His eyebrows tried to climb off the top of his head. There were currently close to two hundred sovereign governments on this medium-sized rock.

The call had originated from a... country... on the other side of the world, making it unlikely that law enforcement would ever involve themselves. This was a common trick on Irth, using a scatter-shot approach. A high enough volume of calls guaranteed a steady flow of cash.

The rest of the context, however, had no need of his suit's CPU. Dexter was trying to hide it but he couldn't stop Gleb from seeing into their minds.

He had strong feelings for her that he pretty much assumed to be hopeless.

He frowned. *What the hells is his problem?* he wondered. *Is this just normal for people who were naturally born?* He shook his head slightly. *This planet would run out of people pretty quickly if that were the case...*

He took a drink and thought it over. An entire planet with free Humans on it. There had to be a wide range of possibilities, of which this was just one. *There must also be people here who take a more direct approach – not quite as direct as I'm accustomed to...*

15

He glanced at Aberdeen who was laughing at the look on Dexter's face. Gleb might not understand the hopelessness of his infatuation but he had to admit, he had good taste.

Thieves – his mind returned to her call. He used his suit to interrogate the local signals. Aberdeen's communications link seemed localised near her left ear. *Some kind of low-tech implant.*

By the standards he was used to, her communicator was rudimentary. It handled basic signals, feeding aural input to her left ear as well as text and imagery to a flexible lens on one of her eyes. Getting into the records was simple enough.

There were a lot of text-only messages and Dexter seemed to send a large proportion of them. Gleb smiled slightly. A lot of them were offers to get her a coffee while he was apparently standing in the line at some shop. *Their workplaces must be close.*

He found her call record and pulled the latest incoming record. Tracing it back through the local communications network was slightly frustrating. *Shouldn't be surprised,* he thought. *With so many political entities, I shouldn't really expect there to be a single network in play.*

He ended up having to work his way through four separate corporate systems before finding the origin on the other side of the planet. There were more than twenty nodes connected from that address. He assumed they were some kind of workstations.

One node was reaching out to banking institutions. He shook his head in amusement. These Humans actually left their funds in the hands of banks.

The suit's computer, always looking out for him, projected a graph of how quickly the bank's fee schedule would deplete a moderately sized account. The interest offered was nowhere close to offsetting the fees.

He closed out the warning. One access window had been open for hours. He could see it was set up with the same address that the

16

calls were originating from. He chuckled, then realized his new friends were watching him.

"What are you up to?" Kace leaned in, squinting at the HUD projection. It would be backwards from his perspective.

Gleb didn't know what his options were yet but he knew he'd need allies. If he had any chance of getting back to his own people – if they were even still alive – he'd have a better chance if he wasn't on his own.

These three were a start. "Aberdeen, you want to talk to your pals from the IRS again? I'm about to crash their systems but I could get them to call you first. You can mess with them for a bit…"

"Dude!" Dexter sighed. "You really expect us to believe you're able to track those guys down while sitting there…" He shrugged at Gleb's raised hand.

Aberdeen's phone rang. She glanced sidelong at Gleb, an eyebrow raised. "Hello?"

Gleb routed the audio through his suit's sound system. "If you don't mind my taking the liberty…" he said as the caller began his script.

"Hello, Miss, this is Agent Steve from the Internal Revenue Services Department of the Justice. I am calling you about an issue with your taxes. You owe us two thousand eCoin in arrears and an arrest warrant has been produced from your local courthouse!"

She smiled but the expression didn't convey anything pleasant. "Agent, are you attempting to warn me that you're under some kind of duress? If so, repeat your name again."

'Miss, this is no joke! We here at the IRS take tax delinquency very seriously! We will only give you one chance to…"

"Confirming agent not under immediate duress," Aberdeen cut him off. "Agent, code in."

'Miss, I… what?'

17

"Code in."

"I don't think you're taking this seriously, Miss. Now, I've tried to help you but..."

"Code failed," she said. "Initiating burn-down protocol. A kill team has been dispatched. Agent, you have three minutes to evacuate the area."

"That sounds like my cue," Gleb whispered. "I'll put up a message on their screens telling them all to remain in place and wait for law enforcement."

Dexter was just taking a drink when Gleb said this and he snorted some of it into his sinuses. He was groaning and laughing at the same time.

"Oh what the hell!" There was the sound of frantic clicking. *"What are you doing, you stupid bitch!"*

"Now let's cut the power," Gleb said quietly, taking care to empty the thieves' bank account first.

"Kill team ETA is two minutes," Aberdeen advised the scammer.

They could hear a rustling sound and a loud thump as the scammer tore off his headset. There was shouting and then the clear sounds of panic as a couple dozen terrified people suddenly started trying to flee from the fictional kill-team.

Gleb was laughing so hard at this point that tears were running down his face and he wasn't alone.

"I can't take it!" Aberdeen was holding her belly with her arms. "I had to pee before this damned call started and now I can barely hold it in!" She killed the call and got up.

Dexter was quick on the draw. He grabbed her mug and looked inside to confirm it was empty. "Another latte?" he asked her eagerly.

"Not right now, thanks." She made her way to the washrooms as Dexter turned to point at Gleb.

"You'll have another?" he asked, slightly less eager, but clearly sincere.

Gleb saw the opportunity immediately. He knew what he was about to do was pushing things but he might pull it off if he kept it between himself and Kace. "Sure, thanks, Dexter."

"Just Dex," the man smiled. He looked at Kace who shook his head, holding up a half full mug.

As Dex walked away Gleb leaned toward Kace. "Can you keep something quiet, just between us?"

Kace was still chuckling. "Probably, depends on what it is."

"Alright, look," Gleb leaned in a bit further. "When I crashed those thieves, I cleaned out their bank account first."

"What? How the hell did you do that? How did you even find them in the first place?"

Gleb chopped his hand to the side in an impatient gesture. "My suit has a pretty decent computer. Don't worry about that. How much do you need for your mom?"

"My mom?"

"Yeah. Aberdeen said you guys were in that contest to win money for her operation." He waved at the white armor Kace was still wearing. "I just took money from thieves. It was easy. Now that I know what to look for, I can practically buy a small country. All I need to do is rob enough of them."

He glanced over to the counter where Dexter was waiting for his order. "Just tell me. What will it cost?"

Dexter shook his head reluctantly. "No, man. I appreciate it but, best case scenario, we're looking at twenty thousand coin at least."

Gleb had just stolen seventy-five thousand eCoin. It was sitting on his wrist implant. "So worst case would be closer to forty?"

"Well, I don't think it would run that high," Kace demurred, "but, even if…" His hand strayed toward his left ear and then he focused on the notification from his data-lens. "Holy shit!" He glanced around nervously, then leaned in toward Gleb. "Dude!" he whispered. "This is nuts! I can't take this!"

Gleb could feel his clear desire to take it. He could feel the hope. His refusal at this point seemed more an ingrained reflex based on politeness. "You just did. It means *nothing* to me. I didn't even have it ten minutes ago, so I can't miss it. Just take it. Help your mom."

The wave of emotion was stronger than anything he'd ever felt before. Kace's reaction was flowing through Gleb's mind, causing his chest to feel constricted, his breath to catch in his throat.

It felt better than killing any Quailu ever had.

"I really don't know what to say!"

"Well then, that's perfect," Gleb said. "Don't say a thing, especially not to the others." He glanced over to where Dex was being handed two drinks.

He looked back to see Kace was slightly confused by this. "This is a little strange, right? I mean, we just met a few hours ago and here I am handing you a pile of credits. I'm serious about the money not meaning anything to me but let's not turn this into a big splashy thing in front of everyone. It would get even weirder."

Aberdeen emerged from the washroom.

"Yeah," Kace nodded as Dex handed Gleb a new mug. "I get that."

"Get what?" Dex asked, sitting.

"Ah, he's just uh…" Gleb gestured toward Kace. "…telling me about his mom."

"Oh, your mom!" Aberdeen sat. "I'm sorry! I totally forgot they put the winnings in my account. They only pay out to the person who signed the entry form. Hang on…" She looked down at the table, concentrating on her lens.

"No, you actually don't have to…"

Gods! He's about to blurt it out already! "Oh yeah," Gleb cut him off. "I won third place but I wouldn't have even entered if not for you three. I'll transfer my prize money as well." He held up a hand to forestall his protest.

"It's only money, Kace. Your mom needs this, *right*?" Gleb said earnestly.

Kace sighed. He sat back in his chair. "You guys are awesome, you know that, right?" He held up his mug.

"To good friends."

Gleb saw Dex raise his mug, so he did the same and took a drink with the other two. He was setting it down when Aberdeen grabbed it and took a drink.

She gave him an apologetic shrug as she handed it back. "Sorry, I didn't have any left in mine." She added in an infectious smile. "Can't let a good toast like that go to waste."

Gleb smiled back to show he didn't mind. He had a sneaking suspicion that she'd just demonstrated a measure of acceptance by stealing his drink.

It was confirmed when he realized Dex was feeling a little jealous. *Might be a workable angle there.* He'd already found a way to get Kace on side; now he could see where Dex needed help.

Aberdeen was at ease with Gleb but he knew she saw him as harmless for some reason. He'd first felt it when she caught him not staring at Ivy.

She wasn't romantically interested. She just felt comfortable around him. Dexter, however, seemed certain that she was falling for Gleb. He also seemed to think it was a bit unfair that some newcomer was suddenly making headway where he'd so consistently failed.

I'd better try to help him out anyway, Gleb thought. *He's not far from turning hostile over this. I'm going to need some allies here. The last thing I need is him resenting me.*

"You gotta show us your workshop," Aberdeen said.

Gleb turned to her. *She's looking at me?* "My workshop?"

"Yeah. We want to see where that suit came from!"

Now he could feel Dexter growing even more morose. He'd put in a lot of work on their costumes. It was the opening Gleb needed. "Sure," he said, "but first, you gotta show me the vacuum forming setup. I remember you saying you built one to make your suits. I'd love to see how you did that."

He could feel an improvement from Dex. Gleb was starting to miss combat.

Things were a lot easier when all you had to do was kill folks.

"Dex set up a shop in the old garage behind his place," Kace explained. "Built the vacuum table from random stuff he bought at the hardware store. When I suggested entering the contest to win money for the medical bills, he cleared out a work-space and just built the damn thing overnight – like, literally overnight."

"Fifteen hours straight," Aberdeen added, reaching over to give Dex's shoulder an affectionate squeeze.

"Now that's a true friend!" Gleb nodded to Dex. "I'd love to get a look at that sometime." *And hopefully alone so we can figure out why you're playing such a weak hand with Aberdeen.* He thought there might be some potential locked away in the back of her mind.

Dex just needed to find it.

If Gleb could help things along, it should firm up his place in this small group.

Useful Idiot

Kitanga System

Shullat entered the great hall and made his usual cheever's-rush for the food. He knew the soft laughter might be aimed at him but he wasn't the only penniless emigre living at his cousin's capital and he'd gotten good at ignoring the currents of derision.

He'd lost Arbella to that old hag Bau, so he could hardly blame the local courtiers for having some fun at his expense. Sooner or later, someone would notice that those who laughed at him tended to die for reasons that had almost nothing to do with poison.

At least as far as anyone could prove…

He loaded up a platter and took it over to a mostly abandoned table. He tried to get the attention of a servitor who walked past with a large pitcher of ale but met with no success. He'd seen the creature look away when he'd waved. It knew Shullat wanted ale and had probably taken great pleasure in ignoring a Quailu lord.

Before he could start in on a suitable revenge fantasy, someone sat on the bench next to him. He looked over before he could stop himself and present the desired show of indifference.

His unexpected dinner partner was Quailu, of course, and he was dressed well but not flamboyantly. *Some prosperous member of the lower class*, he assumed, turning back to his own food.

"They're laughing at you," his neighbour commented casually.

Shullat bristled. *There just isn't enough poison on this cursed planet…*

The servitor came back their way with the ale and Shullat's new friend held out his empty flagon. The creature bobbled its head and stopped to fill his mug.

Shullat was pissed but not so distracted as to forget his own thirst. He reached for his mug and turned back in time to see the servitor's receding back.

He slammed the mug down on the table amid a gale of laughter that was almost certainly meant for him.

"Revenge can be sweet," the Quailu beside him said quietly, "but it's wasted here on Kitanga."

"And where should I seek it," he snarled, "if not here?"

"Do you think anyone would dare laugh at you while you take your revenge on your enemies at Arbella?"

Shullat shuddered despite the heat in the hall. He forced himself not to look; forced himself to toy with his food. "Who are you?" he whispered.

"Nobody," the Quailu answered calmly. "In fact, I'm not even here…"

Insult to Injury
Kurnugian orbit

"Lev," Eth said, looking over at him from the co-pilot seat of their shuttle, "why does it look like we're already docked?"

Their fast produce-freighter had a shuttle attached to the docking ring that they'd left only a few hours ago. Lev frowned. "That junk attached to the dorsal surface..."

And then it crystalized for Eth in a moment of horror. "That's part of a distortion drive," he whispered, though he couldn't say why he was suddenly so certain.

The cold prickling sensation at the back of his neck was telling him not to bother with proof. This was one of those moments when the deeper parts of the mind offered an analysis that the conscious mind couldn't explain in time, encumbered as it was with the need to use language.

"I see no active field," Lev said, looking at a telemetry screen.

"Something that small," Eth said quietly, "couldn't power a field for more than a few minutes. Long enough..."

Long enough to get aboard and kill the crew, trusting the distortion field to strip the Humans of their massive tactical advantage.

"We had four guys on that ship," Lev muttered. "Can't find any of them."

"I can feel two Hasharim, though." Eth took a deep breath and blew it out through his nose. "One of them is nearly dead but I can see the other's perspective, just barely."

Humans like Eth could, with the right training, feel their way back along the fourth dimension, interpreted by our biology as time. There was a connection between sentient beings at that level, kind of like the circles in flatland realizing they were just cross sections of a hand's fingers.

Finding aliens that way was a little harder. They were sentient, of course, but on another hand… or tentacle?

"Follow me in," Eth told Lev and Gard, the last two Humans he had with him at Kurnugia. "I'll try to hold my vision steady for you."

He closed his eyes and reached out, seeing the cockpit of the small freighter, shaded in the odd colors and shadows of alien eyes. The perspective seemed oddly foreshortened and he had to hope there was actually enough room between the Hasharim and the pilot's seat.

He opened them and breathed a sigh of relief that he hadn't become a part of the seat or of the blathering fool who now stood before him, still talking to the holo receiver.

"… so we claim the bounty on these Humans in the name of the… gods!" He leapt back in alarm when his brain finally got around to telling him about the Human.

"In the name of the gods, you say?" Eth tore into his enemy's mind, convincing him he was being eaten alive by the denizens of the underworld. "Nergal may take issue with that idea," he snarled.

Lev and Gard appeared behind him. They growled in anger when they saw the bodies tied up to the bulkhead at the back of the cockpit and Gard pulled an escape bar from its bracket between the corpses of the pilot and the engineer.

Gard had the kind of friendly face that made everyone want to like him but it concealed a dangerous temper and that temper was fully roused now. His features screamed a desire for revenge.

Eth was still inside the Hasharim's mind and he had no desire to linger, not if Gard was about to start using that wicked looking tool. It took very little time to find who this thug worked for and that he'd been transmitting to the entire planet in order to gain face for the Hargindi Syndicate.

He left his enemy in a holding pattern of whimpering terror and withdrew from his mind. The holo-cam was collecting a wide image –

the better to show off the Humans the Hasharim had killed and pinned to the bulkheads. It was also a better angle to show the dark stain spreading from his crotch.

If someone comes after you, crush them, he thought. *If they make it public, make them an example. Make it clear they met a bad end.* He stepped to the side so the cam had a clear view.

Gard hefted the escape tool, a heavy, bladed implement for hacking your way out through the hull. "Not the sharp edge," he told Gard. "Bash him in with the flat of the blade."

He didn't need to tell Gard twice. With a grunt, the big Human swung the axe-like implement and the flat side hit the Hasharim with a sickening, meaty, cracking sound.

Even though he was using the blunt side, he'd hit with enough force to crush the side of his enemy's head by half a hand's-breadth. The skin on the side of his head split open and blood spurted out over Gard's earnest features.

That one blow was enough. The alien fell, twitching on the deck. Nobody said anything about putting him out of his misery.

Eth looked up to the holo-cam. "The Hargindi Syndicate have involved themselves in matters beyond their understanding. They have a new enemy now. Any who deal with them or continue to honor existing bargains with them are also our enemy."

He cut the feed.

"Are we really going to war with a criminal syndicate?" Lev asked, sounding as if he was already certain Eth would say no. It would be a costly distraction for the small Human forces and it would leave them exposed.

It was less than wise to focus on one insignificant group and to do so publicly. Kurnugia would be closely watched by HQE agents as soon as they heard Eth's warning to the Hargindi and Eth knew that.

"No need," he said, sounding tired. "You don't need to kill a syndicate yourself, you just need to put their blood in the water. I've made them look foolish and I've threatened their allies. The delicate balance has been upset."

"Still…" Lev frowned. "… It's no guarantee."

"It's not," Eth agreed with a sigh, "but, for now, it has to be enough. Take the helm and get us out of here."

He wanted to kick something. He was designed to be a leader but he kept leading his people to their deaths.

He'd lost a large part of his forces when Rimush had turned Mishak's Quailu captains against the Humans. Now he'd lost most of the people he'd brought with him for the simple task of cleaning up any traces of Jay's activity on Kurnugia.

Jay was another betrayal he should have seen coming. He wished he'd just kicked Jay to death when he'd been caught selling their equipment. Instead he'd sent him out here as an intelligence gatherer.

He kicked at the alien on the floor. It made a poor substitute for Jay but it helped. He gave the corpse a few more kicks but he was coming up against sharply diminishing returns.

"Uh…" Lev waited until Eth turned to face him. "We have a destination, boss?" He was very obviously not looking down at the body that Eth had been kicking.

"Yeah." Eth took a moment to bring his breathing under control. His thoughts followed the process as well and he realized his self-blaming had been keeping him from seeing the obvious. There was a much more appropriate target for the blame here.

Lev frowned at Eth's sudden smile. "Should I try kicking the bastard? Seems to have done wonders for *you*."

"This bounty on Humans," Eth said, looking down at the body. "We need to put an end to it."

"Ah," Lev nodded wisely. "All this time I thought it was problematic for us, never knowing when someone might blow my head off, but I never came up with the idea of not having a bounty on our heads."

Sarcasm flowed so strongly from his mind that Eth could feel it without even trying.

"So," Lev went on, more serious this time, "I assume you've got a clever plan?"

"I do," Eth confirmed.

And he told him.

Hot Tub Comms Machine

The Odessa Terrace Apartments, San Diego

Gleb sat in a grubby lawn-chair. He stared at the gate separating the complex's courtyard from the street outside but he wasn't really seeing it.

The bubbling water and low voices coming from the hot tub to his right were also failing to register. He was reaching out, seeking familiar perspectives.

He could see countless views of Balboa Park, no more than a block from where his apartment building stood, but he was hoping to find something a little farther away. He closed his eyes and pushed out.

He could see what appeared to be a cramped space habitat, not much bigger than an escape pod. It had a more permanent feeling, though, because there were zero gravity sleeping cubicles in front of him.

He shivered.

This was taking too much out of him. He drew back in with his senses but reached out for a nearby source of heat. The low murmur to his right took on undertones of annoyance.

Don't reach out, he quoted Scylla ruefully. *That's the brute force way of doing it. You have to reach back. That's where we're all connected. It still takes energy, but far less than you need to reach out across the empty blackness.*

He channeled his thoughts along the dimension that biology interpreted as time. He smiled at the familiarity of it. He could sense the presence of old friends.

He'd expected to find Hela or Eth but this probably also had a lot to do with whether he was on the mind of his target, especially at this distance. If not 'on their mind' then, at the very least, somewhere at the back.

There were angry grumbles to his right as the hot tub emptied.

He felt a warmth, an all-over sense of wellness and he drifted toward it. He couldn't quite get there, though. Try as he might, he couldn't see what his target was seeing. He felt sensitized and delightfully filled.

Was it someone having dinner?

Frustrated, he abandoned the link. Shivering, he grabbed the extra hot latte he'd just purchased down the street. The barista had glared at him for such a neophyte request but then, the barista didn't have to deal with the heat loss of a long-range connection attempt.

The drink scalded his throat but it felt good in his stomach. The heat radiated out more effectively than the remote drain he'd set up with the hot tub.

Someone, at least, is still out there, he thought, *but who?*

Blocking

Babilim Station - Siri's Quarters

"What's wrong?" Mel had stopped moving. He looked up at Siri, concern on his face.

"You didn't feel that?" she asked him.

"Umm, I'm feeling a few things right now." He grinned in spite of his concern. "You'd need to be more specific…"

She dropped onto the bed next to him, disengaging. She ignored his sigh of resignation. "It felt as though someone was… trying to connect with me…"

"Are you sure that wasn't me?"

She rolled her eyes at him. "It felt… familiar but I don't know why."

She shook her head. "Probably just my imagination."

"Maybe someone was training with Scylla? Trying to see through your eyes, looking for a place to jump to…"

"Maybe." She sighed. "I don't think you feel it when they're just using your visual cortex, though. This was very vague, but I got a sense of loneliness…"

"That's probably coming from me." Mel chuckled. "Abandoned at a time of great need and vulnerability…" He winced at her playful jab to the ribcage.

She was quiet for a moment, one hand resting on his chest. "Hm… I suppose I could be convinced if you were… persuasive enough…"

Digging In

Balance of Power

Throneworld

Mishak stood at the edge of the balcony. The quarters assigned to the crown-couple were off the side of the throne room, roughly eight hundred meters above the savannah that formed the floor of the gigantic chamber.

He was very close to the edge.

His Varangian guards doubtless thought the same thing. Two of them stood close enough to grab him if he should lose his balance and topple over the edge. *Probably not my physical balance they're worried about,* he thought.

He'd been in a rage for most of the day. He'd seen the video from Kurnugia and that had been the first he'd known of this bounty. Though no direct mention of his name had been used, it had given the distinct impression that he was behind it.

"'Having power and using it are two distinctly different beasts," Marduk had often told him when he'd been fostered to the emperor. In exchange, a minor prince had been sent to Mishak's father so he could learn how to be a miserable bastard.

Mishak had always felt he'd gotten the best half of that deal.

'Those who use power rarely use their *own*,' Marduk had explained. "They find someone with so much power that they won't miss a little, here and there."

Mishak had asked him if that was why he served as the emperor's chief of staff and he'd earned a cuff on the side of the head for his insolence. It hadn't been the first time Marduk had taken a swipe at the young noble but it *was* the day he'd expanded on the scope of Mishak's education.

"Been *waiting* for you to show some sign of awareness," he'd said.

That awareness was making it entirely too obvious that his old mentor was still using the power of others and he wasn't just using the emperor's power. Marduk was almost certainly the one behind the bounty on Humans.

First, Mishak's fleet captain, Rimush, decided he knew better than his master and betrayed the Humans. He felt sure that the dangers represented by the Humans' emerging abilities represented too great a danger for Mishak.

Now the potential danger was a very real one and deservedly so. Through his failure to stop Rimush, Mishak was to blame for the betrayal of those who'd served him.

And now Marduk, no doubt sharing Rimush's concerns, was hounding the Humans in Mishak's name.

He turned from the steep drop and headed back for the doors, feeling the palpable sense of relief from his bodyguards. He stepped into the living room, leaving the guards outside.

It was late. A scensor lay dozing on the couch, the chitinous protrusions on her head slowly smoking. He moved quietly so he wouldn't wake her and passed through the doors to his sleeping chamber.

The anger.

It wasn't his and it was sudden, as if a door had just been opened into someone's mind. He realized with a jolt of fear that Eth was standing by the bed, staring at him.

Standing over Tashmitum.

The implied message was clear. Eth could have killed her at any time while Mishak was out on the balcony. He could kill her even now and there was nothing Mishak could do to stop it because he could kill him as well. He could do it with a mere thought.

The silence grew between them. Mishak knew it would only become more difficult to break as time wore on. He didn't want to be the first to speak, the first to come down from a tactical advantage, but his eyes darted to Tashmitum, her right hand draped protectively over her belly and he abandoned his resolve.

"It wasn't me," he whispered, regretting his choice of words almost instantly. He knew that to be false.

"It wasn't you?" Eth raised an eyebrow. "Was it not you when officers, sworn to *your* service, turned on us at the battle of Kish? Turned on us after we handed you a victory you couldn't have had any other way?

"Was it not you when bounty hunters caught up with us at Kurnugia, leaving only three of us alive?" he continued quietly. "Who are you lying to, me or yourself?"

"Myself," Mishak whispered.

"Remember that when they present her head to you as proof. We had to run for it, so we couldn't bring her body with us. We left her lying there in the street because of you!"

Whether or not Eth was deliberately creating a mental image, the mention of a head in his lap brought back memories of Mishak's brief dalliance with Oliv. His eyes darted back down to Tashmitum as he guiltily wondered if Oliv was the one who'd been killed as a result of the bounty.

Eth offered a grim smile. "Does she know?" He angled his head to indicate the sleeping princess.

Mishak stifled a flare of alarm. Did he mean the bounty or his past with Oliv?

"Let me explain how this works," Eth offered wryly. "For every Human killed over this bounty of yours, you will lose two ships. I'm not saying the HQE will lose two ships. *You* will lose two ships from your own house forces.

"I don't care if this was started by you or if Marduk's been sneaking around behind your back. If he has and you didn't know, then that's your failure, not his. A recording of my terms is being released publicly while we talk.

"That should give whoever's *behind* this pause. Every Human killed for bounty will weaken Prince Mishak, and those who serve you will now be forced to wonder if they're about to die because of your foolishness."

Mishak was stunned. He'd known he'd lost Eth's loyalty but the stark evidence of his outright enmity was something he hadn't allowed his mind to accept and prepare for. It left him speechless.

Eth held out a hand, all fingers extended. "Five of my people killed at Kurnugia. Ten of your ships and crews will pay the price. Now that there's a *personal* interest in this for you..." His voice, still quiet, was laced with more scorn than Sandrak had ever managed to convey. "...I'm reasonably certain you'll finally take action to remedy this situation."

Mishak had never felt more miserable. Sandrak had been hard enough on him but this was far worse. This time he knew he deserved it. "Look, Eth..."

But Eth was already gone.

Mostly not Harmless

India St., San Diego

Gleb was just reaching Aberdeen's apartment building when he got distracted by the large trucks. For one thing, they were wheeled, which he found quaint, but then all ground transport on this world seemed to rely on what had to be one of the Universe's earliest inventions.

His interest had been piqued by their appearance. They looked like giant insects. They had relatively normal operator compartments on the front but the rest consisted of a huge elongated pod that rotated constantly as they sat waiting in a long line.

There were three waiting on Sassafras, just beyond the intersection with India and another two waiting under the overpass for the freeway. He turned to follow the sidewalk under the overpass, moving past the trucks.

The signs on the rotating pods were hard to read without his suit to back him up but at least the locals only used twenty-six letters in their alphabet. The HQE, depending on which stuffy expert you asked, had between thirty and forty thousand characters.

Not that reading helped if he didn't also have the suit feeding him context. He'd been able to use the suit to learn English while he slept and he had the alphabet locked down but he had no idea what 'concrete' was.

He smiled, pulling out the phone Aberdeen had helped him pick out. He wondered if this was what it would feel like to have a sister. Gleb knew she was pretty but he was still intrigued by the vibes he'd felt from Eve.

Aberdeen must have had some abilities of her own, because she seemed to understand that Gleb was only interested in friendship. They'd spent an entirely comfortable afternoon, getting Gleb settled in after his recent move from 'Russia'.

He used the search function to look up concrete. By the time he had his answer, he'd reached the fencing where a pair of armed guards waited. Not much chance of getting a look at what they were doing behind the fence.

He frowned at the large sign behind the guard-post. He looked back at his phone and searched for 'seawall'.

Water now covers five percent of the city? He looked back up at the gate, noticing the tracery of iron rods sticking up inside the site. Some workers were attaching flat panels on either side of the rods. *They need to build a wall to keep out the ocean?*

This planet, if what he'd seen on the local networks was true, had only been civilized for a few thousand years, so it was unlikely they'd have much understanding of the environmental cycles or of their effects on those cycles.

And, without pitch drive tech, they'd rely on sea-borne transport for bulk goods. Imperial cities weren't sited with such considerations in mind. *Hells,* he thought, *Kurnugia only has the hab-ring now, though it must have looked like this world once.*

He turned back, heading again for Aberdeen's building. He pressed his hand on the security scanner on the front door.

"Hi, Gleb!" Aberdeen's voice sounded tinny through the overhead speaker. "Come on up. I'm not quite done getting ready."

He headed up three flights of stairs, still absurdly pleased every time he saw such a thing. After a lifetime among the Quailu, who disdained anything even remotely arboreal, a set of stairs was a treat. They were so much more efficient than those long winding ramps used by the empire's master species.

The door of Aberdeen's apartment unlatched automatically when he placed his hand on the handle. He stepped inside but she wasn't in sight. He could feel her mind, though. She was to his left and a little deeper into the apartment somewhere, glad of his masculine but undemanding presence for some reason he couldn't quite put his finger on.

"Sorry I couldn't meet you at the door," she called out. "Nobody needs to see me in my ratty old shower cap."

"No problem," he assured her. "What's the story on this… movie? The guys said something about several minutes of new footage?"

"Yeah, Kace said it was playing tonight only. We get to see some backstory or something." She stepped out of a door on the left side of the living room. She had on a t-shirt that reached just far enough and held a towel.

"Grab a beer from the fridge. The guys aren't even here yet and Kace is always the last to arrive." She smiled. "Probably so he can work himself up into a frenzy about being late." She turned away and headed for the short hallway that, Gleb assumed, led to her bedroom.

She reached up to gather her hair together behind her neck as she walked.

Gleb's eyes grew wide. Her shirt had ridden up to reveal her buttocks. He'd learned from studying social norms on the network that a gentleman was supposed to avert his eyes at a moment like this.

What kind of idiot would want to be a gentleman and miss this? he asked himself. Friends or not, what he was seeing was too impressive to ignore. *Gentlemen must just be the ones who don't get caught.*

A vase fell from a shelf to his left, pushed off by her cat. He didn't shift his gaze from Aberdeen's backside.

"He can be such a drama Queen," Aberdeen said but then she stopped walking. "Oh, sorry, Gleb!" She turned, deftly slipping an elastic from her wrist over her ponytail. She dropped her arms but not quite fast enough as she faced him.

"The 'Queen' thing," she said. "I don't know how you feel about that. Do you find that derogatory?"

He squinted at her. "Derogatory?"

She shrugged and he had to force himself to keep his gaze on her face.

"Well, yeah. I mean there's this guy I work with at the hospital and he doesn't like anyone saying that." She brightened. "You might like him! For different reasons than me, of course. He's the only guy who isn't sneaking glances at me in the locker-room when I'm getting my scrubs on.

"Sometimes a girl likes to hang out with guys that don't have any expectations," she explained. "You know…" she shrugged again, in a way that Gleb found hard to ignore. "… harmless?"

"Harmless?" he prompted her gently. He was staying out of her mind. Somehow, that seemed more important here.

"Yeah, gay…"

"Gay…" He looked at her quizzically. "You mean, happy?"

She grinned awkwardly. "I… don't know what word you'd use in Russian. I mean… guys who prefer guys over women."

"Prefer…" His eyes grew wide again and he laughed. "Oh, gods! That explains so much!" He shook his head, chuckling. "You thought that?"

"You're not?" She covered her mouth, which was hanging open. "All this time…"

"Yeah," he said mildly. "It probably explains how we got to know each other without any awkwardness. You didn't figure I'd have any expectations, which is kind of true."

He held up a hand. "That's more because of me than you, though. There's someone… back home. She's a friend but there might be potential." He sighed, remembering the battle. "I don't even know if she's still alive…"

40

"Oh!" She gave him a sympathetic look, not knowing how much he appreciated the emotions directly. "She was caught up in the civil war that's going on over there?"

"Uh, yeah, actually." He nodded. The civil war that Eve was caught up in was between Mishak and his family, rather than southern Russia, but it was close enough to the truth.

"No wonder you weren't staring at Ivy's ass," she gave him a sad smile, emanating her admiration at his tragic loyalty.

"Well, I still notice women, and it's not like Eve and I ever really made any commitment."

"Ivy was practically naked," she reminded him.

"That was the only thing about her that stood out, though," he said. "It's not like she was unattractive but, if she was fully dressed, would the crowd have cheered so much? Her costume was, essentially, her nudity."

"Hah!" She went to the fridge and opened the door. "I agree, but I couldn't say it without sounding jealous!" She kept her back straight and lowered herself carefully with her legs to grab two beers from inside the door.

He stepped over to accept the proffered bottle. "You could pull it off," he assured her, nodding at her behind. "You've got a definite advantage going on back there."

"Ew! Gleb! What are you doing, looking at your friend that way!"

"You do remember establishing that I'm not gay, right?" He removed the cap from his bottle and took a drink. "Wait, is this tight t-shirt you picked out for me yesterday a gay thing?" He'd liked it because he was already used to wearing his tight under-armor suit.

"No," she giggled. "Well, it could be, I suppose, but lots of guys with a body like yours would wear a shirt that shows it off, gay or straight."

"What about this busy visual print?" He gestured with his free hand at the shirt he was wearing.

"You're kidding me, right?" She took a drink of her beer. "I literally got this off a rack labeled 'Bold Russian Prints'."

"Oh, yeah," he conceded. *Better get my suit to teach me some Russian before this blows up in my face.* "Hold on… you just said 'with a body like mine'."

"Yeah," she said cautiously, shoulders elevating slightly.

"So that means you noticed my body without having any particular expectations, right?"

The tension disappeared from her shoulders. "Yeah, I suppose."

"So it's the same for me. When I saw your butt a few minutes ago, my response was: 'That's a cute little backside!' followed by: 'Where are the guys? Hope we don't miss the start of the movie.'"

Her eyes grew wide. "You saw what?"

He nodded toward the hallway. "When you were tying up your hair your shirt rode up."

"Gleb!" She grabbed the bottom hem of her shirt, stretching it down. "Why didn't you say anything?"

"I don't know what's normal here," he admitted. "It's not like I'm picking out names for our offspring or anything." He waved his bottle toward the door. "Dex is also pretty good looking. Doesn't mean I have any expectations with him either."

The Universe must have been listening because her security screen lit up, showing Dexter standing outside with Kace.

She set her beer on the kitchen table and headed for the hallway. "Let them in while I get dressed," she told him.

"I'd recommend a longer shirt," he suggested.

She showed him her right fist over her shoulder, the middle finger extended in a gesture that existed in the empire as well.

He wondered if there might be a reason for that. He also noticed that her left hand was holding her shirt down at the back.

He let the guys in, explaining that Aberdeen was still getting ready. Kace dropped into a hammock chair absorbed in a call with his sister. Gleb intercepted Dexter and motioned him into the kitchen.

"Remember what we were talking about a couple of days ago in your garage?" he asked. "I have a phrase you want to keep in mind." He lowered his voice. "What's a fella got to do to be considered harmless?"

Dexter frowned. "I thought you said…"

"What are you guys hiding in here for?" Aberdeen asked, walking into the kitchen and opening the fridge. With jeans on, she didn't have to be as careful reaching for beer. She handed one to Dexter.

Kace noticed the gesture and ended his call, getting out of the awkward chair. He made a beeline for the second beer that she was holding out.

"Hiding?" Dexter asked lamely.

"Oh, I get it!" Gleb grinned at her. "You're worried I'm telling him about what I saw earlier!"

"Ugh!" She rolled her eyes. "You are such an ass!"

"Maybe but not nearly as cute as yours!"

"Wait…" Kace had his beer halfway to his mouth but it stopped moving. "… What did we miss?"

"Oh for…" Aberdeen threw up her hands. "I accidentally flashed my butt at Gleb."

"She wouldn't have been so reckless," Gleb added, "except she thought I was completely harmless."

"Harmless?" Kace lowered his beer, one eyebrow raised at Gleb.

"All this time, she though I was gay."

Aberdeen was giggling now.

"Damn!" Dexter chuckled. "What else can a fella do to be considered harmless?"

She laughed, giving him a light shove. "I need another ten minutes," she told them. She left the kitchen and headed for her bedroom.

Gleb couldn't see her face but he could sense the slightly bemused feeling coming over her. It was so unguarded he didn't even need to try. He was pretty sure she was thinking about Dexter's last comment.

Kace hadn't been completely oblivious. "What are you up to, Dex?" he asked. "You like Abby?"

"'Course I like her," Dex retorted defensively. "She's a friend."

"No, that's not it," Kace insisted. "You also like the fact that she's a *pretty* friend."

A shrug. "And you don't?"

Kace shook his head. "Too much like Ellie."

Gleb looked at Dex. "Ellie?"

Dexter was nodding thoughtfully. "His sister. Now that he mentions it, she's pretty hot. Looks more than a bit like Aberdeen…"

"Whoa!" Kace held up a hand. "You two knuckleheads stay away from my sister!"

Nudge

Human base, Babilim Station

Eth could see for hundreds of miles from up here and the horizon looked oddly flat in every direction. He sat on the edge of what had probably been an observation platform. He couldn't ask the original builders because they'd been gone for tens of thousands of years.

The spire itself was probably some sort of air traffic control facility or it may have something to do with the station's automated defense systems. The space between orbit and a few hundred meters above the surface were still a no-go zone.

For most visitors, the only way to access the station was through the few remaining orbital elevators. The Humans' stealth ships could land, though they'd later found a better way to conceal their coming and going, and that had allowed them to set up a secret base on the far side of the station from the part inhabited by a few million HQE citizens.

Though that didn't sound, at first, like it was terribly isolated, this station was huge. Babilim surrounded a white dwarf star which also provided its power. The radius of the station was roughly at the orbital distance of a typical habitable planet.

Most folks here wondered how the mysterious builders had put such a huge thing together. "Where did they get all the material from?" Eth whispered.

"There's a question to keep you awake at night!" Father Sulak announced his arrival with the statement.

Eth kept looking out at the endless horizon as the Quailu oracle settled beside him. "Y'know, Father, when a fella comes all the way up here, he's probably trying to get a little time alone..."

"And a good spot for it!" Sulak agreed cheerfully. "Great place for a person to hone their focus, I'd think." He waved his hand at the view. "Who gives a damn how this was built? How many solar systems did they *harvest* to build this monstrosity? If you have the capability and the unmitigated arrogance to just take entire systems for your materials, the actual construction's probably not an obstacle."

Eth grunted, letting his agreement be felt by the Quailu.

Sulak glanced sidelong at Eth. "Have you similarly refocused as the leader of this community of powerful, dangerous people?"

"It's a work in progress," Eth admitted. Despite Sulak's species, Eth was fast coming to lean on the oracle. He had a way of nudging people toward sense. "I've been too focused on past failures when I need to be charting a course for our people. We need a way forward, a goal for the species in general."

"That's good!"

Eth looked at him. "Is it?" He grinned. "You just said we're dangerous!"

"You are!" Sulak nodded and turned to gaze out at the horizon. "But I'm your friend, so you're not dangerous to me."

"We're dangerous to other Quailu, though."

"Some, yes." Sulak chuckled. "You were certainly dangerous to Bau's enemies but you pose no danger to the old gal herself."

"I have the feeling you engineered the mention of her name for a reason…"

"Who, me?"

"You're using your oracular wiles on me, Father."

"And what if I am? I'm an oracle, in case you've forgotten."

Eth waited, watching Sulak who still gazed placidly into the distance.

"The Lady Bau?" he finally prompted the Quailu.

Sulak pursed his lips, nodding ever so slightly. "After you saved her life, you've shared a bond of friendship."

There was a long pause.

"Now," Sulak finally continued, "you share a mutual problem…"

Off the Wall

Seawall by the old naval base

Gleb chucked his empty beer bottle over the railing, watching as it plunged ten meters to hit the shallow water lapping at the base of the wall. It went under, hitting pavement almost immediately with a barely audible 'thunk' and nothing more was seen.

He looked up at the sound of gunfire. Looming over the stumps of old buildings, a collection of structures once known by local Humans as 'hotels' played host to communities of squatters.

There were fishermen, sensibly, using the abandoned buildings as a base. The water around them was deep enough that they could build docks from the second floor and easily land their catches for processing and they had more than enough room above for their families.

It would be ideal if not for the drug-traffickers also wanting to use the structures as a base for their own operations.

"You can literally get away with anything out there," Kace told him, holding out a fresh beer.

"The Law Enforcement Choice Act," Aberdeen muttered. "If you can't afford the insurance you're fair game." She nodded out at the hotels where gunshots were lighting up a corner of the fifth floor.

"Those poor souls don't live in any of the networks, so they couldn't buy law-enforcement coverage even if they had the money." She sighed. "Never did trust any legislation that has the word 'choice' in the name…"

"Welcome to the Universe," Gleb said mildly. "That's how it works when you're not a part of the nobility." *Is that a step too far?* He wondered. *I remember reading this country repudiated the idea of a nobility when it was founded…*

"You mean a one-percenter?" Dexter asked.

"A one-percenter?" Gleb turned a quizzical look to the left where Dex was standing between him and Aberdeen.

"Nowadays, we also call them oligarchs like you do in Russia." Dex shrugged. "You know, the guys that are so rich they don't have to worry about little things like laws."

"Oh, yeah." Gleb nodded. "We've got our fair share of that where I'm from."

"Same all over, I suppose," Dex said fatalistically. "No money, no justice, no healthcare... Unless a distant but wealthy relative pops out of the woodwork, that is!"

He leaned over the railing hoisting his beer in Kace's direction. "To Mary's operation and quick recovery!"

They all toasted Kace's mother and settled into amiable silence for a while.

Until Gleb thought of a way to stir the pot between Dexter and Aberdeen.

He leaned back, looking to his right. "That rich relative also saved you from wondering whether you could have endured a little embarrassment to help out more."

"Embarrassment?" Dexter raised an eyebrow.

Aberdeen laughed. "You saw how Ivy won with a few splashes of latex. I was just saying I'd have tried something like that if I knew it would get us more prize money to help with the medical costs.

"Not that it would have worked anyway," she added dismissively. "Ivy was already wearing the bare minimum. If I was trying to beat her at that game, I'd have been arrested before we even got inside the conference center."

Gleb gave Dex a subtle nudge in the ribs.

Dex shook his head. "You're kidding us, right?"

"No," she said. "At least, I don't think so. I'm pretty sure I could have worked up the nerve..."

"No," Dex cut in. "I'm not talking about that. You're one of the nicest people I've ever met. I know you'd put yourself through that for Mary. I'm just finding it hard to believe you think you'd have to out-nude Ivy to beat her."

He waved a hand vaguely. "Hell, you won us second place with your midriff and a pretty smile!"

"*We* won second place, Dex," she insisted, her left hand twisting an errant curl of hair. "There were three of us on the stage, in case you forgot."

Dex chuckled. He jabbed a thumb at Kace. "*We* were just a couple of dudes in white plastic armor that you can buy online pretty easily." He held up a hand at the protest he could see forming in her features.

"Yeah, I know I did an amazing job of making that stuff," he told her, half-jokingly, "but it's not enough for a couple of guys to put it on and goof around on the stage."

"He's not wrong," Gleb said before taking a drink. "I was *practically* wearing a functional combat EVA suit with holo-projectors built in and I only came third."

"Damn right!" Dex nodded. "I'd almost believe that was a real suit he had on! You beat him anyway because nerds love a pretty girl who likes sci-fi stuff!"

"Hah!" she scoffed, head tilted to the left. "Pretty's a bit strong, fellas. I'm okay, I suppose, but let's not get carried away!"

She frowned at Dexter who was simply staring back at her, a perplexed look on his face. "What?" she finally demanded.

"I can't figure out," Dexter began slowly, "whether you're being serious or just being modest, like society expects."

"Serious?"

"Yeah." Dexter turned to face her, leaning his left elbow on the railing. "I've used the washroom in your place, so I know for a fact you've got at least one mirror. You've got to have some idea."

"What... what are you talking about?"

He waved a hand. "Modesty aside, there has to be moments... like when you're brushing your teeth and you look up at your reflection and you think 'Damn, I'm looking good!'"

She rolled her eyes. "Yeah, I just stand there admiring myself..."

Dex looked straight into her eyes, head angled slightly to the side."I might if I were you. Face it, Abs; you're beautiful."

She smiled at Dex, leaning in to give him a kiss on the cheek. "God, you're sweet!" She breathed in his ear. "If we weren't friends..."

Gleb was staying out of her head because he'd started seeing these people as more than just assets in his effort to get back home. He wasn't so scrupulous about Dex, though, because he'd been coaching him on stepping up his efforts with Aberdeen.

If he was going to help the guy, he needed to know where his head was at and he nearly growled at what he was feeling from his friend now. *Numbskull! You can feel her breath on your ear and you're going with sad resignation at hearing the word 'friend'?*

He was unfamiliar with the local intricacies, especially since he'd never had any exposure to the mating habits of wild Humans but he'd had more than his fair share of experience with the unfiltered sexual behaviour of the females in his own social group. Humans wanted what Humans wanted.

He gave Dex a gentle shove from behind, forcing him to step in closer to Aberdeen.

Dex dropped his bottle over the railing and brought his hand up to her face.

Aberdeen sucked in a sharp breath, closing her eyes and turning her face up toward Dex's.

And Gleb decided now was a good time to stay out of his brain. He turned back to the encroaching ocean.

Kace was looking past him at Dex's back, mouth hanging open in shock. He finally looked at Gleb and returned his grin.

He frowned, the right side of his mouth quirking back, the undeniable tell for when he was thinking seriously. "You ready to give me that lift over to the hospital, Gleb?"

"Giving you the what, now?"

Kace jerked his head toward the stairs behind them. "C'mon. We don't want to miss visiting hours." He shepherded Gleb to the stairs.

"You realize I don't have ground transport?" Gleb asked as they started down the stairs.

Kace waved him to silence. "We're off to the *Grace*," he called to the… couple?

It was unlikely they heard him.

Mutual Problem

Arbella System

"Normalizing," the helmsman announced. "We're in position. The local star is behind the belligerent fleets, as requested."

"Very good," Eth replied calmly. "Tactical?"

"As the intelligence suggested, sir." The tactical officer cast a sideways glance at Father Sulak. "Twelve enemy ships, in an eight-and-four mix."

"The Quailu are always going to favour cruisers over smaller ships," Eth said with a hint of scorn. "It works in our favor – fewer ships to fight if this turns into a hairball."

"*If*, huh?" Lev muttered from his position in the nav-bay.

"Something to say, Lieutenant?"

"No, sir. Just glad to see you still have a sense of whimsy." Lev looked at Eth, his expression underlining his concern. "Just so we're clear – this *is* a trap, right?"

Eth raised an eyebrow. "You don't think Shullat has the stones to pull a force together and take his system back from Bau?"

It was clear from Lev's expression that he wasn't taking his captain's question seriously. "Last we heard of Shullat he barely had the stones to beg a crust from his cousin."

"And the last time he tried to take Arbella back," Eth added with a grin, "he was Uktannu's puppet and they used far more ships than this. So... yeah... trap.

"That's why we came. If someone's setting us up, we can't afford to leave them to their own devices. If we failed to show, they might cook up a decent plan B and still hurt us badly."

Lev frowned. "How would they kill us if we don't show up?"

"I believe Eth said 'hurt' us," Father Sulak corrected the nav officer. "Convincing the HQE that the Humans are dangerous, faithless renegades is far more effective than just killing off a few crews."

Eth was pleased to hear the Quailu including himself with that 'us', not because he was flattered to have a member of the ruling species in his group, but because it showed a possible way forward. It showed that Humans might just find a place for themselves in the HQE after all.

"Let's stay alert, everyone," Eth told the bridge crew. "Like Lev said, this is a trap and the first step in evading a trap is to be slightly less stupid that our friend Shullat." He waved at the belligerent fleet on the holo.

"The Varangians are there to adjudicate," he added. "No sign of Lady Bau's forces being here to contest Shullat's claim?"

"No indications, sir," the sensor officer confirmed. "Those rumors about unrest on her home-world…"

"Doubtless they're more than just rumors," Eth said. "Otherwise, Tilsen would be here getting ready to squash this folly. Someone stirred up Enibulu against her and choreographed this little dance party for us."

He turned to tactical. "Since we arrived, what changes have you seen in enemy dispositions?"

"They turned our way when they spotted the drop-out plasma but they haven't been following our movement since."

"So, they probably don't see us." Eth stuck his tongue against the side of his cheek.

Even without the carbon nanotubule coating on his ships, they'd be hard to track at this distance. With the light bouncing down between the carbon filaments and not coming back out, the only way to spot a Human fast-attack-corvette was to notice the absence of background stars.

Sooner or later, some clever Quailu would figure out an algorithm for that. Probably later. Most of them were content to coast along on tech that had existed for thousands of years.

"Launch a message-relay drone."

"Drone away," Comms confirmed.

Eth ran a few scenarios through his expensive mind while he waited for the drone to reach its assigned position. They were great for sending a transmission without giving away your position, as long as they were stationary. Transmitting from a moving drone, however, drew a line straight back to your ship.

By the time the drone had come to a stop, Eth was reasonably certain as to how this would play out. The only problem was that his reasonable certainty allowed for at least three different scenarios, so he'd have to figure out which one he was facing.

He stepped to the middle of his tactical holo and opened a channel through the drone. "Shullat," he greeted his enemy. "Who's using you this time?"

The response took a few moments, giving time for the transmission distance and, let's face it, the outrage gripping Shullat.

"How dare you address me like that, you filthy Mushkennu native? You call me 'Lord', if you even address me at all!"

Eth was far from impressed. There was a time when Humans had lived in awe of the ruling species of the HQE. His own predecessor had even given his own life to prevent the death of some unknown Quailu on Chiron.

That was a long time ago for many of the native species of the HQE. Eth and his people had killed thousands of Quailu and most of those had been better warriors than Shullat.

"You're a lord again?" Eth enquired. "Did your cousin put you in charge of the breakfast buffet?"

He was hoping to tweak the Quailu into blurting out something useful by making him angry. Well, that was at least half true. If he made a really firm attempt at being honest with himself, Eth would have to admit that he was tweaking Shullat because it was funny.

There was a bit of a pause in the conversation.

Shullat must have used the time to calm himself before responding. "You won't be making your little jokes for much longer, Human," the Quailu finally growled. "I assume you've come here on behalf of that thief, Bau?"

"We have," Eth said, "though not at her request or with her knowledge. We've come because she has always dealt *honourably* with us. We have heard that her forces are otherwise occupied and we volunteer to represent her claim to Arbella, with force, if necessary.

"We ask the Varangian commander adjudicating your claim to recognise us as a party of standing in this matter."

"This is Jorunn," a new voice stated. "I represent the Varangian forces in this dispute. I recognize you as a party of standing. If you would approach…"

"I must review a legal question regarding my claim," Shullat cut back in. "There is a technical matter to be examined in the difference between contested and uncontested claims. I ask the party representing the interests of Lady Bau to withdraw to the ninth planet and await our decision."

A sigh came from the Varangian channel. "Ethkennu, will you accompany me to the outer system while Shullat decides whether to continue pressing his claim?"

"Of course, Jorunn," Eth answered quickly, sounding eager to resolve the issue without the need for fighting. He cut the channel.

"So," Lev looked up from the helm. "What's our move?"

"I'd say our most likely next move is to turn on Jorunn and his Varangian ships shortly after we reach the ninth planet," Eth answered mildly.

"And that helps us how?" Father Sulak asked in alarm.

"It doesn't," Eth admitted. "We'll have a force waiting in the gas giant, ready to come out and kill the four Varangian ships accompanying us."

"We will?" Sulak asked, growing suspicious of Eth's light mood.

"Definitely," Eth confirmed, "which is why I sent Noa with five ships before we left Babilim Station."

"Gods preserve us,"Sulak muttered. "I'm not fussy about which ones, as long as someone takes on the j0b."

The trip was fast. Both the Humans and their Varangian escort used path drives rather than using pitch. As soon as they returned to normal spatial geometry, Eth nodded at Lev. "You have the helm. I'm going to visit with Jorunn before the shooting starts."

"Be nice!" Father Shulak said earnestly. "Compliment his ship or whatever it is that you captains love the most."

"Don't worry, Father," Eth said. "It will all work out in the end."

He reached back, looking for the link to the Varangians but they were tough to find, perhaps because they weren't originally from this Universe. They did have a Quailu aboard, though.

The Quailu turned to Jorunn, who was speaking. There were several paces of unoccupied deck between the two and Eth slid into place there.

"Gods!" the Quailu exclaimed, followed by the sound of a quick backward shuffle of feet.

"Ethkennu," Jorunn nodded politely.

"Commander," Eth nodded back. "I assume you were... expecting me?"

"I was." He nodded to Eth's left. "That's Militun, Lady Bau's governor on Arbella."

"Lord," Eth greeted him politely. He was, after all, Bau's representative and the Humans were hoping to maintain good relations. Her people produced excellent weapons.

"The governor..." Eth gave Militun a polite incline of the head before turning to Jorunn. "... is here to witness the treachery, I presume?"

"He is."

"And you've already taken steps? Sabotaged their weapon systems, perhaps?" He was hoping the Varangians, with their knowledge of future events, would have already protected themselves from a surprise assault.

"That isn't how we operate," Jorunn said.

"Here we go," Eth muttered.

"Though matters involving Humans are always clouded," Jorunn explained, "we have reason to believe you're up to the task."

"Great," Eth said dryly. "That's just great. We're all flying blind out here." He frowned. "You might have to fight before this is done, you know."

"It's always a possibility," Jorunn conceded.

"Yeah, well..." Eth jabbed a thumb at Militun. "... You better get him into an EVA suit before you have to rig for combat."

Jorunn's eyes widened. "Fornication!"

"Right?" Eth spread his hands. "How foolish would you have felt, stopping a false-flag attack but having to explain to Bau that you got her governor killed?

"Well," Eth said, already reaching back to his own bridge crew, "I'll be off. Got bad guys to kill and all that..."

He opened his eyes on his own ship again. "We're still on full combat alert?"

"Yes, sir," Lev confirmed. "Any news from our Varangian friends... victims?"

"They have confidence that we'll do as expected."

"Ah. That's nice. Isn't that nice, Father?"

Sulak frowned at Eth. "Is it?"

Eth sighed. "It'll have to do. In the meantime, we should be seeing something happen soon. Now that we're here, they'll be eager to get on with it."

Almost as if his words had triggered the event, the tactical officer announced six shapes emerging from the gas giant below them.

"Are they transmitting our recognition codes?" Eth demanded.

"No codes at all," Comms answered.

"They're descending again," Tactical warned. "I'm losing them!"

"What the hells?" Lev sounded offended that the enemy weren't offering combat. "They just pop out for a quick look and then bugger off?"

"It's called reconnaissance," Eth said, the hairs on the back of his neck standing on end. *Whoever they did that for is the one we need to worry about!* "Comms, get everyone moving! We can't just coast along like practice targets. Random course patterns, now!"

"Reading pressure waves consistent with last known tracks of the six hostiles," Tactical announced.

"That would be Noa's group, blinding the enemy for us." Eth threw out his left arm for balance as the ship performed an evasive maneuver, her three pitch drives temporarily overloading the grav emitters in the center of the bridge.

"Missile and kinetic rounds coming out of the gas!" Tactical said in a loud but calm voice. "Our ships are fast enough to evade but most of the weapons appear to be targeted at our Varangian escort vessels…"

"And those cruisers are slow," Eth finished for him. "C'mon, Jorunn, let's see some of that Varangian 'luck'."

"I have a projected course for the enemy ship firing on us," Tactical announced, adding a new overlay to the central holo. It showed a line through the upper atmosphere of the gas giant. Smaller vectors sprouted off from the line at regular intervals, becoming the current trace of each inbound missile and kinetic round.

"Gotta be a cruiser, to put out that volume of fire so quickly. I have a brace of *Bau-Specials* ready to fire."

Eth's lips slid apart in a silent snarl. "Fire!"

The Bau-Specials, missiles produced on one of her worlds, used mass-attenuation technology to reduce the mass of the weapon during the acceleration phase, allowing near relativistic velocities.

The weapons streaked away from the Human ship, striking their target almost instantly, eliminating the need at such a close distance for any target-leading calculations. If there was a way to evade such a missile, Eth had never heard of it.

Just before impact, the MA field generator reversed itself, increasing the mass of the weapon for a brief instant, though it was mostly overkill. At the speeds involved, a clipped fingernail would still punch a cone-shaped hole straight through a cruiser.

The enemy ship was most likely out of action and on its way down to the crushing depths of the gas giant. Meanwhile, its missiles and kinetic rounds were still tracking their way toward the Varangian ships.

"Dammit!" the tactical officer growled. "Get those slow shit-piles out of the way!"

The five Varangian cruisers scattered but they were almost certain to take hits. The kinetic rounds were like dice; cast and forgot, they couldn't change course.

The missiles, nowhere near as fast as what the Humans were using, could still home in on a designated target.

The Human corvettes, using three pitch drives each to reinforce their gravitational waves, had no trouble dancing their way through clouds of missiles but the cruisers were far too slow. A cruiser, given enough notice, could evade one missile easily, two with a bit of cleverness…

But the Varangian cruisers were facing a brace of five missiles each.

"Not a single missile aimed at us," the tactical officer said, his tone almost offended.

"Not as effective for us to murder the emperor's Varangians if we're not alive as symbols of Human perfidy," Eth said tersely. He was leaning forward, urging the Varangian ships on, pretty much all he could do at this point.

"They're taking hits!" Tactical opened new sub-windows near each ship in the main holo. The Varangians were showing damage estimates now as the missiles impacted.

"The *Niall* took the worst of it," Tactical continued. "Engineering took three warheads. They're drifting."

"Launch shuttles to search for survivors," Eth ordered. He opened a channel to the *Grimdallr*.

"Jorunn, can we assist?"

"An engineering team would be welcome on the *Niall*," Jorunn said. "Thankfully, we were hit by conventional missiles instead of those demonic things you use. You're lucky to have Lady Bau as a friend."

"I'd say you're lucky she gave us those missiles as well," Eth told him.

Jorunn laughed. "You should know, Shullat has pulled up stakes and scampered. I suppose he must have just found out what happened."

Eth nodded. "I doubt he knew why he was really here." His eyes darted to the right. "Noa just reported in. He has prisoners, some of them senior enough to be credible witnesses."

"I told you we had confidence in your ability to handle this." Jorunn disconnected.

Eth pinched the bridge of his nose. *It's like dealing with oracles.* He remembered Jorunn's expression when Eth had pointed out the danger the governor was in.

"You don't see everything, do you?" he said quietly.

Coming Clean

The Odessa Terrace Apartments

Gleb opened his door. "Ah, good! The three of you came together!" He stepped back and waved them in, smiling nervously at each as they passed.

"What's the big secret?" Aberdeen asked on her way past.

He gestured to the couch. "You'll see soon enough."

He moved to stand opposite the coffee table from his three Irth friends. "Grab a seat, everyone, and get one of those shots into you."

They sat but then they just looked at him expectantly.

"Seriously," he urged, "have a shot. It's called vodka – it'll help, believe me."

Kace chuckled, reaching out for one of the small glasses. "It's called vodka," he told Dexter, raising his glass in a mock toast.

Smiling, Aberdeen and Dexter followed suit.

Then back to looking expectantly at Gleb.

He took a deep breath. "Okay, this will sound crazy," he warned, scratching the back of his head, "but I'm not from here."

"Wow!" Aberdeen replied. "I suppose we should have seen the signs. You know, stuff like your accent, your lack of knowledge about our customs…" She leaned forward. "…Or the fact that you *told* us 'I'm not from here, I'm from Russia!' the day we met you!"

"Oh shit…" Gleb sighed. "No, look. I'm not from this world…"

Kace rolled his eyes. "You're not far wrong, there, buddy."

Gleb just looked at them for a moment, mouth pressed into a grim line of resignation. Then he remembered why he'd put a half dozen mugs of hot coffee on his side of the low table.

"Y'know," he said quietly, "I've learned a lot about perception over the last few lunars. I've learned how our biology takes a terrifying thing like the Universe and layers a comfy little construct over it so we don't go insane."

He nodded at Kace. "Kind of like those tea-cozies that Mary collects, except seeing a bare teapot isn't all that scary. The point is we can make ourselves see whatever we want to. We're better at it than we think."

He gestured to Aberdeen. "If we can make ourselves see the Universe the way we do, it's not such a stretch that Abby, here, doesn't see how pretty she is.

"And it's also easy to ignore some pretty compelling evidence. You've been here before. You've all taken a turn at trying on my EVA suit – which screws up the calibration by the way – so thanks for getting my nuts pinched last week when I tried to reset it."

He tilted his head forward, looking at them with his eyebrows raised. "Do you guys really think I made that thing in some garage workshop? There's nothing on this planet that even comes close to the tech in that suit."

Aberdeen sighed. "Gleb…" She sat up straighter. "What the hell?"

"Try explaining this away," he said from behind the couch.

"Holy shit!" Dexter jumped off the couch and turned to face him. "He's a vampire?"

"You're messing with me, right?" Gleb asked. "I just told you I'm not from this planet and, the minute I show you proof, you go with 'vampire'? How the hells do you reach a conclusion like that?"

"It's probably that movie he made us all watch a couple of months ago," Kace explained, turning his head to track Gleb as he walked around the couch to get at the hot coffee. "Because vampires are supposed to be eternal, they've eventually figured out a way to… well, do what you just did."

"Yeah," Dex said, eyes glued to Gleb. "They teleport."

"No," Kace insisted pedantically, they have super-speed. They developed a special relationship with time…"

"Oh my god!" Aberdeen nearly shouted. "I get that you two are geekier than I am – by a pretty wide margin – but our friend just outed himself as a self-teleporting alien and you somehow turn that into an argument about movie lore?"

"Right?" Gleb nodded his agreement but he held up a finger. "Though alien is probably a bit strong, unless you mean it like immigrant or something. I'm still a Human, just like you guys."

He sniffed with disdain at Kace. "Super-speed!" He turned to Dex, shaking his head and waving a hand at Kace as if to say 'can you believe this guy?'."

He was about to take a drink but realized he hadn't really used much heat. He smiled. Scylla had given him a hard time for trying to brute-force his transpositions rather than doing what she called reaching back.

She'd be proud.

"I'm new at the whole teleport thing myself," he told them, "but at least I'm getting better at following the right method. Don't even need a coffee to replenish my body heat this time.

"I must have shifted a hells of a long way to get to Irth. Thank the gods I did it properly, too, or I'd have done more than just freeze that swimming pool; I'd probably have killed myself and most of San Diego."

Aberdeen's mouth fell open. She turned to look at her friends and then back at Gleb. "That's how you froze the pool?"

Gleb nodded. "It was during a battle," he said. "We'd just gained the upper hand over our enemy..." His face darkened, fists clenched. "One of the enemy ships figured out a way to track us.

"We knew it would happen, sooner or later. One of our own people betrayed us to our lord's brother, told him how our stealth ships worked but only one ship seemed able to find us. The Quailu are loath to acknowledge anything other than a straight up, toe-to-toe fight, and they certainly don't want to believe another species might be better at anything.

"Having half their fleet knocked out in the opening minutes of the fight must have made at least one of them think otherwise…"

"You had a lord?" Kace asked.

"I come from the Holy Quailu Empire," he explained. "Our lord commissioned the Meleke Corporation to produce Humans for use in economic raids. We're designed for combat."

"There's a lot to unwrap in that sentence," Aberdeen said. "And I don't know about you guys," she added, glancing at Kace and Dexter, "but I'm still processing the whole 'I'm from another world' thing."

She looked back at Gleb. "You were *designed* and *produced* by a company?"

"That's right," Gleb said, sitting in a chair opposite the couch. "I was a combat slave for the Lord Mishak, an elector of the HQE."

"You're a slave?" Kace asked tentatively. "You're from an interplanetary empire that *allows* slavery?"

"Why wouldn't it?" Gleb asked. "You think the wealthy Awilu – the ruling class – would outlaw one of the things that made them wealthy in the first place?

"The way they look at it, they're doing us a favor. Only extinct species can be sold as slaves so, in a way, they're bringing us back to life."

"Okay," Dexter said hesitantly, "but you said only extinct species." He spread his hands. "We're definitely not extinct."

"Yeah," Aberdeen agreed. "We'd probably have noticed something like that."

Gleb took a deep breath. "Look, guys, the Chironans stocked Humans here. I have no idea why but they're illegally procuring Humans for something they referred to as 'Project Irth'. I don't know how long this has been going on but…"

"Gleb," Kace cut in. "This is where we're from. If you're really a Human, then this is your home-world."

"Fossil records go back a long way," Dex added. "And that Genome Kit I did a couple of years back shows that our species, as you see us now, has been diverging from an origin point in northeast Africa for the last hundred thousand years."

"Huh!" Gleb stood there, staring at Dex or, rather, at a patch of wall that would have been visible if Dex hadn't been in the way. "A hundred thousand years is a long time," he admitted. "It's about twice the age of the HQE… the empire," he added, seeing their confusion at the acronym.

"But their civilization, including pre-imperial history, goes back for nearly a quarter-million years. The Meleke Corporation has its roots in a handful of companies that used to operate in the time of the middle kingdom."

He set his coffee down and grabbed a shot. "They could have seeded our species on Irth back then. Just dropped us off to fend for ourselves, hoping the new challenges would result in new genetic aberrations that they could harvest for use in the commercial market…"

"But that doesn't explain the other humanoid relations that died out," Dex countered. "Their records go back even further."

"How far?" Gleb tossed back the shot.

"Maybe a quarter million years for Neanderthals."

Gleb shrugged. "Still plausible. The early kingdoms that got swallowed up by the Quailu were around back then."

"Yeah, well…" Dex stopped, staring at Gleb. "Really? A quarter million years? Of continuous civilization?"

"More or less, why?"

"'Cause a few centuries is considered long around here," Aberdeen told him. "We only know a fraction of our history on this planet." She held up a hand. "Let's get back to the main point. You're from this… empire but you've come here to Earth. Why come here and not to one of your lord's ships? I mean, they had to be a lot closer, right?"

"I think it had to do with density," Gleb said slowly, reaching down for another shot. "I find my way by seeing through someone's eyes at my destination. It's easier if I'm viewing through a Human and there were a few hundred at the battle, a few thousand down on Kish…" He looked up at his friends. "… There are Billions of us here, and I think Scylla may have given me a bit of an assist."

"Who's Scylla?" Aberdeen asked. "Is she the one you want to find again?"

"Well, yes and no." Gleb shrugged. "I think you're referring to Eve, though. We're new to the whole relationship thing, but I think there might be potential with her."

"New to relationships?" Kace raised an eyebrow.

"Yeah. Our genomes are incredibly expensive. Accelerated healing, improved cognition, enhanced endurance… We emerge from the maturation chambers with sterility implants to protect the Meleke Corporation's intellectual property. Sex for us carried less baggage than it does for you."

He drank the shot and set the small glass down. "Eve and I have had sex before, when we were still Mishak's property. It was almost like… exchanging massages except for the massive hit of endorphins."

He leaned back in the chair, staring down at the empty shot-glass. "When we were freed, though, folks started to think about what it would mean to remove our steri-plants."

He waggled his head. "Sex with someone wouldn't just be recreational, it would be *pro*creational. It takes on a whole new dimension when your genes might be shared with someone to create a new life."

"Hmm." Aberdeen gave a little half-laugh. "You don't hear talk like that from men very often on *this* planet. When the blood-flow to their brain suddenly gets competition from south of the beltline, they aren't thinking any farther than the next few minutes."

"I think you might be generalizing a little there," Dexter said mildly.

She gave him a fond smile. "You're right," she admitted, putting a hand on his thigh. "Some men can handle themselves quite well."

"Um..." Dexter's face reddened.

Kace sniggered.

Now Aberdeen reddened as well. "Not that... I mean, I don't mean he's been handling... not that he shouldn't..."

"I'm just going to cut in here," Gleb said, sighing. "My people are developing a little baggage around sex but you Irthers have built up an entire luggage store around it!" He got out of his chair and started pacing.

"I think I need to partner up with a local oligarch," he told them. "Someone with the financial resources, personal influence and tech base to help me build a ship."

"You'd have to offer them something in return," Kace said. "Make it worth their time."

"You've got a city on Mars," Gleb replied. "How long does it take to get there?"

"With the new engines they've developed," Aberdeen said, wrinkling her nose as she searched her memory, "about four months."

"Hah!" Gleb slapped his thigh. "If they work with me, I can cut that down considerably!"

"That's definitely valuable!" Aberdeen looked at Kace and Dexter. "Who better than the one whose granddad put Humans on Mars?"

Their eyes lit up.

"Oh, Maeve!" Dex exclaimed. "Yeah, that's actually perfect!" His gaze took on the focus of somebody who was using his lens.

"Day after tomorrow," he muttered. "She'll be visiting a site where you might find a quiet moment to talk."

The Way Ahead

The Missile is the Message

Kharko System

"Mel," Eth greeted the engineering tech. "You've got something odd to show me?"

"Sir!" Mel jumped up from the missile he was tinkering with, slamming himself to attention.

Mel was one of the crewmen he'd inherited from Gleb's ship when he'd rammed her into an enemy at the battle of Kish. Gleb had taken him and Siri from the ship of Mishak's renegade half-brother.

He still had a strong fear of authority figures.

"Easy, Mel!" Eth grinned at him. "You'll strain something."

"Yes, sir. Sorry, sir."

Eth held up a hand. "Just relax. Show me what's going on with the warheads."

"Yes. Um… well…" Mel held out his hands in front of his belly, fingers splayed as if he were holding a small globe. "It's the AI units, sir. They're…" he counter rotated his hands a few degrees and moved them closer together, "…talking to us."

"Talking to us," Eth said flatly.

71

"Yes, sir." He nodded eagerly. "Ever since we arrived in system, here at Kharko. They've been at it non-stop since we dropped out of path."

"So something local is causing it?"

Another nod. "A steady broadcast, if I don't miss my bet, sir. Set to get the warheads talking."

"And what are they telling us?"

Mel activated a routing link from the missile.

Eth accepted the link and a non-descript system-voice came to life. "The luggage I didn't touch. The sad story that opened my eyes. Let me open yours. 345633-23-5456-12... The luggage I didn't..." Eth cut the link, frowning.

Lady Bau.

When he'd saved her life at Arbella, her ship had been going down into the same gas giant where he'd just foiled the ambush against Jorunn's Varangians. They had crash-landed on an old gas-harvesting platform in the upper reaches of the atmosphere.

She'd nearly touched an abandoned piece of luggage but he'd stopped her before she could set off its alarm. There were hostiles crashed on the platform as well and they were keeping a low profile.

She'd seen the owners of the luggage shortly after, a native child and its parent, left to die when the platform had been abandoned by the Quailu. They'd found other bodies, proof that the company harvesting the gas couldn't be bothered to provide anything more than minimal evacuation transport at the end of their harvesting contract.

Her shock had renewed Eth's faith in the Quailu, at least in her case. If she could feel shame at how the Quailu treated a native species of the empire, perhaps there was some hope after all.

Mel was looking at him. "D'you think it's for us, sir?"

He nodded. "It's for someone using Lady Bau's missile tech, someone who'll recognise the context of the message."

Mel squinted. "She's the Imperial Grocer, isn't she?" His eyes grew wide when Eth looked at him. "Sorry, sir! No disrespect meant, I just…"

"Easy, Mel." Eth waved a dismissive hand. "You're on a Human ship now. No need to worry that word of your *insolence* will reach Melvin the Bastard anymore."

Mel looked away, his ears red.

"Look at me, Mel," Eth urged, waiting until he met his gaze. "Say 'Melvin the Bastard' for me."

Mel grimaced but his captain was staring intently at him now. He took a deep breath. "Melvin the Bastard."

"There," Eth leaned back spreading his hands. "You just made fun of a Quailu and you didn't magically drop dead!"

Mel nodded. "Melvin the *Bastard*," he repeated with far more feeling.

"Now you got it!" Eth slapped him on the shoulder. "Those jackasses bleed just like everyone else. Melvin's an enemy. It's your job to put a hole in him if you get half a chance, so making fun of his name is hardly a big deal anymore."

"It's still a big adjustment," Mel admitted. "Thinking of them as targets – as enemies."

"Yeah, well, some of them *are* enemies, so we're supposed to kill them. Some of them are our friends." Eth looked down at the missile.

"So I suppose we'd better go ahead and trust them…"

One

Rapiqur System

Mishak stared at the holo-projection standing in front of him. He was fighting to control the shock and rage. He realized his fists were clenched and he forced his hands to open. His emotions followed the example of his hands and he found himself able to speak again.

He knew he owed his awareness of physical cues to Oliv, who may have been killed by bounty hunters for all he knew. He forced that thought aside to deal with the current crisis.

"Say that again, Gibbal," he grated.

Gibbal, the minor lord of a neighboring system, the aggressor here at Rapiqur, leaned forward. "I asked you why either of us should listen to a lord who can't even be trusted to keep the faith with his own subjects." He said it loudly and slowly to ensure the insult was properly shoved in Mishak's face.

"Fornicate trust!" Mishak snarled, surprising even himself. He stalked forward, the two holograms retreating before him. "Don't concern yourself with what I've done. Worry about what I might do to *you* right now!"

"Slow, now," Eth urged, leaning over Lev's shoulder. "Remember to keep an eye on those sensor sweeps. We don't want any pitch waves active when they're looking right at us."

"Right, right," Lev muttered. "Y'know, it's not like I've been doing many stalking exercises since Hela qualified me. Last time I've even been in a shuttle was…" He trailed off, not wanting to mention Kurnugia.

"Nobody's been doing them, unless they work directly for Hela," Eth said, "and we didn't have time to bring any of them with us. So just do the best you can."

"They must have just arrived," Mel said. He was holding a mine and staring up at a holo-projection that mostly showed telemetry on his engines but also had a link open to the bridge so he could provide any useful engineering perspectives that might occur to him.

"Tons of path-residue still coming off their mains and the startup interference from their pitch drives is still all over the place. We got lucky. Should be fairly blind in the baffles."

The baffles, the hot mess of mixed spectra that made it so hard to see what was behind a ship, was a perfect approach vector for Human stealth ships and Hela's scouts spent endless hours practicing against large vessels. The Quailu, preferring honourable, face-to-face slugfests, paid little attention to the rear of their ships.

Or, at least, they didn't in the past…

"Reading a towed array!" Mel warned.

"Bet they made that SOP after you went and told them you'd kill two of his ships for every Human killed by bounty hunters," Lev said.

"Towed array's still not going to get a return off our hull, especially not in this soup," Mel said, sounding *relatively* confident.

"Can they use it to look for a hole in the soup?" Lev asked.

Mel just frowned.

"Sweep coming," Eth warned.

Lev cut power to the pitch drives again. "Should be able to coast the rest of the way in," he said. "We'll need to fire up again to avoid a collision, though. Timing it with the next sweep."

"So it's your choice," Mishak told Gibbal. "Either pack up and go home or our fleets will be firing at each other as soon as this transmission ends. I've had enough of these minor fights!"

To his horror, Eth shimmered into view next to Gibbal.

Eth held up a hand. "Looks like you've got a deadly game of hound-and-cheever going on here, so I won't keep you for long." He looked at Mishak. "I told you, two ships for every Human killed over that bounty."

This was the last thing Mishak needed right now. "I found who initiated that bounty and had it rescinded!"

"You did," Eth nodded, "but not before five of my people were killed at Kurnugia. That's ten ships you owe me. I'll take one today."

An alarm sounded.

"Lord, the *Stellar Storm*! She's broken in two!" the tactical officer shouted, spreading a feeling of alarm throughout the bridge. "No missile traces, no kinetics on the trace…"

"Well, I can see you're busy," Eth said. "I'll see you later, when I decide which ship will be number two." His holographic image glitched and faded, indicating the sender had just pathed out while still connected.

A blinking icon caught Mishak's attention. He was still broadcasting the conversation in the open…

To all the ships in the system.

Getting in the Spirit

Texas, Gulf Coast

Maeve sat atop the oldest of the test gantries, watching the sun set and trying to come to a hard decision. Her family had already exceeded the vision of a sustainable presence on Mars.

She'd driven some ground-breaking advances in propulsion but it seemed more of a side-note compared to what her predecessors had accomplished. The smart money insisted that doubling down on the red planet was the thing to do.

She took a long drag.

The smart money had just finished talking her ears off in a boardroom down nearer the ground. She was developing the opinion that it was more of an ironic name.

Now that there were millions of people living in two Martian cities, the trade routes were ripe for exploiting. She knew she could fill every ship to capacity in both directions. She had already put it in motion.

"But what's the challenge in that?" she asked the breeze.

She was raking in money but it seemed wrong to just leave it sitting in an account. The very thought made her feel restless. She wanted to put it to work.

She wanted Venus.

Mars still had its problems but the Martians didn't need her to sharpen their focus. They were dealing with issues such as bone density on their own and they were highly motivated, all things considered.

Venus. A chance to step away from the legacy of her family and make her own mark. Do something new and unexpected.

The sun was almost at the horizon.

She sucked in a sharp breath, eyes wide and fixed on the person she'd suddenly realized was standing on the steel-grid platform in front of her.

Gleb opened his eyes. She'd definitely taken note of his arrival, which he'd deliberately arranged so as to start off their talk with proof that he wasn't just some nutcase pretending to be from outer space.

His friends had been a little leery of the idea but they'd had to admit they were very skeptical (or downright disbelieving) until he'd teleported himself to a spot behind them in his apartment.

"Hi there," he began in a friendly tone. "I don't have an appointment, but if I could just have a moment of your time…"

Maeve looked at him for a half-minute, then took a long hard look at the hand-rolled joint in her right hand. Finally, she shrugged, turning a neutral gaze back to him. "Like it's gonna be of any use to say no to a hallucination…"

"Oh, well, I'm not…"

"So, you tell me what my spirit animal is or something?" she asked. "'Cause I need to be at a logistics meeting in half an hour, so we need to move this along."

"What the hells is a spirit animal?" Gleb asked her, completely flummoxed by her reaction.

"You call yourself a spirit guide?" She arched her eyebrows at him. "You new at this or something?"

"I… What?" Gleb replied helpfully. He shook his head, waving off her question with both hands. "Look, I'm not a… spirit-guy. I'm just a regular guy…"

"Who suddenly appears in my vision without making a single sound on that noisy steel grating?" She nodded sagely. "Yeah, that sounds totally legit." She tossed the joint. "Definitely not the Sonoma-Green making me see things…"

"You use that stuff before a meeting?"

"You did hear me say it was *logistics*, right? I have a whole division of experts to handle logistics. I'd be an idiot to think I should be telling them about their own specialty. They're a good team; they just need to see me from time to time so they feel like I'm keeping an eye on them."

"Okay." Gleb took a breath and launched into the points he'd worked on. "I'm not a hallucination. I just have the ability to teleport myself..."

"So," she cut in dryly, "just a regular guy, as you said..."

"All right," he conceded. "Maybe 'regular' was a bit of an overreach on my part but that's not what I came here to talk with you about."

"Really?" she replied in a tone that made it more of a comment than a question.

"Really," he confirmed. "I'm offering you tech in return for some help with researching and developing a prototype..."

She held up a hand. "Let me cut you off right there," she said. "You want me to make you a hover-car, don't you? I can't be cooking up fake inventions every time some hallucinatory spirit guide shows up. So why don't you just give me the spirit-questionnaire on how you did today and I'll promise to give you top grades as long as you just piss off?"

Gleb pressed his lips together grimly, sighing through his nose. *Why must the Universe always amuse itself at my expense?* "Look, this isn't the right time for this discussion. How about we reconvene in a day or so, when you've got a witness with you?"

She gave him an appraising look, suddenly not quite so sure. Finally she nodded. "Day after tomorrow, three o'clock, my office in L.A.."

He grinned, nodding. "Remember to have a witness. Preferably someone with a strong tech background."

"That doesn't really narrow things down, you know," she told him. "Not many of my employees lack experience with tech."

"Tech *development*," Gleb amended. Then he disappeared.

Maeve realized her bizarre visitor was gone. She looked down to where an office block waited for her, up the coast.

"Knew it," she said, half disappointed.

Problematic

Throneworld

Tashmitum and Mishak stood quietly, not quite sure if the elevator to Marduk's offices was bugged. Mishak's hand inched over and touched hers. She slipped her fingers around his and gave a gentle squeeze.

The doors slid open and Marduk's aide looked up, emanating mild annoyance at a sudden, unannounced visit. He quickly brought his feelings under control when he realized who had arrived.

He stood and bowed over his desk. "You were expected?" he asked politely.

"Not officially," Mishak conceded as they headed for the door. *Not at all, actually.* He managed a quick knock before his wife opened it and led the way in.

"Uncle," she greeted the emperor's Chief of Staff. "We have a serious problem."

Marduk cast one last glance at the holo-projection he'd been working in and then turned to face his unexpected visitors. He left the projection open, though, doubtless assuming that if he couldn't trust the emperor's daughter and son-in-law, then there wasn't much hope for the empire anyway.

"We?" He tilted his head, leaning toward them. "*We* in the personal or imperial sense?"

"Imperial," Mishak said. "Meaning my father-in-law may find himself out of work very soon if we don't sort this out."

"Speaking of my father," Tashmitum eased herself into a chair with a sigh, one hand coming to rest on her abdomen. "Where is he?"

"The emperor is… on a religious retreat," Marduk said stiffly.

Mishak opened his mouth but then shut it again with a sidelong glance at his wife. The frustration, however, was clearly felt.

Over the last few decades, the phrase 'religious retreat' had come to refer, euphemistically, to the emperor's habit of going into hiding when his paranoia got the better of him. No one questioned the phrase, not even the heirs apparent, who refrained more out of respect for Marduk.

The emperor, after all, was his oldest friend.

"No need to disturb him with this," Tashmitum said, "but it must still be dealt with. There is a risk of fracture. The empire is on the verge of breaking up."

"Separatists?" Marduk asked, surprised. "There are always a few houses pining for independence but they're hardly a threat. Once others see a separatist's holdings parceled out to his rivals, they lose their appetite for rebellion."

"We're not talking about isolated brush-fires," Mishak insisted. "We're seeing too many converging data-points for something so simple."

"What are you talking about?"

"We've been comparing intercept traffic from our forces as well as the data you've got access to," Tashmitum told him. "Really, Uncle, you should be more creative with your passwords!" She exuded a mood of gentle teasing.

"We've been seeing the same turns of phrase among houses that rarely, if ever, talk to each other," Mishak said, "and at least half of them have been engaging in suspicious activity – arms purchases, shifting procurement plans to new vendors closer to home…"

"Rumors of secret meetings," Tashmitum added. "Hints of serious backing from someone in the upper reaches of the nobility…"

"What would they eat?" Marduk demanded. "If we embargoed them, Bau would…"

He nearly stepped back in the face of the concentrated irony flowing from the two young nobles he'd practically raised by himself.

"Dear Gods, no…" he whispered. "She wouldn't! Certainly not when you stand to sit the throne one day? You saved her!"

"Eth saved her," Mishak replied quietly. "You know he did that on his own initiative when he figured out where my uncle was headed after the battle at Heliopolis."

"She's no fool," Tashmitum said mildly. "I'm sure she knows to whom she really owes her hide. She's even had one of them knighted."

"And she's been providing them with her advanced warheads," Mishak added darkly. "*Them*, not *me*. I'm sure you've noticed that they used those same warheads to deal with Shullat's latest folly at Arbella, but they were careful not to use them against me when they took their first installment of revenge…"

Marduk felt a surge of indignation at this recrimination from his former protégé.

"You're angry with me?" Mishak flared. "First, Rimush used my name to betray my best forces and then you use it, however obliquely, to launch a bounty on their heads?"

The anger grew. "I was cleaning up a mess you left untended!" Marduk growled.

"A mess that I didn't create but one that I might have other plans for!" Mishak snarled back.

"Enough!" Tashmitum shouted, startling them both into silence. "Folly is folly! No amount of argument can change what has been done. We need to focus on the future, on a very real but still undefined threat to the realm."

They looked at her for a long moment, then they met each other's gaze, contrition flowing.

Marduk sighed. "Send me the data you have on this. I have some people who might be able to find us the answers we need."

Trading

Maeve's office, just outside of L.A.

Gleb could see a man with slightly graying hair and a dark knit shirt, a plastic badge hanging around his neck. He slid back, reaching into the dimension that biology insisted was time and flowed back down into the space he'd seen.

He opened his eyes and the man was standing in front of him. "Did she warn you I might drop in?" he asked him.

The man dropped the file he'd been holding and leapt backward. "What the shit?" His hand went automatically to a weapon he wasn't wearing.

"I'll take that as a no." Gleb took note of the conditioned reflex and turned to Maeve who was sitting behind her desk, one hand on a keyboard. Her faint smile was hard to read.

"You're seeing this, right?" he gestured at her startled employee, who he then turned to. "You see me, right?"

"How the hell did you do that?" the man demanded.

"Do what?" Gleb feigned innocence.

The man shook his head, spreading his hands. He looked to Maeve for support.

"I'm just messing with you!" Gleb chuckled. "Some of my people can… relocate themselves with their minds. Sorry for the dramatic entrance but, if I'd just walked into your front office and demanded an appointment so I can trade world-changing tech with you, you'd think I was off my algorithms."

He turned back to Maeve. "So, I'm real, right?"

"Jury's still out," she muttered. "What do you think, John?"

"You know what's going on here?"

"Not by much more than you do. This is… What's your name?"

"I'm Gleb."

"She looked back at John. So, Gleb, here, appeared in front of me when I was in Texas a couple of days ago. I figured it was the Sonoma messing with me."

"Hey," John protested. "My brother grows that in a controlled environment. It's top-quality stuff!"

"C'mon, John. If you'd just blazed one before you walked in here, you'd be wondering too."

"I don't bring the stuff to work," he sniffed.

"Of course you don't," she agreed. "It's a legal intoxicant. When I met this guy, it was after hours, I had to get through a long, late meeting where somebody was bragging about how they fixed the EOQ for inanimate carbon rods and, more importantly, I *own* the company."

"Alright," John conceded, "fair enough but…" He nodded at Gleb. "… What are we doing here?"

"Gleb said he was offering to trade tech in return for help building a prototype," she explained. "Gleb, this is John McAdam. He leads one of our rapid-prototyping teams."

Gleb, coached by his friends, shook hands with John and Maeve, even though the HQE had a strong taboo against such casual contact with strangers.

This was the moment where John noticed the visitor was armored, including his hands.

Ironic that we have no qualms about sex with people we know, he thought, *but these people, despite their hangups, will touch anyone's skin as a greeting. Have they eradicated all viruses or simply abandoned common sense?*

"What sort of tech are we talking about, Gleb?" John asked carefully.

Gleb knocked a hand against his armored chest. "I brought my suit as a demonstration. It's based on nanites. They're entirely

85

reprogrammable." He held up his right hand and activated a code he'd set up that morning.

The armored glove flowed out of the way, exposing his hand. The nanites flowed like a tumbling river around his forearm before racing back into place, recreating the articulated plates that sealed his hand in from the vagaries of space.

He closed his helmet, a flow of nanites carrying the non-nanite elements with them. They created the housings for sensors and projectors and locked down the whole assembly in less than two seconds, leaving Maeve and John staring at the white Human skull patterned on the face of his armor.

It reopened just as quickly. "The nanites are controlled by an on-board processing unit and a programmable logic controller that passes the patterns to the nanites."

"Okay…" John stared at the suit. "And where, exactly, did you say you're from?"

Gleb frowned. "Don't think I said, yet. I'm from the Holy Quailu Empire."

Maeve came out from behind the desk, walking slowly over to Gleb. "Where is this… empire?"

He spread his hands. "I wish I could tell you. I came here, to Irth, the same way I arrived in your office. I think I came a long way, though. Coming here from San Diego barely took any energy at all but I froze the pool at a hotel when I travelled to your world."

"Our world," Maeve said quietly. "Who rules this Holy Empire of yours?"

"The Quailu rule," he said. "Why?"

"The processor in your suit, it was programmed by these Quailu… by aliens?"

He nodded.

"How do we know we aren't about to unleash an alien virus in our computers and shut down the whole damn planet?" she asked him.

"A virus?" Gleb frowned. "You mean harmful algorithms?" He shook his head. "That's not like the Quailu. They love to play their little games of intrigue but they use people, not programming code.

"Most code is locked down by the vendors anyway." He gestured at his armor. "This suit, for example, is covered by strict intellectual property rights. Any attempt to fiddle with the base code would result in a ban on any further sales."

"So we wouldn't be able to make any changes?" John asked.

"Oh, we make tons of changes," Gleb grinned. "Our lord ruled over a back-verse dust-ball where he picked up a few bad habits. He'd rather have effective, victorious forces than an honorable field of debris. He lets his Humans fiddle. We were cut off by most of the vendors a while ago."

"Aren't you undercutting your argument?" John asked.

"Not really. He lets us mess with the coding for ships." Gleb jabbed a thumb at his chest. "Us. His Humans. And we're mostly just making a few improvements to his capital ships or developing new classes of warship for our own use. We don't create any planet-crippling viruses.

"Our lord prefers a stand-up fight but he doesn't mind if we sneak around to the side in stealthy ships and slit a few throats, if it makes that stand-up fight a little easier. All those years on Kish have made him into a bit of a pirate."

"You keep mentioning your lord," Maeve said. "I'm definitely intrigued by your tech offer but I think you'd better start by explaining the political situation."

She gestured to a small boardroom table in the corner of the office. "After all," she said as they walked over, "we're just learning there's life out there and that it's organised into some kind of empire."

She moved to a machine on a sideboard against the wall of windows that gave a view of L.A. in the hazy distance. "Do they drink caffeinated beverages where you're from?"

Gleb nodded slowly, frowning. "Yeah. They have coffee, just like you have here. I had some the day I arrived and it was an eye-opener in more ways than one."

"So…" John moved over to the coffee machine, nodding his thanks at Maeve for the mug she handed him. "… You teleport yourself across the galaxy, assuming even that you're from *this* galaxy, and the first thing you do is pop into a coffee shop?"

"'Course not," Gleb retorted. "Before that, I was in the ComiCon costume contest. Came in third."

They both laughed, but they noticed he wasn't laughing along with them.

"Y'know," Maeve said speculatively, "I think he's serious."

"Got me a few hundred credits," Gleb admitted. "Doesn't matter where you are, a fella needs some coffee-money."

"And they have coffee," Maeve asked, "where you come from? How is that possible?"

Gleb took a deep breath, glancing up at the ceiling for a second before meeting her eyes. "I think the empire is already meddling with Irth. We know the Chironans were growing Humans earmarked for use on this planet. We just don't know why."

"Growing Humans?" John blurted.

"In a maturation-chamber," Gleb confirmed. "Very illegal."

"I should hope so! Are the… Chironans… different from the, who did you call them?" John asked.

"Quailu?"

"Yeah, those guys."

Gleb shook his head. "No. When I talk about the Chironans, I'm not referring to the natives of Chiron; I mean the Quailu nobles that rule the system. They might just be here to harvest new genetic data from a wild source."

"So…" John smirked, "… they're the guys behind all those stories about abductions… probes…"

"I've met one of the Humans they'd had illegally created. She said the others they had at Kwharaz Station for a new program were all female." Gleb shrugged. "Given my gene harvesting theory, it would seem there's a simpler way to get the… data… without arousing suspicion."

"Well, that got gross pretty quickly." Maeve handed Gleb a mug of coffee and waved him to a seat.

"The Chironans – are they aware of your presence here and will they try to interfere in your technology swap with us?" she asked as she sat.

Gleb lowered himself into a seat and took a drink to give himself time to think. "I'm pretty certain they have no idea I'm here," he finally said. "I didn't even know I was coming here. I was trying to escape from my ship during a battle. I'd set her to ram an enemy and I was trying to teleport to safety. Somehow I ended up here."

He shrugged. "As to the second part of your question, they probably would try to intervene if they knew I was talking to you. It would impact their local operation if you suddenly got too powerful to control."

Maeve and John exchanged a glance. "Powerful?" she asked.

Gleb nodded. "This tech," he said, gesturing at his suit, "is the basis for a lot of things. We use these nanites to grow ship's hulls. We can use them, in an emergency, to take the place of our gravity emitters, which allows us to create a weak engine, nowhere near as powerful as a proper pitch drive but it would get you to Mars, for example."

Both of them sat up straight at this. "You can show us how to make a ship from nanites that can reach Mars?" John asked. "How much acceleration can you give us?"

Gleb grimaced. "If we're using local gear to control it, I'd want to keep it down to something manageable, just so we don't cause the ship to fly apart on us. Maybe two standards?"

"What's a standard?" Maeve asked.

"Oh, yeah, sorry." Gleb sub-vocalised a command and a holographic image of Throneworld sprang up from his suit's projectors. "All measures are based on Throneworld. Imperial Standard gravity is roughly six percent higher than Irth's."

John whistled. "Just over two Earth gravities for constant thrust? That would take…"

"Less than two days!" Maeve finished for him. "At least when Mars is closest. Hell! We could even go at superior conjunction and not take more than a week!"

"Better hit the gym, though," John advised. "Be a long time to be pinned down by double gravity."

"Hang on." Gleb set his mug down with a grin. "You're missing out on an important fact. We can localize the effects of the propulsion plating."

"Yeah," John said. "That's how you make the ship move, but if it's moving at a constant 2 G's and we're inside…" He slapped his thigh. "Son of a bitch! 'Localised' you said. You can cancel out some of the acceleration inside the cabin?"

"Now you see why I want to go easy on the acceleration," Gleb said, grinning. "We need to see how far we can trust your local processors before we try something higher."

"Is it feasible to use this approach to provide full gravity in our Mars habitats?" Maeve asked. "We run into problems with bone density, which leads to no end of problems where pregnancies and childhood are concerned."

Gleb nodded. "That's no biggie. Mining colonies do it all the time on small moons, though they use proper emitters which give a better field. You'll want to avoid jumping too high or you'll hit your heads."

"How hard will this be to build?" John asked. "How hard is it to make the nanites?"

"Not hard at all," Gleb said. "In fact, that's the easiest part. My suit is designed for combat, so it has all the latest escape and evasion algorithms built in.

"As long as the processor is working, the logic controller is passing the instructions and at least a small amount of nanites are functional, you can use the suit to *produce* all the nanites you need." He nodded out the window. "We can go outside and make you a block of them right now if you don't mind a hole in the ground."

"That's handy," Maeve said. "So where do you see us needing to put in the most effort?"

"I'd say the power source. I've been looking at the tech on this world and it looks like nine Gigahertz is the top end for CPU's here. That's not quite what my suit is capable of but I figure a ship with a simple pattern can be held together and controlled with a couple of your CPU's. The pattern emitters can be cobbled together from commercially available components.

"It's the power generation that's going to need the most development." He shrugged. "No way around it. You guys are nowhere close to meeting the energy requirements."

"Hey," John protested, though he was grinning. "Fusion is just ten years away, it has been for fifty years!"

"This is what I'm talking about," Gleb shook his head. "Rubbing two atoms together like some savage in the forest…"

"You don't use fusion?" Maeve asked.

"Not unless I'm marooned on some ball of rock and need an emergency energy supply," he waved the idea away. "Our suits are programmed to build them, if needed, but don't waste your time on that…"

"Half a century our people have been trying to build a working reactor and you tell us not to waste our time?" John blurted out. "I think it might be kind of useful, all the same."

"Fine," Gleb threw up his hands. "When we set up a data transfer from my suit, I'll make sure you get the specs but I'm telling you it won't be more than a side project. I'm talking about *serious* energy, guys. Real 'meaning of the Universe' type stuff."

"The one thing I don't get," Maeve said slowly, "is what you plan to do with one of these ships once we've built them. You just gonna putz around the solar system? If you've come as far as you seem to think, I doubt a 2-G ship would get you home before your bones have decomposed."

"You're not wrong," Gleb admitted, "but you forgot to account for the Chironans. If they're here, I want to find them. They've got some way of getting out here from the empire and I want to slap them around and take it away from them.

"It's also a safe bet they've at least got some shuttles for getting to Irth from their hiding place. They might even have a few bigger ships, like a frigate or a cruiser or even a freighter." He chuckled.

"I could get us real engines, real grav-emitters. I have the patterns in my suit for a fast-attack corvette. I was commanding one up till the moment I found myself in that swimming pool in San Diego…"

"Hold on there," John cut in.

"Yeah," Maeve added. "Now you're talking about a military build-up and direct conflict with someone from your empire? I'm not sure we're ready for that. What the hell do we know about space-combat? When I woke up this morning, it was still considered quite the achievement that my family flies rockets between Earth and Mars and you want us stealing cruisers and building fast-attack corvettes?"

"Pretty much. Look, guys, the empire is a hot mess right now. My own lord is in line for the throne, *his* father is trying to carve out a small kingdom for himself and the corporation licensing the genomes of extinct species is on the verge of collapse because it's turning out they were selling rights to species that haven't died out at all.

"Whatever the Chironans are doing out here would hardly cause a blip in the news cycle. It's only a matter of time before they realize this for themselves, even though they're not particularly astute. I'd give it a year at most before they're parking a force in high orbit and demanding your surrender."

"I call bullshit!" John said angrily. "I mean, how do we know you're not just trying to scare us into helping you?" He set his mug down, the hot liquid splashing out onto the table. "I'd be surprised if…"

The mug shattered.

John jumped up from his seat but he still got hot coffee all over his crotch.

Gleb drained his mug, shivering. He pointed at the mug. "That's why they'll come," he told them. "Because they know some of our people can hop around the Universe like they have built-in path engines.

"And that we can kill with a thought."

Maeve stared at him. "Are you saying you did that to John's mug with your mind?"

"My mind and all the heat in your coffee pot," he said, nodding over her shoulder.

She turned and looked at the pot. It was covered in a tracery of frost on the outside, though it was already starting to melt from the bottom where the heat-pad was. She jumped in alarm when the glass shattered from the pressure of the frozen coffee.

"Energy is never free," Gleb said, "and neither is power. The Chironans must have realized by now that they're sitting on one of the most valuable resources in the Universe. Our people are the only ones who've ever shown this ability. Soon they'll try to bring us under control so our power will serve them.

"The price of our ability is either slavery or the fight for freedom." He gazed at the mess on the sideboard.

"Really regret breaking that coffee pot," he muttered, crossing his arms over his chest to conserve body heat.

Maeve was still staring at Gleb but it took her a while to notice how cold he was. She touched her ear. "Jules, our coffee pot broke. Can you bring in a fresh pot from the cafeteria? Thanks."

She got up and walked over to the sideboard, grabbing the huge chunk of brown ice and dropping it in the garbage. "You're sure the Chironans will try to seize Earth?" She turned to him. "It doesn't really leave us with a choice, does it? We're forced to fight."

"Well, there's no guarantee they'd enslave us," Gleb said, "but they'd take over, either way. You'd have to defer to any Quailu in any matter, as a member of a subject species…"

"Second-class citizens on our own world?" she growled, eyes flashing. "Tell me now, Gleb. Do you think we can actually stop these guys? I mean, we're not exactly a spacefaring people yet. We're barely on two planets as it is."

"It's not all doom and gloom…" Gleb trailed off as the door opened and a young man came in with a full coffee pot. He set it on the sideboard, then grabbed a paper towel and wiped up most of the glass shards.

He slid the pot into the brewer and turned to find Gleb standing next to him.

"Thanks!" Gleb said. "Really needed a hot drink."

The man smiled, glanced once at the strange armored suit the visitor was wearing and then left without another word.

"I like where you were headed before Jules came in," John prompted. "Let's make sure you finish that particular train of thought."

Gleb had drained a full mug by now and was pouring another. He nodded. "The Chironans sound frightening from your perspective because they're able to reach Irth and you can't reach Chiron."

He sat again, this time nursing his drink. "I've seen them humiliated before. They showed up at Kish, leading a coalition against my lord but the very fact that they had Human genomes in their data banks – something one of our Human teams found during a raid on Chiron – was enough to neuter their aggression, such as it was.

"Chiron is a minor house. They possess little force and even less sense. If you're going to get attacked by any faction in the HQE, you couldn't have picked a better one.

"They won't come with many ships, nor would they think there was any need to." He nodded to Maeve. "You said it yourself. You're crawling around the inner system with rockets. One cruiser, hells, even a single frigate would be enough to pacify this world."

He waved a hand over his head. "Park one ship in orbit, make a demand for surrender and then start blasting a few cities with kinetic drops… You got anything here that can stop them?"

"No!" Maeve said without missing a beat. "So, how do we?"

Gleb grinned. "Something small, I think. Understated… We get in close before they notice us, not that those improvidential lack-wits will think to look for hostiles here. Once we're in their baffles, we close, board and turn their ships into *our* ships."

He leaned in. "That's why we need this first ship, this barely working shit-wagon that can get us to wherever the Chironans have their base of operations for Irth. If we can steal enough gear from them, we have a chance of holding out against an attempt to incorporate us into their fief."

Maeve sighed. "This is a hell of a choice to drop in one person's lap," she said.

"We could present this to Congress…" John suggested archly.

She snorted. "Might as well have a giant welcome mat put in orbit. By the time they finish tacking on riders to the funding bill, we'd already be slaves."

"The government isn't effective here?" Gleb asked.

"Regardless of party, they pass laws to favor whoever gives them the most money. They even pushed a court case to make the process legal," Maeve scorned. "I have no qualms about ignoring them. They're the reason so many cities have been lost on the coastlines. Miami was half flooded before they finally started taking it seriously."

"You know," Gleb said, grinning, "this world might just be a good match for Chiron. If the other hundred or so governments on Irth are as bad…"

"Hah hah," Maeve replied dryly. "I'm in. Let's get moving on this right now." She turned to John. "Get your team to clear the decks. Toss whatever they're working on now and get us a working power plant."

John frowned slightly, darting a quick glance at Gleb. "Are we sure we're doing the right thing here? It feels like we're jumping in with both feet when we still don't have the full picture."

"That's a pretty accurate description," Gleb admitted, "but you may not have much time to think it over."

"We'll start work now," Maeve decided, "and keep asking questions as they come up." She looked back at Gleb. "Have you approached anyone else about this, any other corporations or officials?"

"No." Gleb shook his head emphatically. "My friends told me the best bet was to come straight to you. If I spoke to anyone else, they'd just slow things down."

She nodded. "I like your friends," she said. "Smart folks. You ready to start on this today?"

"Um… yeah. Sure!" Gleb looked at John who was getting up from his seat, looking a little shell-shocked. "I'll coordinate with John, then?"

"Yeah," John confirmed. "You said you're from San Diego, right?" He squinted. "At least, you're *currently* from there?"

Gleb nodded. "Got a place there."

"Perfect. My lab is under the old Scripps Ranch, just north of the city. I'm taking the loop there now, so you can hitch a ride with me."

A.G. Claymore

Council of... War?
Babilim Station

Eth looked out the window of the large conference room. Outside, the gigantic cargo yard stretched away into the hazy distance, the far side of the purpose-built commercial crater barely visible. Teams of Humans were bringing storage containers, abandoned for hundreds of thousands of years, to inspection platforms to find out what treasures might lay within.

He turned from the window. *They're busy, but that doesn't equal a purpose.* "So that's what we know," he told the assembled senior officers. "Bau has invited us to something but we don't know what it is."

"We don't think it's a trap, right?" Noa looked around at the others. "I mean, we like her, right? She's always played straight with us."

"She's still Quailu." Oliv took a meal-bar from the table. "I trust her as far as we can avoid testing her loyalties to the empire."

"Which is why we refrained from using her weapons against Mishak's ships," Eth said, walking over to stand at the end of the large table which had just had its legs cut down by more than a full cubit in order to fit its new users. "We don't want to imply she's hostile to anyone we're attacking."

"Except for Shullat," Father Sulak muttered absently, rooting through the upper reaches of his filthy oracle's robes. He pulled out a moldy strip of river-dragon fat with an expression of satisfaction.

Of all the empire's various intoxicants, fermented fat was the most common by far. Some versions even had a carefully cultivated mold that enhanced the flavor.

The strip in Sulak's hand, however, was just moldy from being kept near his armpit for gods knew how long.

"I don't think she'd be angry that we used her warheads to defend a part of her own fief," Eth replied, grimacing as the Quailu oracle took a bite, "and it reinforces our continuing bond. We risked our lives for her yet again."

"Even if the whole thing was cooked up to make us look bad in the first place," Sulak observed. He held up his hands. "Hey, I'm just playing Nergal's advocate here."

"Whoever set that up was attacking us both," Noa put in. "Does anyone doubt that Throneworld's fingerprints are all over it?"

"Maybe that's why she's reaching out," Eth mused. "I think all the separatist talk lately is leading back to her. After the last few months, she may see Mishak and Tashmitum as simply more of the same old empire."

"Effective rule by Marduk?" Sulak asked.

Eth nodded, a gesture the oracle had learned to recognize. "He's almost certainly behind the bounty on our people and he's been known to meddle in her business in an attempt to weaken her power as the 'empire's grocer'."

"We'd make an effective ally if she's building some kind of coalition or power-block," Hela said. "So what's our move, boss?"

Eth took a moment to consider his response, conscious of the eyes on him. He was designed to be a leader. The other Humans in the room were filling leadership roles of their own but they were still predisposed to follow his lead.

"I don't think she'd try to trick us like this," he finally said, "and, frankly, we need her as much as she might need us."

"We *are* running low on her advanced warheads." Noa shrugged.

"And we need her help with food," Sulak added. "She could probably help set us up with some automated farms here on Babilim. We have quite a few natural spaces within a day's walk of this room."

Eth nodded. "We're sending a delegation to Arbella."

"Are you sure you don't want to run that past Kolm first?" Noa smirked.

"That sphincter-face?" Oliv shuddered. "He'd just say no and blather about concentrating on our own problems rather than running off to get involved in someone else's troubles."

"So…" Noa turned his sardonic expression on her. "… He'd start saying we need to stay here and keep our heads down when he's been complaining that we're only staying here and keeping our heads down?"

"You have a politician in your midst," Sulak warned. "Few things are more dangerous. He'll keep throwing fat at the bulkhead until something sticks." He took another bite of the strip of moldy intoxicant.

"It always comes back to fat with your analogies, Father," Eth teased. "But you're not wrong. He wants power, which is the first hint that he isn't fit for it."

"In the old kingdom, political agitators were taken outside and shot with frozen balls of their own excrement," Sulak said helpfully. "You should consider it for this Kolm fellow."

Undertaking

North of San Diego

Gleb stepped off the loop-car, convinced now that he'd picked the right people to work with.

Maeve had been open-minded and decisive. Good qualities in a leader and she seemed to have good people working for her.

John had brought him here on a small transit vehicle that ran in a near-vacuum tunnel. It was open to the general public between San Diego, Los Angeles and San Francisco.

What wasn't open to the public was this small sub-station under the hills of an old ranch, just north of San Diego. The surface belonged, currently, to the Air Force – a quaint military branch, from Gleb's perspective – but the dirt beneath the base was another matter, especially for a company like Maeve's, considering it had built the loop circuit in the first place.

They walked through the embarkation airlock and across the broad platform where several pallets of cargo waited. Four armed guards were there, two at the main lab entrance and two patrolling the platform.

"Hi, John," one of the guards greeted him. "Thanks for the heads-up about our visitor." He nodded at Gleb. "Sir, if you'll just step over to the intake room, we'll get your retinas on file for future access."

Gleb followed him into a small office, taking the seat indicated by the guard.

"Just put this on and we'll be done in a few seconds." The guard handed him a headset with a dark gray assembly on the front that had two lenses.

Gleb put it on and did his best to hold his eyelids open. He heard a surprised grunt.

"Okay, you can take it off," the guard told him. "S'funny. Never saw such a… regular looking retina before. Seems denser than usual…"

Gleb took off the assembly and stood. He turned for the door to find John standing there, looking at him quizzically. Rather than ask questions, though, the prototyping director just jerked his head to indicate Gleb should follow him.

"What's the story on your retinas?" he asked quietly as they crossed to the main doors.

"I'm designed for combat," Gleb told him. "They made a few tweaks to the standard genome."

"Designed?"

"Yeah." Gleb shrugged as they came into hearing distance of the guards at the door. "Long story."

They took turns putting their faces in front of a scanner that stood on a pedestal to one side of the entrance and the guards waved them through.

John looked like he was about to ask another question but he was accosted the instant he passed through the doors.

"What the hell kind of sick joke are you pulling here, McAdam? Why'd you order every single lab to stop and clear?" a man in a light-blue isolation suit yelled. "I need those parts! Twenty percent efficiency boost, remember? What could possibly be more important than a gain like that?"

John chuckled. "You're about to find out, Eddie." He kept walking, Eddie falling in beside him.

"Not if I'm gone," Eddie said darkly.

"Don't be silly," John said. "We're not firing you! We're just taking this group in a new direction. One you'll be telling your grandkids about one day."

"Firing…" Eddie stopped for a heartbeat, mouth hanging open, then trotted to catch up with John and Gleb. "Dammit, John! I've been working on this idea for months and you shut it down just as we're about to set up the production systems?"

"Patience, Eddie," John soothed. "When you see what our new friend has to show us, you're gonna forget all about that manifold. Get your team and the other four groups assembled in the main auditorium. We'll be in shortly, and Eddie?"

"John?"

McAdam chuckled. "If you have an extra pair of shorts in your locker, bring 'em along. You might just need 'em."

He led Gleb into his office. "You up for a short teleport?" he asked, turning on a monitor on the wall opposite his desk. It showed people filing into a large room with rising banks of seats arrayed in front of a podium.

"Shouldn't be a problem," Gleb said. "You looking to convince them with a shock appearance?"

"Yeah. They're smart people but this is beyond anything in our experience, so it would mean a lot of talking before they take this seriously." He nodded at the screen. "When I introduce you, you can appear?"

"Sure, as long as you don't mind me seeing through your eyes first. I can't just jump in blind."

"The view on this monitor isn't enough?"

"No." Gleb gestured at the image on the screen. "Where the hells is that room from here? I need a Human link. I need to connect with your perceptions before I remove myself from here and replace myself in that room."

"That's wild." John shook his head. "Hold on…" He frowned. "Is that how you got to Maeve's office this afternoon?"

"Yeah, why?"

"She had to go to the can ten minutes earlier," John said. "That's why!"

"The can?"

"Yeah, you know, food goes in one end and…" He tilted his head, squinting at Gleb. "You guys have to eat, right?"

"Oh, hells!" Gleb covered his mouth. "I got lucky, then."

"Yeah, I'd say so," John agreed. "I doubt we'd be standing here right now if you'd been a few minutes early. I think we need to make that a new social protocol for this partnership of ours. If you plan on using our perceptions, you need agreement and a timeframe.

"If I know you're about to show up, I can hold it…"

"Sounds good."

"Alright, everyone settle down!" John shouted as he walked into the auditorium. It was an optimistic demand, he realized. Every team-leader in the room was shouting for his attention.

Next time we get a visiting Human from an alien empire and decide to start a revolutionary project with him, he thought wryly, *I'll have the meeting first, rather than telling everyone to shut down while I'm still halfway here on the loop.*

Drawing on his formative years in the military, he braced his belly muscles, filled his lungs and committed all that air to just two words. "Shut up!" he roared.

The clamor died but he knew it would start again very quickly if he left room for it. "This is an emergency situation! Now shut your cake-holes and sit down!"

It was the kind of tone he'd used on the parade square. It wasn't the sort of thing you used with a room filled with creative geniuses but he figured they would get over it once they heard what he had to say.

"Everybody in this room has a level-three clearance at the very least, given the kind of contracts we handle for the government." He stepped to the middle of the stage, ignoring the podium and its microphone. He felt it would take away from the moment to use it.

"Keep in mind that what I'm about to tell you is highly classified information. Not a single word about it outside this facility or I'll hear about it, understood?"

They all just exchanged quizzical glances.

"I asked if you understand," he said, pointing at Jenkins, in the first row on the right. "Jed, stand up and tell me if you understand."

It might have been overkill, but he'd rather make sure he started off with a strong impression.

Jenkins stood. "Whatever you need, John. You know I take security seriously." He gestured at his seat, a questioning look on his face, and John nodded for him to sit.

"Thanks, Jed. Now let's finish the first row and work our way through to the back. Emma?"

Emma stood and made the same declaration, though her expression indicated a healthy dose of skepticism over the need for this performance.

By the time the last staffer sat, John had sorted out his plan for this meeting. Another deep breath.

"A few hours ago, I was talking with the boss in her office," he said. "It suddenly became apparent to me that there was someone standing between us." He paused for a moment.

"It's disconcerting, believe me. I thought I'd lost my marbles but, all of a sudden, there was this guy standing there, four feet away, in some kind of armored suit."

He grinned at them. "By now, I'd be disappointed if most of you didn't think I'm off my rocker. Like I said, the same thought crossed my mind. The thing is, Maeve was talking to the guy so, either we're both crazy and can somehow share some kind of mutual hallucination, or…"

He had to chuckle at the looks on their faces. "Or it's real. Now's a good time, I suppose. Nobody's going to absorb anything else until we get buy-in. Gleb, I'm just gonna settle my eyes on this spot to my right. Any time you feel like showing up…"

It was just like earlier in the office. He just suddenly noticed that Gleb was there.

So did everyone in the room. After a moment to realize that what they'd just 'noticed' wasn't at all normal, there was a buzz of voices and a rustle of mildly startled movement.

John gave Gleb a friendly nod then turned to the audience. "See what I mean?" he asked them. "Not necessarily frightening but it's definitely unsettling."

He gave them a moment to regain some calm, though the buzz only dropped so far on its own. "Here's the broad strokes," he said loudly, bringing the group under control again. "There's life out there.

"Our friend, here, is from something called the Holy Quailu Empire." He looked at Gleb. "I got that right?"

Gleb nodded.

"One of the empire's factions is up to shenanigans here on Earth and it probably won't be long before they decide it's a good idea to openly take over and enslave the lot of us."

That wasn't strictly the only possibility but he figured it would help keep them motivated. "The good news is that Gleb has some pretty impressive tech and he's willing to work with us to develop that tech into working ships.

"There's a chance," he added, holding up his right hand, thumb and forefinger a half inch apart from each other, "a small chance that we can stop the meddling bastards. Apparently, we're dealing with one of the less impressive groups in this empire.

"If we can build a power-plant from the specs Gleb has on his suit's CPU, we can take the first steps toward saving the planet. We won't go into any further details on the overall strategy because, sooner or later, someone talks. Someone always talks."

He turned back to Gleb. "Everybody, this is Gleb. Gleb, this is our team. You want to explain what they're going to be working on?"

"I'll give it a try." Gleb turned to the crowd. "Keep in mind that I'm not an engineering officer," he warned the assembly, "so don't expect any detailed explanations. I'm just a ship's captain."

He activated a holo interface and re-sized it to fill the space over the center of the stage. The room broke out in a collective gasp of astonishment as an image of a ship's generator sprang into three-dimensional view.

It was faded and slightly glitchy because an EVA suit's emitters were never intended for large-scale projections but it had enough resolution for everyone to get a good initial look at their new project. Gleb set it to an exploded view, showing the interior structure.

"This, essentially, harvests energy from the vacuum of space," he explained.

"I hope you're not trying to sell us on zero-point energy," a smug voice cut him off. "That's not possible!"

"Really?" Gleb asked mockingly, eyes wide. He held a finger to his lips. "Let's keep that quiet, OK, cause if my fast-attack corvette had known she wasn't allowed to harvest energy from space itself, she would have stopped working long before she got destroyed at the Battle of Kish!"

"Harry," John said in a warning tone, "what did we say about using absolutes to shoot down ideas in this facility?"

Harry fumed amidst the laughter of his colleagues. "We're not supposed to…"

"And what will I do if it happens again?"

Harry sighed. "You'll kick my smart balls so hard they'll plug up my smart mouth for me?"

"So I'm giving you a choice, Harry. How about you listen to the guy who crossed the vastness of space using only his mind?"

"Hey," Harry blurted, suddenly surprised. "Why does he look so Human?" His hands dropped to cover his crotch as he darted a glance back at John.

"Because we *are* Humans," Gleb replied. "The empire believes us to be an extinct species, so they've been growing models like me for thousands of years. If they had any idea how many freely reproducing Humans there are on this planet, they'd be… very concerned."

"Satisfied, Harry?" John asked sweetly. "Good. Now, Gleb, what sort of tolerances are we looking at for these parts?" He waved up at the exploded view.

"Long story short, John, the equipment to make this generator doesn't exist on this world. I looked for it before coming to you." Gleb nodded at the assembled teams. "These guys need to make the machines that make the machines that, maybe, make the parts.

"It's like giving you a stone hammer and telling you to make an integrated circuit."

"But knowing the path gives us an advantage," John mused. "We don't have to stumble through the random advances of the industrial revolution; we can just jump to the exact steps needed." He looked up to where Fran Holloway was sitting.

The manager of the Archimedes Team had a light in her eyes. "We'll need to draw up a machine-bloodline," she said eagerly.

"Starting with the ones that build the final parts, then we work back from there."

"That leaves the ship's processors and the interface that transmits the ship's pattern to the nanites. I want us using second-gen gear; none of that newly released garbage that still isn't stable enough to keep a computer working properly. The last thing we need is for the hull to dissolve on us while we're halfway across the solar system."

"What about propulsion?" a voice called from the back of the room.

Gleb projected an image of a pitch drive and exploded the parts. "This is a pitch drive. It's about twice as difficult to manufacture as the generator, so we won't be wasting our time on it just yet."

He changed the image to show a scout-ship but with a plate of nanites attached to the front like a shield. "We can use basic nanites, in a specific arrangement – the closest term in your language would be meta-material, though it's not exactly what we're doing here – to create an artificial gravity field."

He looked at a woman in the front row and reached out with his right hand. "Can I borrow that fruit?"

She glanced at the person on her left then, with a shrug, handed over the apple she'd been about to bite into.

Gleb activated an isolated code fragment from his Escape and Evasion menu and tied it to the nanites covering his right arm. The room sighed in appreciation as the previously solid armor suddenly flowed like a granular fluid.

It set up a flat plate, roughly a half-meter squared, supported above the floor by four organically-branching trusses of the same material. A single, flexible tendril of nanites kept the assembly connected to the power-cell in the suit.

"This will be a very short demonstration," he told them. "I don't want to drain my power-cells."

He activated the newly formed gravity plate and placed the apple beneath it. The room exploded with excitement as the apple floated between the plate and the floor.

Gleb reached for the apple but it tumbled through an anomaly in the projected field and bounced out onto the floor. He shut down the plate and recalled the nanites. They flowed back onto his right arm as he bent down and retrieved the apple with his left hand.

"Sorry about that." He handed it back to the woman.

"Now keep in mind," he said, holding up a warning hand, "that I'm just a combat-guy trying to explain something that our engineer described for me once when we were heavily intoxicated. Imagine you trying to explain one of your rockets to that guy with the stone axe that you've asked to build an integrated circuit."

He grinned at them. "No offense! I'm the guy with the axe in that analogy."

They chuckled, most of them indulgently.

"When you channel energy through a properly configured emergency grav-plate, it creates a false signature. It fools the Universe into thinking there's a lot of mass in front of the plate."

"But how does it work?" the woman with the bruised apple asked him.

"I asked Noa the same question," he told her. "I'm probably making the same face that Noa did at the time."

He stared at the apple in her hand. "Noa told me that gravity is not so much a force as it is an outcome." He looked up, meeting her eyes.

"A function of probabilities," he added.

Her eyes widened. "The probability of a quantum particle to be in a given position?"

He had to wait for the suit to translate 'quantum'. He nodded. "Yes. That and information. Every bit of space, every little chunk of matter has its own information, like a manufacturer's data-sheet. It's like advertising. Everywhere you go in the Universe, you're bombarded with information.

"A particle might find itself in an adjacent position at any given instant but it needs a place to go. The 'advertising' is what lets it know what the options are."

"So you use your grav-plating to…" she smirked at him, "…put up a few billboards?"

He smiled. "That's how I would have explained it," he agreed. "But then Noa would have spent hours correcting me with a more exact description. Anyway, that advertising has a limit to its range. The closer you get to a massive body, the denser the data gets, hence the acceleration as you fall down a gravity well."

He looked up at the rest of the group. "Any questions?"

Silence.

"Well, that is a first." John glanced up at the ceiling. "This group with no questions? Hope the camera caught this!"

He clapped his hands. "Alright, now you know why I tossed a dead rat in your stew. Clear the decks and get ready to build Doc Holloway's first designs. Harry, set up an interface with the processor in Gleb's suit and get the specs onto our server, then I want you figuring out how to create our own control scheme for the nanites: CPU's, pattern transmitters, backups…

"You all know the drill, people! If you aren't already assigned to something, put your name on the list and somebody will snatch you up. Even if you're just doing a pizza run or popping out to Compu-Shack to grab some wifi repeaters, you're still helping to save the planet! Let's show some energy!"

The assembly broke up into small groups moving to the exit, chattering excitedly. More than one glance was directed Gleb's way.

Harry came over, hand out. "Name's Harry," he said, "though I think John already mentioned it. Let's get you linked up to our network."

Gleb fell in beside him as he headed for one of the less-crowded exits. "Does John really kick people in the balls?"

"Hmm? Oh, that's just a figure of speech, probably…"

"A figure of speech?"

"Yeah. Kind of like 'I'd like to lure you to my wine-cellar with the promise of a rare vintage and then brick you up in a back corner where nobody can hear your screams'…"

Gleb walked in silence for a few moments.

"You have some strange customs on this world…"

Fitting In
Bau's Palace, Enibulu

Urukh shoved the dead bodyguard into a reclamation chute. The body would be identified as organic matter and automatically sent to a composting vat. He stood and did a few quick stretches to calibrate his victim's armor to his own body.

"Firmware," he ordered the suit. It was already cleared for system access by its former wearer but one scan of Urukh's retinas and it would go into a full lockdown, trapping him inside.

Those scans happened several times a day, so he had to move quickly. He pulled the suit's on-board copy of the dead guard's retinal scans and replaced them with his own, stored on a small data-dot in his sinuses.

There was still the central system's copy of the proper retinal image but it was less secure than the software vendor's claims might otherwise indicate. With the right snippets of code, the new image could be piggybacked on a security-check from central.

The new retinas could be sent back with a pre-emptory priority coding. The image would replace the original one mere nano-seconds before the comparison took place.

He set aobut altering the armor-wearer's history creating a background for himself as a new backup member of Bau's personal security detail, but one who now sat at the top of the call-up list. Like the image of his retina, the new data would slip into the central system without detection. It was the perfect cover.

She'd just lost a guard, after all…

He took a deep breath and then stepped out of the small sleeping room that had belonged to the former owner of his new suit. The suit, before he'd altered it, had shown a summons for her team. As soon as the dead guard was found to be absent from the team, Urukh would be getting an urgent call.

The Lady Bau was going somewhere and he'd be in the perfect position to hear what the old bat was up to.

Bad Timing

The Odessa Terrace Apartments

"Gleb... You in there?"

Gleb opened his eyes. He looked at his clock. *Fornication!* He hadn't set an alarm last night but he didn't expect to sleep till eleven in the morning.

"Yeah," he called out, "Slept in." He stretched.

Kace popped his head around the door-frame. "S'alright," he announced. "He's decent... enough..."

Kace, Dex and Aberdeen trooped in.

"So lesson one," Aberdeen teased, "is that a big important ship's captain can sleep whenever the hell he wants to?"

"Sorry, guys." Gleb sat up, taking care to keep the bedsheet in place on his lap. "I don't know why I overslept. I never do that."

"I might have the answer to that," Kace took a pen from the nightstand and leaned over, using the pen to pick up something from the floor like a detective with a piece of evidence.

He straightened, a black pair of soft cotton panties dangling from the end of the pen. "Cute but not overly racy," he offered in a clinical tone. "Possibly suggesting a chance encounter..."

"Gleb," Aberdeen exclaimed, "I get that the girl you left behind was still just a friend but, with everything that you've got going on right now, stranded on Earth..."

"Working to build a functioning ship," Kace added.

"Planning a *war* with the Chironans," Dex said.

"And teaching us about Imperial politics and ship-to-ship tactics," Aberdeen continued, "where do you even find the time to hook up with some local girl?"

"Yeah," Dex grinned. "Who is she? Someone from this building?"

115

Gleb looked helplessly at the flimsy garment dangling from Kace's pen. *Who indeed?* No wonder he'd slept in. No wonder he felt so relaxed or, rather, he *had* felt relaxed.

For the second time that morning and more appropriately to the evolving situation…

"Fornication!" he muttered in Imperial Standard.

"Huh?" Dex tore his gaze from the underwear to look at his friend.

"It's happening again." Gleb sighed, shaking his head.

"What is," Aberdeen demanded, "girls throwing themselves at you?"

"No," he said, suddenly tired again. "When I was on an enemy ship, pretending to be one of their contraband Humans, someone thumped me on the head pretty hard. It has to be what caused this because, after that, I started blacking out."

"Blacking out?" Dex glanced at the others. "You mean you pass out and fall down, or…" He darted a glance at what Kace was still holding up. "Were you still doing things and couldn't remember?"

"Still doing things," Gleb admitted. "I sabotaged a door-control so a jackass would get a bad shock and I think I set up some kind of under-market deal with a junior officer as well.

"Sometimes I'd be walking toward someone and suddenly find myself three paces closer. It also temporarily dampens my… abilities each time. I don't think Other-Gleb knows about them.

"The last time this happened was at the Battle of Kish. I'd just set my ship to ram the enemy and nearly didn't make it off in time. I was starting to hope it was over with."

"What's the last thing you remember?" Aberdeen sat on the edge of the bed.

Gleb stared at the foot of the bed. "Someone from the lab dropped me out front. I came inside, pressed the button for the elevator…" He squinted, his right hand coming up to his ear.

"There was heat," he said cautiously. "My right ear… someone's breath…"

"And then?" she prompted gently.

"And then…" He looked up at her. "And then, I heard you calling my name this morning." He saw the look on her face and he blushed. "Calling to see if I was in my room, I mean. Just now…"

"So you don't remember her at all?" Aberdeen asked. "She could be anybody, from anywhere… The person who dropped you off from the prototype lab, even…"

Gleb shivered. "Gods, I hope not! Even my alter ego wouldn't like the sight of Harry in those." He nodded toward Kace.

Kace laughed. "We must ride throughout the kingdom!" he declared with gusto. "When we find who they fit…"

"Stop waving those around, you idiot!" Aberdeen was leaning back. "Put them back where you found them for God's sake!"

"What the hells is he even talking about?" Gleb turned to Aberdeen, assuming correctly that she was a better barometer of local custom than either Dex or Kace.

"Is that acceptable behaviour on Irth? If I go down to the courtyard and ask random women to try those on, will I find our mystery woman?"

"Yeah," Aberdeen confirmed. "She'd be the one that punched you in the face." She turned to glare at Kace until he finally returned the garment to where he'd found it.

She turned back to Gleb, leaning in to put a hand on his shoulder. "Promise me that you won't take any advice from these two idiots about anything related to this girl or any items of her clothing you may find, OK?"

"OK," he agreed, "but this is just a whole new level of complication I didn't need."

"That's putting it mildly!" Kace blurted. "You need to pay close attention to the people around you now. Somebody smiles at you and you just nod and keep walking, you might have just insulted your mystery girlfriend."

"He's right." Aberdeen sighed. "After a random encounter like this, she's probably wondering if it was a mistake. Should she say hello? Why didn't you say anything when you bumped into her in the lobby later today?"

"Yeah," Kace nodded solemnly. "She's gonna be all fragile and vulnerable…"

"Gleb?" A voice, deep but delicate and smooth, called from his living room.

Everyone turned in time to see an attractive young woman with dark brown hair in a blue camouflage uniform step through the door. She was tying her hair up into a bun. "Hope you don't mind," she said. "You insisted on giving me a biometric pass last night…"

"Well…" Gleb was flailing desperately. "…Seemed like the least I could do, considering…"

She laughed and somehow it was both deep and high-pitched at the same time and Gleb felt like his eardrums were getting a massage. His shoulders relaxed a fraction.

"You're gonna claim you owe *me*," she asked. "Last night was enough to keep a girl going for at least a week… if she *had* to, that is…"

She stepped past Dex. "I think I left something here in my rush to get ready for work earlier. I was hoping to sneak in and get it back before you thought I was marking territory or something…"

She edged past Kace and reached down. "Yep. Right where you tossed them last night." She put them in a cargo pocket on her leg.

"You know I had to climb up on the dresser to get my bra off the ceiling fan?" she asked. "Thought for sure I'd wake you but you just kept snoring away."

"Umm…" Gleb said wisely.

"I gotta get back to the base," she said, edging past Kace again. "Supposed to be in the air in less than two hours…"

She stopped at the bedroom door. "Don't be a stranger! Love that hair, by the way!"

This last was to Aberdeen who flushed. "Thanks!" she called to the woman who was already at the apartment's main door.

"Then again," Kale muttered, "some gals are a little more pragmatic…"

"You might want to tell her everything," Aberdeen suggested.

"Because his alter ego had wild monkey sex with her?" Kace grimaced. "We might end up having to tell half the women in San Diego."

"What?" She wrinkled her nose at him.

"He's only been here a few weeks and he's already found himself a beautiful Latina goddess. What if Alter-Gleb goes full jock and starts chasing after every girl in sight?"

"So…" Aberdeen finally looked from Kace back to Gleb. "… I'm suggesting you tell her because of her uniform. She's a Navy lieutenant and she's an aviator. If you're looking for a potential new recruit for the ships you plan on stealing from the Chironans, she's probably a good choice."

"Oh," Kace started to cut in, "she's definitely…"

"Don't!" Aberdeen warned. "Still, she does deserve to know who she was with last night. I'm not sure it'll bother her all that much, though. She seems very…"

"Like the women I'm used to back home," Gleb said. "Maybe that's what triggered me to glitch again. Too bad it didn't wait to happen until after…"

"Can't say I blame you." Aberdeen glanced at the door the young woman had just left through. She looked back to see the three men all looking at her. She flushed.

She cleared her throat. "So, you ready to run us through some basic ship-to-ship tactics now or are you all worn out from the freaky night you don't even remember?"

"You gonna get out of my room and let me get dressed first?"

On the HQE's Decline
Arbella System

"Getting a tic through the platform's beacon," the communications officer announced. "Looks like the others have arrived for the meeting."

The 'tic' was a simple bit of very specific static that Eth's advance scout had sent up using the ancient gas-harvesting platform's locator beacon. One tic was the pre-arranged signal to indicate the attendees had shown up.

Eth closed his eyes and reached up through the fourth dimension, finding the common connection between himself and the Human he'd sent down to the platform yesterday. The connection he made allowed him to see the scout's report, typed onto his HUD, as if the intervening thousands of kilometers of swirling gas didn't even exist.

A quick scan of the report showed him the numbers. He looked past the HUD to the tiny figures disembarking from their shuttles.

The scout was on the same tower they'd used for overwatch when they'd rescued Bau from this station during a previous fight with Shullat and Uktannu.

Using his scout's vision, he selected a spot ten meters in front of Bau and slid into it.

She and her entourage kept walking for a few moments until they realized Eth was now in front of them.

There were rumors. Urukh had mostly scoffed at them. The part about some kind of empathic or even telepathic ability was absurd enough for a native species like Humans but the ability to suddenly appear out of thin atmo? Utterly ridiculous…

And yet, a Human was suddenly standing a few meters ahead of them and he wasn't there a heartbeat ago. *Some trick of optics,* he told himself but it did nothing to dispel the flood of supernatural dread coming from his 'fellow' bodyguards.

Even if it was nothing but clever trickery, it was damnably effective. The mood eased, taking its cue from Bau who, though just as startled as the other Quailu, had no fear of this Human.

Urukh inclined his head toward her. *No,* he thought. *That's not quite right. She's genuinely fond of this wretched creature!* He fought to keep his disgust from showing and fell into step with the rest as she resumed her progress.

The Zeartekka Queen and her entourage, walking to their right, might as well not exist at all. No emotions came from their notoriously closed minds, if they felt any emotions in the first place. Half of her guards, fliers, swooped around her group in intersecting patterns.

He schooled his emotions, bringing them under strict control so he could have the mental privacy to concentrate on his job. Most Quailu mastered their emotional output by the time they reached their first decade but an operative like Urukh had to take it to the next level.

All Quailu possessed the unique ability to put half of their brain to sleep at a time. Some were able to use that discrete functionality to partition one side of their brain as the 'open' half, giving off the expected emotions while the other half did the scheming in private.

Marduk would be very interested to know he was right. The old gal was consorting with Humans, just as he'd surmised. They'd saved her life, right here on this very station, and she seemed to have developed some irrational sentimentality over the incident.

Any decent Awilu would have simply accepted such service as their due, feeling no reciprocal debt from natives not even a part of their own fief. It was a possible point of attack if Marduk decided on a bit of old fashioned character assassination…

He nearly stopped walking when he realized the Human was staring directly at him. Urukh shuddered. This one was as much an empty shell as the Zeartekka. What quirk of fate had drawn its attention?

Eth fought the urge to smile. It was a mistake to stare at the infiltrator but he'd picked up his thoughts and wanted to make sure he knew which face went with the treachery.

He turned to Bau, releasing complimentary emotions. "My lady! It's been far too long! I'm gratified by your invitation, all the more so by the clever way in which it was delivered."

He turned to the Zeartekka Queen and bowed.

"Your grace," Bau said, "allow me to introduce Ethkennu of Kish."

"I counselled against your invitation," the Hive-Queen said bluntly. "Though some of your species are rumored to have access to impressive abilities, your numbers are few and likely to dwindle quickly, if it comes to a fight."

Eth allowed a smile at this. If you needed one constant in this Universe to hang your faith on, you could do a lot worse than the blunt nature of the Zeartekka. The Queen would never dissemble or lie to advance her aims.

A Zeartekka always said what it was thinking and screw you if you didn't like it.

"Your grace," Eth greeted her, bowing once again. "I hear you're embarked on a path that will almost certainly lead to open conflict."

"Where did you hear that?" the Queen chittered in consternation.

"From you," Eth said, "just now." He turned back to Bau, who was amused by the exchange, but mostly out of a need to ease the stress of the moment.

"You're into something risky, my lady." He gave her a roguish grin which he was pretty sure she could recognize. At least, she should be able to tell that he was grinning, if not discern the specific flavor of the expression. "If you're thinking of including my people in it, then I'm flattered!"

She laughed at this. "You're part of the reason for what we're doing," she told him. "My people are complacent. It comes from being on the top of the heap for so many millennia.

"The last time we were here, you changed that. You forced me to re-examine my own attitudes."

"And what have you found?"

"Our people need to face new challenges. We're stagnating, falling into decay so gradually we don't even notice. New ideas terrify my people…"

"I have some experience with that," Eth interjected dryly. "When some of my people began to change, the empire turned on us with a vengeance."

"We're breaking from the empire," the Zeartekka Queen buzzed. "We also know what it is to be reviled by our 'betters'."

"And what, your grace, do you need from Humans?"

"Varangians," the Queen hissed. "The emperor has his Varangians. We need to balance that."

"You want us to hold off a Varangian incursion?"

124

Bau shook her head, a very Human affectation for a Quailu noble. "The Varangians keep the peace in the empire. If my house forces or the Queen's troops try to fill that role in our new republic, then those who consider joining us would see us as just another group of tyrants.

"What objections would they have to you as the keepers of the peace?" Bau concluded.

Eth had promised himself that he would maintain a level of detachment from whatever Bau had in mind. He didn't want to get dragged into some futile venture when his people were still struggling to find their way forward in an empire that seemed to want them all dead.

And here was Bau, dangling a damned good future in front of him. It was more than just a place to belong, it was a crucial role for his species. What the Varangians did for the HQE, Humans could do for Bau's republic.

This was no futile venture. If Bau and the Zeartekka were backing this, it would probably be too big for the empire to put down.

If Eth and his people joined it, they could probably dictate terms to the emperor...

He liked the idea. There was no thought of bringing it back to Babilim for discussion. Eth was designed for leadership and his people were designed to accept his role.

They could fill the leadership role as well but they each had their own specialties. Eth was one of the few purpose-grown leaders in his small renegade group and he was, by far, the pre-eminent member of that small cadre.

"We're in," he said simply.

"Oh!" Bau floundered slightly. Having been ready to sell Eth on the concept, she was suddenly caught between gears but the Queen rescued her.

"Perhaps I was wrong about you," she croaked, chittering with amusement. "Your kind are more decisive than I anticipated. Now that you have joined us, there are more decisions to be made."

"Indeed, Your Grace, but first…" Eth raised his right arm and pointed toward Bau's entourage. "…That one is not what he seems."

Urukh felt the hairs on the back of his neck stand on end. The Human was aiming a finger straight at him. *How does it know?* His hand started to drift automatically toward the grip of his sidearm but then it froze in place.

He tried to look down at his mutinous hand but his head had apparently joined the rebellion as well. The fear swamped him now, the sweat prickling his skin like thorns of ice. His body began to shiver.

"How do you know this?" Bau demanded, her surprise mingling with that of the other bodyguards.

"Sources and methods, my lady," the damnable Human admonished her gently. "If we are to support each other in this venture, there will be things I cannot reveal without rendering them useless."

Bau turned to the captain of her guard. "How long have you known this operator?"

"He's a replacement, mi'lady," the commander admitted, clearly nervous. "I'd never seen him before we boarded your ship to come here."

A loud, deep thrumming sound assaulted Urukh's ears.

He gasped in pain as viciously sharp talons sank into his shoulders, easily piercing the gaps between his armor plates and sinking into his flesh. He'd thought the pain was intense but it seemed to increase a thousand-fold as the Zeartekka guard lifted him from the decking with a deeper buzz of wings.

"Lady Bau," the Hive Queen rattled angrily. "If you have no objections, I will dispose of this traitor for you."

Bau looked to the Human, who shrugged. "He's from Marduk," the horrid thing told her. "We know all we need to about him. He serves no purpose that we care about."

The indignity of it! Urukh nearly forgot about the searing pain as he was borne away from the group by the unreadable flying bodyguard. *A princess of the realm hands my fate over to a native Human?* The doomed spy even managed to overlook that he was being dispatched by a native Zeartekka, so angry was he at the insult.

The pain in his shoulders lessened as the talons were withdrawn but his relief was short-lived. He'd been tossed toward the atmospheric shielding along the side of the massive station.

He passed through the energy field, his suit snapping shut just before the transit, and then the gravity of the gas giant took over. The suit had saved him from the toxic gasses outside the station but knew it was only saving him for a far worse fate.

He fell, accelerating at a slightly faster rate than Imperial-Standard. The suit, may it rot in the underworld, projected a helpful estimate of the time left before it would fail.

It wasn't even very long. His life wasn't flashing before his eyes but, even if it were, he doubted he'd have gotten through much of it.

The buffeting was getting heavier, the gas getting denser. The pressure on his suit was increasing rapidly.

The joint at his right knee failed first, a jet of highly pressurised gas searing through bones and flesh before the shockwave filled the rest of the suit, shattering him in an instant…

"You destroyed one of Mishak's ships." Bau turned to Eth as the guard returned to hover near his Queen. "I noticed that you didn't use my weapons."

"The entire empire would have noticed if I had," Eth replied, sensing her approval of his explanation. "His betrayal didn't involve you. I had no wish to imply that our revenge does."

"You will have to set your revenge aside," the Zeartekka Queen rattled. "As our military leader, your actions now reflect entirely upon all those who join us."

"That's not a problem." Eth shrugged. "I've already got his crews wondering if they'll be the next ship destroyed. Sowing fear among his people was the real goal and destroying one ship seems to have done the job admirably."

Bau laughed and the Queen… Well, she was probably laughing as well. Her entourage were also chittering loudly.

Just as suddenly as she'd started her strange probably-a-laugh, she stopped. "Memnon. We must use him to further our own goals. A strategic application of force in the right place and at the right time can help advance his goals, rendering the emperor weaker and more amenable to our own aims."

Eth nodded. "To business, then. I partially agree."

"Partially?" Bau asked.

"Memnon is of use to us," Eth conceded, "but making him more dangerous at a time when we also represent a threat to imperial authority might force Mishak into an emotional decision, which is harder to predict than an analytical one."

He turned to Bau. "What is the broad outline? We intend to separate?"

"We do," Bau confirmed, "but we will carry on selling food to the empire, if they wish."

"Which they certainly would wish," the Queen rasped, "considering their aversion to mass-starvation."

"It would be a serious blow to the empire," he warned. "We need a better marketing plan."

"Marketing?" they both asked in disharmonious shock.

He nodded. "We're selling something the empire doesn't want... yet. But what if we use Memnon as part of the sales-pitch?"

"How do you propose we use Memnon?" the Queen croaked.

"Helping Memnon would provoke a strong emotional response in Mishak and set us down a path we can't predict." Eth turned to the Queen. "And it sends the wrong sort of message to Throneworld.

"I would rather provoke another response, one that's more effective for a new organisation like ours, a group that needs to build up the right kind of..." He grinned at the insectoid monarch.

"... Buzz."

"And what response is that?" she rattled. Her guards edged closer, heads cocked to hear the response.

"Curiosity."

Just a Scratch

North of San Diego

"Ready?" John asked, poking his head into Gleb's small office. "They're probably halfway through printing the test part already."

"Sure. Let's go." Gleb got up and followed him down the hall to the elevators.

He wasn't terribly excited or, at least, not nearly as excited as John. The test part was a calibration exercise. They were hoping this morning's print would confirm that the next stage of measurement tolerance had been met.

It was important but Gleb simply saw it as a necessary milestone that had to be achieved, rather than any great cause for elation. He'd been more excited about the printer they'd cooked up.

Someone had realized that the majority of the equipment needed to print the generator parts was indifferent to tolerance requirements. They'd essentially discovered that they had to make a printer, then use it to make progressively more accurate printer heads that could replace the heads that made them.

The resulting reduction in the overall timeframe had seemed far more exciting to Gleb than this measuring process. They stepped into the elevator, riding down even lower than the main office, which was already thirty meters below the surface.

"By the way, we did find some unexplained activity on the far side," John said. "Sent a rocket on a plausible slingshot course, passive sensors only, and found movement in one of the smaller craters."

"Seemed a safe bet," Gleb replied. "If I were running some kind of secret operation on this planet, I'd want a base you couldn't easily get to but not so far that it takes hours to get down to the surface in an emergency. Your moon is ideal, especially the far side seeing as most of your facilities are on the near side."

"Made for easier communication." John shook his head. "We didn't figure there'd be anything on the other side but more moon, so why bother spreading out?"

He held up a hand, warning Gleb. "We'll save the rest for when there are fewer ears around."

The elevator doors chimed and slid open.

"Goggles," a guard by the print-room door insisted, handing a pair to each man before opening the door.

"Almost done printing." Fran Holloway waved them over. "One more round and we might just start on the generator but I'm not entirely happy about the pressure in the melting chamber."

John looked at her. "It's showing fatigue?"

She nodded. "The optic fibers in its walls are showing micro-fractures. We should probably…"

As if in agreement, the chamber in the print head, responsible for melting the alloy and pressurizing it enough for the nozzle, blew apart.

The melted metal was stopped by the safety shield but several chunks of the chamber itself punched through the shield and carved out a few head-sized pieces of the concrete wall behind them.

Gleb looked at the wall. "Good thing we had these goggles on," he muttered.

"Gleb!" Holloway exclaimed. "You're hit!"

As Gleb reached up to the sting on his cheek, John ran across the room to grab a first aid kit. He had it open before he'd re-crossed the room and he slapped a gauze pad over the wound.

"Keep pressure on it," he snapped but Gleb pulled the gauze away.

"Appreciate the help," Gleb told him, using both hands to press the edges of the cut together, "but I don't want that stuff stuck in the wound."

"Stuck in the..." John went quiet when Gleb stopped holding the wound closed and used the gauze to wipe away some of the blood.

The three-inch long, half-inch deep cut was gone.

"Well now," John said in a half whisper, "that *is* interesting."

"We're designed for fast healing," Gleb explained. "It's considered a valuable combat feature. Plus we have a small army of medical nanites in our bodies. They're a little more advanced than the ones we use for suits and ships."

"Why the difference?" John stepped closer, peering at Gleb's cheek.

"There's strict laws about letting medical nanites self-produce, for one thing. Their group-think ability is pretty basic but you don't want to run the chance of them accidentally making themselves smarter and running amok.

"There's also the fact that their enhanced abilities require more exotic materials. They're damned expensive. Cost more than a whole planet to make a ship out of them and it wouldn't be any better than a standard ship anyway."

"Well..." Holloway was leaning in now to take a closer look at the nearly invisible wound. "... Holy shit," she added in a matter-of-fact voice. "You need to let me have a look at your little helpers, one of these days."

She turned to her crew. "Alright folks, clear the printer, check for damage and let's try Mick's plan."

"Which one was Mick's plan again?" John asked her.

"Same melt chamber but lower pressure." She pointed at a case on the other side of the lab. "We'll be using a heated nozzle to keep the alloy's viscosity high enough for proper placement."

"Why wasn't that plan A?"

"Because forcing the alloy into place under higher pressure and lower temperature was resulting in a harder part surface." She nodded at the printer, now billowing with smoke. "The explody part was an unrequested design feature."

"Well," Gleb muttered, looking around, "at least I'm still here."

"No kidding," John added. "A few inches to the left and that would have shot through your brainstem."

"I'm not talking about that." Gleb lowered his voice. "I was having blackouts, back in the empire. They stopped when I came here but I had one again yesterday."

"Blackouts?" John hissed, stepping in closer. "And you're just telling me this now?"

"Really, John? This happened yesterday so, yeah, I'm telling you now. You think I should have thrown some pants on and taken a cab over here immediately?"

"Well, I... Pants?" He grinned. "You mean you keep doing stuff but you don't remember any of it?"

"Yeah. I seem to keep acting mostly like myself but I don't have any memories of it. At Kish, I went down to the magazine to arm our mass-attenuation warheads and just... glitched from one end of the room to the other. Turned out I'd armed all of them but didn't remember doing it at all."

"Hm." John scratched at his chin. "At least it's not like you're going to suddenly go ape-shit and start killing us all, right?"

"Uh, I don't have my suit on," Gleb said. "So, having to guess at the context for 'ape-shit', I think I can safely say it's not gonna happen."

"Alright." John nodded. "I'll talk with the team-leads, spread the word about this so no crazy accidents happen down here." He turned for the exit but stopped and aimed a finger at Gleb.

"Keep your pants on when you're here, got it?"

In the Dark
Throneworld orbit

"Didn't you say we'd have heard something by now?" Tashmitum demanded.

"If anyone can get us our answers," the holograph of Marduk said, "it's Urukh. We just need to give him time."

"Is this the same one you used to stir up Shullat a few cycles back?" Mishak turned from the view of Throneworld afforded by the large portal in their quarters. "I thought he was searching for Tashmitum's cousin."

The *Dibbarra* was provisioning for imminent departure. The sounds of luxury food items being stowed in a cooler next to their living room were probably audible to the emperor's Chief of Staff, underlying the urgency of the call.

"The same, yes. He's one of my best operators." The hologram turned to face Mishak. "Have your people heard anything?"

"About Bau? No, we've been focusing on my half-brother. He's up to our father's usual tricks, though it's still unclear what his aims are this time." He thrust his head forward.

"We've left the separatist matter in your hands because it needs a lighter touch." *The old fellow may be losing his touch,* Mishak thought with growing alarm.

For almost his entire life, at least since he'd been fostered to the emperor's court as a youth, Mishak had viewed the Chief of Staff as an almost omniscient being. There was no plot he was unaware of or, for the most part, *uninvolved* in.

Now he seemed to be playing catch-up at every turn. *And this Urukh is almost certainly dead by now,* he thought morosely. "We know Bau convened a meeting in the Arbella system. Who else attended and what was discussed is still a mystery but it's dead certain that my half-brother has heard of it as well.

"He'll see it as an imperial weakness. If he didn't take advantage of the uncertainty to advance his own fortunes, I'd be amazed." Mishak moved to stand by his wife.

"We're preparing to break orbit," he told his former mentor. "We're headed for Arraphka. Intercepts are starting to indicate Memnon has an interest there. Let us know if you find anything further on the separatists."

"Yes, yes," Marduk waved absently. "I'll take care of it." He shimmered out of view.

"I'm no longer certain that you can, Uncle," Tashmitum muttered quietly. She slid her hand into Mishak's and gave it a gentle squeeze.

It's for Science

The Odessa Terrace Apartments

"Are you bullshitting me?" She was holding the front of her uniform-shirt's collar together with her right hand but finally let go to accept the glass of wine that Gleb was holding out to her.

It was definitely less convenient than the fermented fat common in the empire but he was acquiring a taste for wine.

"I wish I were," he said with feeling. "I don't remember a thing about the… other night. I didn't even know it happened until…"

He'd almost said 'until Kace found your undies' but he realized that was probably a bad idea. "Until you showed up again in my room," he finished.

"I had no idea!" She moved along the couch, making room for him to sit next to her.

He sat next to her. "You and me both," he said. "A beautiful woman walks into my room looking for the clothes she left there the night before? Do you have any idea what it's like to be jealous of yourself?"

She laughed. "Must have been weird, asking me over to explain something like this!"

Gleb took a drink and set his glass on the coffee table. "Believe it or not, it gets weirder."

She shook her head, a sly smile on her face. "I almost said you already know that I don't mind weird but, then, you don't remember, so…"

"Yeah well…" He forgot what he was about to say. His mouth was hanging open, so he decided to put it back to work. "Y'know, later, you should really get me caught up on what I missed because it sounds very… interesting.

"First, I should tell you the rest." He stood and walked over to where his suit sat in a neatly stacked cube of nanites with two depressions for his feet. The specialised components were tucked safely in the center.

"Let's just take it as a fact that you won't believe me at first," he stepped back into the footplates and the nanites began flowing onto his body. "Until a few weeks ago, I'd never even heard of this planet. I came here by accident during a battle."

"That is really cool," she said, watching the armor take shape, "but, yeah, the rest sounds crazy. It also seems self-contradictory. How did you come here if you'd never even heard of Earth?"

"It's based on awareness, on perception. For me to travel the way I did when I ended up here, I need to see where I'm going. I need to see through someone's eyes."

He nodded his head at the living room window. "There are a lot of people here. It drew my focus in the middle of an emergency."

"During a battle, you said?" she asked flatly.

Gleb desperately wanted to look inside her mind to see how he could convince her but he knew it would cross a line he'd started holding since he'd begun making friends on Irth. He pushed his tongue against his cheek. *Did Alter-Gleb use our ability to get her into bed? Can he access minds?*

He held up a hand. "I'm going to step over here," he said cautiously, knowing she was worried about his sanity. He moved to the door by the washroom.

"Now just look over at the bedroom door." He waited until she did, then he closed his eyes.

He found her quickly and he saw the other side of his apartment from her seated perspective. He placed himself there and opened his eyes, hearing her gasp of surprise.

She was still holding her glass of wine but it was starting to tilt.

"See?" he asked, smiling. "I'm not nuts after all!"

"Shit!" She jerked the glass upright but not before spilling some on her uniform. She stared at it accusingly for a moment before setting it next to Gleb's glass.

"OK," she said slowly. "That was pretty compelling. So… you're an alien?"

"Legally, I suppose." He shrugged. "But I'm a Human, just like you." A chuckle… "Well, I doubt there are many Humans just like *you* but you know what I mean."

She raised an eyebrow. "So you're a Human but you're from some other planet? There are Humans on other planets?"

"Not as many as there are on *this* one, but yes."

"How did they get there?"

"We've been in the empire for tens of thousands of years."

"Thousands…" She trailed off, then fixed him with a sharp gaze. "How do I know who I'm talking to?"

"What?"

"Are you regular Gleb or are you the Gleb that lasted for three hours with me and my roommate two nights ago?"

"Your roommate?" he burst out in shock. "Both of… hang on!"

He walked back to the couch, sat and gave her an accusatory look. "You're pulling a fast one on me! You don't *have* a roommate!"

She was already laughing. "All right, you caught me!" she admitted. "But I had you for a few seconds there! It's a good thing you're cute 'cause you're an awfully easy mark for a spaceman!"

Her eyes grew wide. "Hey! Is your memory coming back?"

"No, why?"

"You knew I don't have a roommate…"

He waved that off. "I saw you on your balcony last week. That whole row of the building is bachelor apartments only."

138

She smiled. "Friday afternoon. You saw me alright. Quite a few times. I thought you were going to walk straight into the pool with your clothes on."

"What do you call that tiny thing you had on?"

"A bikini." She brushed her fingertips across her collarbone. "You *really* aren't from this world, are you?"

"No," he confirmed, "but a guy could get used to the place." He picked up his glass and leaned back with a comfortable sigh.

"Bikini," he said, liking the sound. "And all this time, I thought the difference-engine was the highpoint of sentient civilisation…"

She giggled. "I'll civilize you yet!" She took his glass and put it back on the table. "Maybe we can jog your memory as well."

He let his hand rest on her back as she leaned over him. "What do you have in mind?"

"I think it might be therapeutic for us to re-enact our previous encounter," she purred in his ear. "See if anything rises to the surface…"

Gleb woke with a start. He reached up, touching the arm draped across his chest. He looked down at the mass of dark brown hair framing a delicate face resting on his shoulder. A light sheen of drool cooled his chest when she exhaled.

His mind raced. *Her name is Luna, she's a pilot in one of Irth's military forces, though it's a water-based branch for some reason. She looks so good in a bikini that I nearly walked into the pool…*

Last night, we were talking. I told her where I'm from and then we were going to… re-enact our first encounter…

He compressed his lips in a tight line, blowing out an angry breath through his nose. "Son of a harpy!" he cursed in Imperial Standard.

Gods-damned Alter-Gleb!

Building Buzz

Arraphka

Eth opened his eyes. He was in the missile control-room aboard one of Memnon's cruisers. He grinned at the startled missile-rating whose eyes he'd had to use to get aboard. It was a wasted expression on the Quailu but Eth was enjoying himself.

"Don't mind me," he said, reaching out to take the heat from his enemy's body, converting the heat into kinetic energy in a way that only someone like Eth could understand.

Having been taken to a space between the Universes by Varangians, he'd had his comforting illusions stripped away. Matter, energy… such comforting fantasies…

It had nearly driven him insane.

He released the kinetic energy, focused on the *radix callosum*, the connection between the two independent hemispheres of a Quailu mind. Without that connection, the two sides couldn't communicate, which was worse than it sounded.

The two sides were in constant communication, even when a Quailu was letting one side sleep while the other remained awake. They were continuously updating a check-file of sorts. A backup to keep the two sides up to date with each other.

Without that data transfer, a whole host of detrimental effects would result. The most useful here was severe aphasia. This crewman would be unable to communicate, which meant he couldn't spread the alarm after Eth left and it avoided the need to dispose of a body on an enemy ship.

If found, his crewmates would assume the aphasia had been caused by a cardiovascular event.

Eth turned to look at an open space in the small room and held up his hand in front of his vision, thumb and forefinger extended in the standard 'all is good' signal.

After a few moments, he suddenly noticed that Mel was standing in the open space. This time his grin wasn't wasted. "See? Not so hard if you have Human eyes to look through."

"I suppose," Mel allowed, dubiously. "Still… goes against the grain to go *to* one of that asshole's ships."

"Yeah, well you're *here* to mess with him, so let's get to it. Get linked up and load the new program." He waved to the weapons control console.

It may have taken a little help for Mel to transition to this ship but he needed no help with his assigned task. Eth knew he had potential and, as one of Gleb's rescues from Memnon's own ship, he wanted to see how far he could go. That was why he was taking a personal interest in his training.

Mel stepped away from the console with a feeling of satisfaction. "Good." Eth nodded. "Don't forget the psychological component."

Chuckling, Mel pulled out a small plasma torch, set to the lowest temperature, and began scorching a message on the wall in cuneiform.

"Follow me when you're done," Eth told him. "I've got to go see a very frightened Quailu about a very necessary gesture."

Oliv opened her eyes. Siri stood in front of her, eyes both eager and nervous and no wonder. They were in Memnon's private quarters.

Their particular role was to prevent the *DeathStalker* from firing any weapons. That required access to his personal terminal.

"Not bad!" She beamed at her protégé.

"I've been here a few times," Siri said quietly, glancing nervously at the door to the bedchamber where steady snoring indicated the enemy was close.

"You mean he…" Oliv trailed off, skin beginning to flush with anger.

"No," Siri insisted. "At least, not *me*, but several of the Quailu crew were brought here… I was detailed as a personal attendant for them. You know, be there with a towel for after, refreshemnts. Mostly, I think we were there to reinforce his disdain for us, like it didn't matter if we were in the room." She shuddered. "His tastes don't trend native at all, as far as I know."

"We already knew he was scum," Oliv said quietly. "His 'combat games' with Human slaves on Kurnugia made me want to skin him alive."

She nodded at the terminal. "Get the thing done."

She found herself drifting over to the bedchamber door as Siri worked. She nearly jumped when Siri appeared at her elbow.

"Done," she whispered, eyes on the door.

Oliv nodded then jerked her head toward the door. "Can you feel his mind?"

Siri nodded, eyes wide.

"Think you can keep him under?"

"Sure. I can keep Father Sulak under for the full test duration, so…"

The Quailu oracle was a mostly willing volunteer for some of the more advanced training exercises, as long as Scylla had cleared each trainee for live testing.

Oliv walked in and, after a moment of hesitation, Siri focused on Memnon's brain and followed her in.

Oliv was staring down at the sleeping Quailu. Like most of the empire, he slept in the nude and the sheets were balled up in a corner of the bed.

"He's no Mishak," she said softly, looking down with amusement.

"So that's the Quailu you were involved with?" Siri asked absently, still concentrating on keeping her target unconscious.

"I shouldn't have said that," Oliv muttered. "Well, it's not like I owe that bastard any discretion anymore. Screw it."

"Phrasing," Siri mumbled.

Oliv almost laughed out loud.

"You're sure you can keep him under?"

"You could kick him in the face and he won't wake up."

Oliv looked down at Memnon for a moment. "No," She said, "he'd notice when he woke."

She pulled out a grease pencil. They were handy if you needed to mark something while floating in the vacuum of space so most Humans had a few with them at all times. She kneeled next to Memnon's sleeping form and leaned over.

They were also handy if you wanted to have a little fun with a degenerate megalomaniac...

"Normalizing," the helmsman reported. "Stellar nav shows us well within margin of error for our chosen arrival corridor."

"Very good." Mishak took a step closer to his tactical holo. "All call-signs, full tactical alert. Confirm."

After the Battle of Kish, he'd dispensed with the old custom of lords relying on fleet captains to manage their forces. Rimush had been an excellent leader but he'd taken too much on himself.

Thinking the Humans' new strength translated into a fatal weakness for Mishak, he'd issued secret orders in an attempt to wipe them out in one surprise stroke. It had failed and Rimush had been executed on the spot by his lord who now had to live with the results.

His Humans would have been useful now, if he hadn't lost their loyalty at Kish. They would have slipped in ahead of his main force, letting him know what awaited them…

"Populating the trace now," Tactical announced.

Mishak nearly took a step back at what he saw.

It was eerily familiar. Lugalbandu, the lord of Arraphka, had his forces stretched in a thin, patchy plane between his only world and Memnon's forces. Memnon had brought a lot of force.

"They have us outclassed by fifty percent, lord," the tactical officer advised.

"Indeed they do." Mishak silently cursed Rimush. Eth and his Humans would have had Bau's missiles waiting to wipe out half of Memnon's force in the opening moments, and that was just so the other half would leave in a state of fear.

Perhaps Tashmitum was right, he thought morosely. The Humans were too much power for an emperor to wield, especially when he had the Varangians at his disposal. The electors would never tolerate him on the throne if he could take them all on with the kind of ease he was just contemplating.

And so we must find a way to lead without force, he told himself. That, after all had probably been a major factor in Memnon's calculations. Memnon would have known his half-brother would seek to act with a light touch in this matter.

Memnon could have brought far more force than he had. He was sending a message. He was telling anyone who cared to see that message that he could calculate imperial response and play it to his advantage.

As if on cue, his half-brother appeared in front of him holographically, accompanied by Lugalbanda. "What brings the prince presumptive so far from the comforts of Throneworld?" Memnon sneered.

Mishak squinted. *What the hells?* He took a step closer, peering up at Memnon's forehead. A shiver ran down his spine. *Could it be?* He kept staring until Memnon broke back into his thoughts.

"What the hells is wrong with you?" he growled.

"Just… glad… to see you, brother," Mishak stepped back, nodding to Lugalbanda. "I might ask the same question."

"What?"

"What brings you so far from the distractions of Kurnugia?"

"Ah." Memnon glanced at Lugalbanda's holographic form. "I've come for Arraphka. I should have thought that was obvious."

"You're concerned about your food supplies?"

Arraphka was a back-verse dust-ball, like Kish. Its only claim to prominence was that it produced synthetic foodstuffs, designed chiefly for disaster-relief operations.

"My reasons are my own," Memnon said smoothly. "By the end of this encounter, this system will fall under my rule or I'll leave behind a sterile ball of rock."

Mishak stood still. Memnon had improved on his game since their last encounter. No bluster, no misplaced anger – he was coming straight to the point.

And now Mishak was left hanging in the breeze. He was expected to respond to this provocation, to find a way through this mess. As the presumptive future emperor, he was supposed to keep the peace of the realm and here his brother was about to show him up for the fool he really was.

How to save this situation, though? *I could slip back in later and retake the place with a larger force,* he thought but that, of course, presupposed the other end of a bad bargain... *I can't just slink away...*

With almost perfect timing, Lugalbanda saved Mishak from having to come to his rescue by screwing the situation beyond all recall. "I place far more trust in the prince-presumptive," his hologram said scratchily, "than I ever could in some grasping adventurer like you, Melvin the Miniscule!"

Lugalbanda's holographic image turned to Mishak and... he winked at Mishak?

That tingle in his spine returned. *What the hells? How does he know an obscure native facial gesture like that?* He resisted the urge to look to the tactical trace for any hints of a stealthy force.

The starscape here was filled with enough dark regions to hide ships. The Humans could easily be sitting out there, hidden from both sides of this dispute, and there'd be no way to find them.

And there was still the matter of his brother. Some muted laughter was coming through his holograph but Memnon wasn't the least bit amused.

He was looking to the side, listening to someone, and then he wiped his hand angrily across his forehead, pulling it away to glare at the palm. He pulled his sidearm and shot whomever he'd been talking to.

"Destroy Lugulbanda's flagship!" he roared.

No matter what else happened here today, Mishak knew he'd just failed. If Lugalbanda died, then Mishak would have failed to protect him from aggression. It made no difference that the fool had made an inflammatory insult in the face of overwhelming force.

Something was wrong.

By now, Memnon should have been watching his missiles streaking toward their target but nothing was happening. His holograph darted a look to the left. "What do you mean 'locked out'?"

Something indistinct in reply.

"I locked it out? *I* did?" He raised his hand, still holding the pistol, and executed his weapons officer. "Fleet-wide channel," he ordered.

"Destroy Lugalbanda's flagship!" he shouted.

As commands went, this one was pretty vague. He hadn't clarified who he wanted to do the destroying and Lugalbanda's flagship probably had a name or, at least, a target designation, just to avoid accidents…

Three cruisers and two frigates fired missiles. They left odd, sparkly trails as they sped away and then curved around gracefully to smash back into the same ships they'd come from.

Five of Memnon's ships were gone. Definitely not a good look when you're planning to slap someone *else* around.

He looked away again. "They said what?"

More indistinct words.

"Burned into the bulkheads?" He turned to glare at his half-brother. "This isn't over!" His projection faded.

"And yet," Lugalbanda's projection mused, "it feels so much as if it *is*." He bowed to Mishak. "If you'll excuse me, Prince Mishak, I have a nervous population in need of reassurance."

And Mishak stood alone in the central holo.

A.G. Claymore

Sparring

The *Reaper*, enroute to Babilim

Eth looked up from his lunch as Scylla set her tray on the table.

"I need you," she said, settling into a seat opposite him.

"Excuse me?"

"I've had the modules for hand to hand combat ingrained but there's been no time to 'bring it all out'."

"Ah!"

The training modules could place knowledge in a Human brain but it worked kind of like something you'd recently forgotten. When you needed the knowledge, it sprang up from the depths as needed.

That was fine for something like replacing a crewmate who'd died at the nav station in combat, but for something that relied on fine motor-skills, practice was needed.

"The other crew are a little too in awe of me," she said. "They'd be terrible training partners. You, on the other hand, wouldn't go so easy on me."

Eth wasn't entirely sure about that but it was for other reasons. "Um, sure. We could figure out a time to hit the mats…"

"How about now?"

"Well, you should probably at least finish your…" He looked down, frowning, reasonably sure there'd been a pile of food on her plate when she had sat.

He shrugged. "Sure, let's go."

Smalltalk

The Truck-Fights, San Diego

Gleb loved the air on Irth but this was taking it to a new level. The Truck-Fights was an arena, if only metaphorically, where various food trucks came to 'do battle' for customer dollars.

A large circular paved road had parking-spots and hookups for twenty trucks at a time and, according to Luna, it was one of the best places to pop his cherry – her words – on the planet's best food.

He held his breath for as long as he could and then treated himself to another. It was a symphony! There was good food in the empire but it was all native to other worlds. What he was smelling now was the product of millennia of experimentation by Humans cooking exclusively for Humans.

Luna grinned at him. "You were shivering like that two nights ago; should I be jealous of the food?"

"Seeing as your question is making me jealous of myself for not having access to those particular memories then, yes. Yes, you absolutely should!"

"There they are!" She grabbed his hand and dragged him through the crowd.

He realized he was a little nervous. This was entirely new for him. Luna had made light of it but he knew she took a lot of pressure from her family for being single and concentrating on her career as a naval aviator.

Now he was about to meet her older sister. *No biggie,* she'd said at the time though she'd clearly been nervous about asking him to do this. She had seemed worried that he'd disapprove somehow.

He was fascinated by the idea of meeting anyone's sibling but to meet Luna's sister… He was wondering how they'd be alike – how they'd differ. In the last few hours, however, it had occurred to him that she might be nervous that her sister wouldn't approve of him.

That confused him to no end. *I'm practically a sociopathic killer,* he thought as a lovely dark-haired woman with Luna's sparkling brown eyes turned and gave them a smile. *Why the hells would I care about this Adelina's opinion so much?*

It hit him as they arrived. *I care because Luna cares. I don't remember a single time we had sex but I care based entirely on the time we've spent together.* He shook his head. *What sorcery is this?*

"Gleb," Luna began in a rush, "this is my sister Adelina and her daughter Gabriella. Guys this is Gleb."

Gabriella was so fascinating that Gleb forgot how nervous he was. She was young, maybe two-thirds the height of her mother. *Does that mean she's two-thirds her age?* "Ladies." He gave them the fractional bow common in the empire as a polite greeting. "I've been looking forward to meeting some of Selar's family."

"Selar?" Adelina wrinkled her nose the same way Luna often did.

Did I lapse into Imperial? He smiled. "Ah, that's what we call the lunar goddess, back home."

"Really?" She tilted her head. "You mean in some old mythology? I thought you guys were mostly Orthodox."

"Yeah," he agreed, having stupidly forgotten what planet he was pretending to be from. "It does seem to fit her though." He shrugged. "Same idea, just different languages."

The sister nodded. "He'll do," she admitted. "Easy on the eyes and he's already picked out a cute little nickname for you…"

"Adelina!" Luna's eyes flashed.

Gleb wasn't sure why but he could feel a shouting match building. *Am I accidentally reading their emotions?*

"Are you guys a couple in the biblical sense?" the daughter asked him.

"Gabriella!" both women exclaimed in shock and near-perfect unison.

Gleb laughed. He didn't know, exactly, what the young woman meant by 'biblical' but he could make a pretty shrewd guess based on the two sisters' reactions.

"Ai!" Adelina exclaimed. "Why do I bring you anywhere?"

"She should ask the same about letting you out in public," Luna declared, "trying to embarrass us like that! The apple never falls so far, does it?"

He realized he was still holding Luna's hand and so he gave it an affectionate squeeze. He nodded at her relatives when she looked at him. "I have no secrets, as far as I know…" He thought he saw the beginnings of a knowing smirk on her face at that comment. "…If it's appropriate in your culture to answer that kind of question, I have no objections."

She rolled her eyes. "Look, I know you think that helps, but now it's even more awkward."

"I don't see why," Gabriella said, her large eyes flashing with mischief. "It's not like Mom hasn't been wondering as well…"

Now it was Luna's turn to laugh as her embarrassed sister turned deep red and subjected her daughter to an angry rapid-fire tirade in a language Gleb didn't know. *Is this the language Luna grew up using?* He wondered. *How many languages does this planet have?*

The sister finally trailed off and looked toward a large tarp that hid a food truck. The truck was a recent qualifying entry and was, for the moment, a mystery.

"Nosy little *interrogadora*!" Luna leaned in, lowering her voice. "In the *biblical* sense… Yes. But…" She held up her hand to emphasize her point. "… We take precautions!"

"Yes," Gleb confirmed with an exaggerated gravity. "Seatbelts!"

Gabriella snorted.

"So," Luna said, pointedly changing the discussion, "what's the big surprise? You finished the project?"

"It's back there." Adelina nodded at the tarp. "Just got certified last week. The buyer can back it up to the loading bay at his restaurant and use it as a kitchen extension during peak hours. Then he can send it out for street service the rest of the time."

"And you still won't tell me who bought it?"

"You'll see in a few minutes." She frowned down at her watch. "Any second now, really."

"Ow! Dammit!" a muffled voice came from behind the tarp. *"Who the hell left this here?"*

Adelina grinned. "Sounds like he's here, at least."

Luna started asking her sister probing questions about the truck but she wasn't making much headway if she was trying to ferret out who bought it.

"What about this tarp, guys?" the voice continued. *"It drops. Then what? People climb over the damn thing to get to us? I gotta say, we really didn't think that part through..."*

There was an indistinct mumble from somewhere behind the tarp.

"Nobody's blaming you," the first voice insisted. *"I said 'we', didn't I? It's like the royal 'we'. It means I didn't think it through."*

Gleb glanced over at Gabriella, noticing how she looked more like her aunt than her mother. It almost felt like he was looking back in time, seeing Luna as a younger person. "What's it like," he asked her, "being young?" *Dammit! Stupid thing to ask! I'm supposed to know that, idiot!*

"That's an odd question, don't you think?" She raised an eyebrow at him. "You're an adult. You're supposed to be telling me what it's like, saying it's the best years of my life and all that horse-shit…"

"It's not?"

"Shit! No, just get me that tape." There was a splash followed by sizzling. *"No, I'll fish that out; just get the other roll of tape! Ow, ow, dammit!"*

She made a wry face. "Are you kidding?" She gestured to her face. "Acne, definitely not a girl's best friend. I can never get my hair to do anything even remotely acceptable and, at this age, your body always has something humiliating up its sleeve.

"Mean girls, jackass boys, demanding teachers and several hours of homework every night." She nodded sarcastically. "Yeah, best years."

He didn't need to read her to pick up on the insecurity. *I might actually be glad I came from a maturation chamber.* "That doesn't sound like 'best years' to me."

"No shit?" She turned to look at the tarp when a crash of pans came from behind.

"Forget it," the voice behind the tarp urged. *"Just toss all that behind the truck and we'll take care of it later. No, no, not the back end. Behind as in the opposite side from the public. Yeah, over there."*

"So that means you must have some good stuff to look forward to," Gleb suggested.

"I'd better," she growled, crossing her arms. "Though it's hard to imagine what form any of that will take."

"Well, I barely know you but you seem pretty smart."

She snorted again. "Yeah, that and about forty cats will be a great comfort to me."

He tried to make sense of that on his own but he had no idea what kind of plan might involve so many of the small creatures. As far as he could tell they seemed to be utterly indifferent to Humans. "You like cats?"

She laughed at that. "Oh God, no!" She shook her head, uncrossing her arms. "They're the assholes of the pet world. Mind you, they do prove the Flat-Earthers wrong."

"How's that?" He'd heard of the movement. People who thought the planet was flat, rather than round. He wasn't entirely sure but he suspected the Chironans might be using the movement to identify which segments of the population to avoid.

He'd be surprised if they had any genetic samples from members of a group like that.

"Seems obvious," she said. "If the Earth was truly flat, cats would have pushed everything off by now."

He laughed, remembering Aberdeen's cat. "So why would you derive comfort from so many cats if you don't like them?"

"It's standard procedure for hideous old ladies. Don't ask me why, it's just the law."

Gods the legal system's a mess here! "I doubt you'd be subject to that particular injunction," he said. "You already look a lot like your aunt. I don't see any cats in your future."

She looked wistfully at her warrior-aunt.

"More importantly," he lowered his voice and leaned a little closer. "You're smart. Humanity is quickly approaching a point where they're going to become a multi-planet species. There's going to be a need for smart people to help set up shop on new planets, not just Mars but proper, habitable worlds."

"Let's not get carried away, Gleb." Gabriella gave him a tolerant look. "Once they figure out how to keep kids healthy on Mars without having to spend half their time in rotating orbital stations, maybe then we can start finding new worlds."

"You scoff," he said, "but changes are coming and they're coming soon. If you want work off-planet, you'll have it."

She opened her mouth but whatever she was about to say remained unsaid. The tarp dropped, revealing a shiny new food truck with a large neon sign that simply said 'Best!' above the serving window. A dark-haired man was helping his crew gather up the tarp and pull it out of the way. Half his fingers were patched up with blue tape.

The crowd started buzzing with excitement.

"No way!" Luna turned a shocked expression on her sister. "I love this guy! I grilled his yakitori recipe on my balcony a couple of weeks ago!"

"Uh huh?" Her sister looked askance at her. "In that tiny bikini, no doubt."

"I like that bikini," she protested.

"A little mystery goes a long way, chica."

"Not as long as a little lycra," Gleb suggested.

Adelina narrowed her gaze. "I'll be keeping an eye on you…"

"Who wants a delicious, gigantic cheese-skirt burger?" the truck owner yelled.

The crowd went nuts.

It was slightly cooler in Luna's apartment than it was outside but her air-conditioner was a sad little thing. "Get me something cool to drink?" She nodded Gleb toward the refrigerator as she closed her door. "I'll be in the shower. I smell like I've been playing basketball in a forest fire."

He opened the fridge, taking a moment, shivering with pleasure at the wave of cold. He grabbed two bottles of porter and closed the door with no small amount of reluctance. He turned to head for the bathroom but jumped in mild alarm when he realized she was standing right behind him.

She already had her shorts in her hand, so she tossed them on the counter to take the beer.

She popped the cap and took a long drink. Gleb took a moment to appreciate the way her light shirt moved when she raised her arm. His approval of her wardrobe was inversely proportional to her older sister's disapproval.

He remembered she'd tossed her shorts on the counter and started shifting his gaze but she was lowering the bottle.

"We need to talk about tonight." Her voice had a slight waver.

"Ok." *What did I do?*

"I don't want you to freak out that I'm introducing you to family after just a few weeks," she said. "It's just that they harp all the time about me finding someone, about starting a family of my own while I'm still young…" She shook her head angrily and took another drink.

This time, Gleb kept his eyes on her face.

"Ok," she continued, "not really getting my point across here. Look, I'm not saying I was just using you as a prop or something; it's just… this isn't easy. My job isn't conducive to relationships.

"If it wasn't for the reactor problems on the *Fauci*, I'd be somewhere in the eastern Mediterranean right now. This is the longest I've been involved with someone." Her shoulders slumped. "Every guy I've ever liked has moved on after a few weeks of me putting back to sea."

"That seems kind of stupid," Gleb said, hurrying to explain when he saw the storm cloud building in her eyes. "What kind of idiot wouldn't wait for you?"

And Eve? he thought. *I suppose it was never more than a possibility that might or might not have worked out.* It had been little more than the standard, pre-freedom flirting that had always gone on.

She's probably moved on to something else anyway. Meanwhile, there's something very real happening here…

He moved a little closer. "I'm kind of in the same place you are. I've never even been in a relationship because that's not something Humans *do* in the empire. I really like being with you, meeting the family of someone I care about…"

She set her beer on the counter and he did the same, reaching out to put his arms around her waist. "Hells, caring about anyone at all is kind of new territory for me. I was designed for combat. Finding out I can be normal is a bit of a surprise."

She rested her head against his chest. "You might feel differently after I've been deployed for a few months." Her right hand slid down and Gleb sucked in a surprised breath. "This might have other ideas."

He froze, not wanting to give her a reason to stop. "I don't think so," he finally whispered, his eyes closed. "I kind of like the idea of having you to miss…"

"That's a good answer," she purred. "A very good answer. Let's go make that shower the kind you won't remember…"

She took his hand and led him across the living room. He let his eyes drift down as they walked.

The birds were singing in the large tree outside Luna's balcony. The heatwave was finally breaking and a breeze blew over them, bearing a sweet, resinous rumor from the large eucalyptus trees in the courtyard.

He ran a hand down Luna's back and she murmured, nestling in closer. He closed his eyes.

Dammit! He lay still, not wanting to disturb her. *What is it even like with her? It would be hard to believe that I didn't enjoy it…* He tilted his head slightly, admiring the sublime curvature that began just below where his hand was resting.

But what about her? he wondered. *I'd like to think I'm holding up my end of things but what does she think, afterward?*

Making a Difference
North of San Diego

"I expected it to be bigger," John muttered. He glanced over at Gleb, noticing he was wearing his EVA suit this morning. "Unlimited energy… Something like that you'd expect to be a little bigger than a filing cabinet."

Gleb kept looking through the thick glass. The final part of the shell was being attached. Workers in isolation suits were clearing the rest of the lab of tools and packaging.

The test was about to start.

"That's the last plate." Holloway's voice rattled the cheap overhead speaker. "Everybody do a final sweep and then clear out!"

"I expected it to *take* longer," Gleb said.

"Well, your original analogy might have been a bit extreme." John smiled grimly. "We're not just a pack of savages with stone hammers. We're a pack of savages running an experimental stone hammer prototyping lab. But let's not pat ourselves on the back just yet."

"Third time's the charm," Gleb said casually.

"You realize that's more a hopeful figure of speech, right?" John clasped his hands behind his back. "It's not a fundamental law of the Universe or anything."

"Yeah," Gleb acknowledged, "but the Universe has to cut us a break every now and then. The first two assembly labs are still being repaired. The Universe wouldn't blow up our last room, would it?"

"The Universe doesn't run tabs, my friend. It's the most mercenary capitalist I've ever met. It will happily take the shirt off your back and then call the cops on you for public indecency."

"Y'know, John, I was feeling a lot better about this test before you started flapping your gums."

John laughed. "You're sounding more like an Earth-man every day!"

Gleb fumed silently, staring through the glass at the now-empty room. He was turning into an Irther. It wasn't so bad, he supposed. He was sort of in a relationship with Luna and the sex was great, or so she told him.

It was nice to be on a planet where he wasn't a second-class species. Even the loud-mouth idiots who'd yell at him for being a foreigner didn't faze him. Their irrational dislike was because they thought he was a Human from a different country, not just because he was a Human.

He didn't read his friends but he made no such distinction when some slack-jawed moron would accost him in public. It was incredible how many of them thought they'd be captains of industry if only it wasn't for all the damn foreigners.

Still, this was a good place to be a Human. He just didn't quite feel like he belonged here. At least, not here in one corner of the planet. He missed his team, he missed his ship and he was steadfastly trying to ignore the growing unease he'd been feeling about Mishak.

Their lord had been uncomfortable with them since learning about the changes they'd undergone. Even worse, he and others had noticed heightened levels of tension from the fleet's Quailu captains. Rimush, especially, had become very remote, going to unusual lengths to avoid the Humans in the fleet.

Gleb needed to get back to the empire. He couldn't shake the feeling that something bad was brewing and he wanted to be there to help protect Human interests, if they ever happened to diverge from Mishak's.

Holloway exited the room's airlock and came over to the control panel, pulling off her hood. "Room three is clear," she announced. "Sealing the doors now!"

There was a low rumble as pins slid from the door-frame into corresponding holes in the edge of the heavy, inner door. The red light inside turned green.

"Flow-limiters are green across the board." She touched the control screen and slid her finger down. "All busses set to one percent."

Ten percent had seemed like a good idea for their second test. The lab's in-house fire department had unleashed a few choice words about that sentiment after they'd extinguished the blaze.

"Halon system is active," she reached out and touched the plastic safety cover over the red 'fire' button.

"The plates are all reading in the green," a technician next to her announced. "We're good to go, Doc."

She pulled out a small sculpture on a chain around her neck and gave it a kiss before turning to Gleb and John and giving them a wink. "Third time's the charm, right fellas?"

"I tried telling him that," Gleb said, "and he just got all gloomy."

She didn't seem to notice what he'd said. She turned back to the window for one last glance, though if they'd missed anything during a check inside the room, she was hardly going to find it from out here.

"Okay." She took a deep breath, reaching out to a large physical switch covered by a safety cover. She flipped up the cover and brought her forefinger to rest against the switch. "Going live in three, two, one, zero…"

She flipped the switch.

Everyone was holding their breath. Everyone kept holding their breath…

Gleb finally exhaled.

"The shunts are holding this time," Holloway said, mostly to herself as she leaned over the main screen. "No heat buildup either!"

She smiled at the tech beside her. The man had oddly clear brow-ridges where most folks had eyebrows.

"You were right, Carl! It's not just about the material listed in the schematic, it's how the individual molecules are arranged! There doesn't seem to be any resistance at all!"

"So no boom?" John asked.

"Not at one percent anyway," Holloway told him. "Let's ramp it up a bit, see if we can push some power back into the state grid and cut our monthly bill. Going to two percent."

She looked at her telemetry feed. "Temperatures are all still in the green! Still no heat. Going to five percent."

"CalPo is gonna owe us money at this point," the tech exclaimed. "At five percent power, we're the third biggest co-generation partner in the state!"

"Let's see if we can take the top spot." Holloway looked at Gleb. "Anything over eight percent should be enough for your small ship design, right?"

"Yeah, as long as we take it easy."

"OK." She put her finger on the slider control. "Carl, watch the temperatures for me, I'm gonna start ramping it up."

She moved her finger. "Seven percent."

"Still no change on temperature," Carl advised.

"Ten."

"Still good."

"Fifteen."

"Maybe we should ease up here," John stepped in. "We finally managed to turn one of these things on without burning a lab or frying off somebody's eyebrows. Let's not push this one to the failure-point in the first ten minutes of operation."

"Spoil-sport!" Holloway took her finger off the slider.

"Anyway…" Gleb rubbed his hands together. "…Fifteen percent is more than enough to give us propulsion and grav-control."

"Yeah," Holloway agreed, nodding. "Of course, twenty-five is going to give you a little extra leeway."

"Doc!" John warned.

"Too late, John. I already had it up to twenty-five."

"Fine." John threw up his hands. "But no higher, for now. We'll let it run at quarter power for a bit, while Gleb sets up a large grav-plate, so we can see how the temperatures look under load."

"About that, John…"

The director turned to Gleb. "If you're gonna start a sentence like that while we're busy stealing energy from the Universe, you should at least be handing me a couple of heartburn pills. What reckless scheme is bouncing around in that skull of yours?"

"Well, we already have a full grav-plate set up in the *Holy Shit, What's That?*. She's holding a pattern on those power cells you got us. Why not just use her to run the next set of tests?"

"For starters, the engine is up here and our ship is over in Newton's lab." John waved at the window. "We haven't even worked out the mechanism for moving the engine to the ship and getting it installed."

"No need to over-think that part, John. Combat's my natural environment. You got any idea how many times my people have had to cobble together an emergency ship from parts? Hells, I'm not even getting shot at!"

"What are you suggesting?"

"My suit. I just tell the CPU that I want that engine in our new ship. It has all the necessary algorithms and enough leeway to see past obstacles. It can leave the CPU and the pattern emitters on me but hand over the nanites to the engine.

"Drawing power from the engine – a good test in its own right – they'll form a grav-plate, lift the engine, carry it down the hall and hand it off to the ship for installation. We've already loaded the standard codes into the ship's processors, so the install should go off without a hitch."

"Should? How well is this code tested?"

"Been in use for thousands of years – since before you guys figured out how to use fire. I doubt we'd be making good use of time by devising any new tests at this point."

"Are we sure this is wise?" Holloway asked. "This may all be old news to Gleb but I'm pretty sure this is the first time a difference engine has been built on this world and the last attempts were kind of messy."

"Yeah, but this one isn't messy, Doc." Gleb gave her a formal court bow. "You sorted out the heat problem. You're giving us more than enough power to do what we need to do."

"The Chironans *are* out there, somewhere," John admitted, turning to look through the window at the engine.

"And we don't know when they're going to stop sneaking around but they will, sooner or later." Gleb held up his wrist, a holographic menu floating above it. "Best for us to get out there and start taking what we need from their covert teams, while we still can."

John looked down at the holo. He took a deep breath. "Alright, dammit. Go ahead."

Gleb activated the control and most of his suit flowed down his body and over to the wall of the lab. The helmet-ring and a chest harness were the only parts that remained on his body and a thin line of nanites kept the rest connected to the power cells on his back.

The nanites spread across the concrete and glass, harvesting their way through it, replicating as they went.

Both John and Holloway took a step back. "That's still damned unsettling." John shivered. "If even one of those things went viral and started eating our planet…"

"As much as we ignore the rules on nanite-pattern copyrights for things like ships, that is one thing we never mess with." Gleb shook his head. "Their firmware is hardwired, you might say. There's only one place in the Universe known to have the ability to do anything with that coding and it's under guard by a whole squadron of Varangians.

"The guys who invented nanites were evacuated from their moon shortly after they presented their results to the Imperial Society of Science. The emperor granted them a permanent royalty on all sales related to nanite use but he locked down the facility for the very reason that has you so concerned."

By now, the nanites had latched onto the engine's mounting brackets and they were lifting it to make room underneath for a grav-plate to form.

"What about mutations?" Holloway asked pointedly. "Every self-replicating system runs the risk of the code being transcribed incorrectly."

"Each nanite runs a self-check. If it can't transmit a clean bill of health to its neighbors, they slice it up and re-use the material." Gleb stepped out of the way as the impromptu grav-plate lifted the engine off the workbench and started moving toward the hole in the wall.

"More than twenty thousand years of constant widespread use in the empire," he said as the engine drifted past them. "Not a single incident has ever been reported of them going wild on us."

"Not *reported*, huh?" John's voice had a slight edge to it.

Gleb shrugged at him. "Information does get locked down sometimes but, if a bunch of nanites went wild and ate a planet or a moon, folks would talk.

"Speaking of talking, can you call Doc Newton and get her to open the doors to her lab?" Gleb nodded at the hole in the wall. "The nanites will follow the most logical path but they clearly don't recognize your doors for what they are if they're closed."

John sighed. His focus drifted from Gleb. "Hey, Doc, it's John. Can you open your lab doors right away? We've got a delivery inbound." He laughed. "Yes, the engine. I don't suppose it used the door?" He nodded. "We're on our way."

"C'mon," he urged, jogging down the hall. "This might be everyday stuff for Gleb but I've never watched a power generator install itself into a spaceship before!"

They got there as the engine was sliding its way through the side of the hull. The nanites of starboard side flowed back into place as it disappeared from sight.

"Whoa, hey!" John reached out but failed to grab Gleb before he could climb up into the small craft.

"Thought you wanted to watch," Gleb called from inside.

After a moment's hesitation, John followed him in through the forward boarding hatch. The engine was settling into place and the small vessel's secondary systems started humming to life.

"This is how we develop our own ships," Gleb said absently. "We put in modifications and then observe first-hand as they're executed. The folks who commercially design cruisers or frigates never bother to watch them grow but they're idiots."

He pointed to a hole in the upper hull. "See how it uses some of the hull, temporarily, to get the job done? That's why we watch. We know we need more nanites if the hull breaches. We ought to add in a few bulkheads and prioritize them for stuff like this so we can maintain hull integrity."

"Does it matter?" John asked. "It's not like you need to worry about venting atmosphere in Newton's lab…"

"We usually do this kind of thing in the black." Gleb brought up a telemetry feed on his main holo. "You never know when you might have to make changes on the fly so it's best if we're used to the conditions that can arise from unexpected problems."

John stared at him. "You want to take this thing out for a test flight right now, don't you?"

"What are you nuts?" He gave John an incredulous look. "It's almost lunch. It's Taco Tuesday…"

Head-Scratcher

The *Dibbarra*

Mishak stood at the window, staring out at the indiscriminate patterns of color that enveloped a ship during path-flow. "You know the thing I really don't understand?" he asked his mate. The feeling of gentle amusement from her was almost instantaneous.

"You've narrowed it down to just one thing?"

"I have absolutely no doubts that Eth was there, at Arraphka," he said, leaving her gibe unchallenged. "What he did was useful to us when you'd expect them to throw in with Memnon, just to keep us even *more* off-balance. What's his game?"

"And he didn't take the opportunity to destroy a second ship," she added. "Of course, that may just be a way of drawing out the time your crews have to live in fear of a meaningless death…"

"Not long after we hear that Bau was near Arbella at the same time as the Zeartekka Queen, we find the Humans at Arraphka, acting strangely." He turned from the window to face her.

"They *are* renegades in the empire," she reminded him. "If they have no place among us, the idea of an autonomous entity under Bau might be tempting…"

"For Bau as well," he agreed. "Having their abilities at her disposal would increase their chances of secession by an order of magnitude."

"That would change their behaviour." She winced, placing a hand on her growing belly. "They can't serve as a military arm for the separatists and still pursue personal vengeance."

"And they would probably expect us to figure that out," he said, moving over to the couch and sitting next to her. He stared down at his empty mug.

"You think?"

"They were sending a message," he insisted. "I just can't figure out what the message is. Are they offering peace? Are they warning us somehow?"

She sighed and leaned against his shoulder. "Messages are rarely that comprehensive. I doubt we'll be able to pick this one apart and find answers to all our questions. Best to rely only on what it seems to tell us."

"Hmmm…" He closed his eyes. "They may be in league with the separatists who, possibly, may have an interest in helping me keep peace in what remains of the empire?"

Tashmitum snored softly in response.

A.G. Claymore

Floodgates

Field Trip
Maeve's Office

Maeve looked up. "Hey, guys. Didn't know you were coming…" She jumped up from her chair, a grin forming. "Shall I assume, from the fact that you're both suited up and that you've got an extra suit with you, that you've got our ship flying?"

"She's on the roof," Gleb confirmed, "and one of your guards seems to have guessed her name without any help from us!"

John handed over the suit, one of their own models designed for the Mars crews. "Flight here was easy enough, though the inertial dampening is a little sketchy."

"It's improving, though," Gleb insisted. "The system will take feedback as we maneuver and update the control for the grav-plating. It just takes time to calibrate."

"Still…" John offered his boss a shoulder to lean on while she struggled into the suit. "…Seeing the ground lurch around while you fail to actually feel most of it… Your stomach tends to feel like it's being left out of all the fun. Damn near wasted that taco…"

He helped Maeve with the zipper on the back and handed her a holstered pistol.

She looked pointedly at the weapon and then up at her two visitors.

"The minute we break atmo," Gleb explained, sliding his own sidearm out and hefting it, "we become active combatants, as far as Chiron is concerned. If they spot us, they'll be curious enough to want to run us down and capture us."

"You sound kind of eager about that." She pulled out the pistol, ejected the magazine and pulled back on the slide to confirm it wasn't loaded. "You want us to get caught?" She checked the full magazine before sliding it back into the weapon.

"Quickest way to find them," Gleb said.

"Except for the part where we're their prisoners…" She put the weapon back in the holster and clipped it to a strip of utility webbing on her thigh.

"I find that 'prisoner' is really a matter of perspective." Gleb grinned putting away his own, more advanced sidearm. "I was once a prisoner on the Lord Sandrak's flagship. I still walked away with a couple of his shuttles and his entire comms database."

"Do that kind of thing all the time, do you?" She took her helmet from John.

"It's what I was grown for, plus… I have the ability to project thoughts into the minds of the Quailu."

"What?" She looked at John. "Did you know about this?"

"No!" John looked at Gleb, face unreadable. "When were you planning to tell us about this?"

"Now." Gleb replied mildly. "Obviously. I'm telling you now because you might find yourselves in a position where it's relevant later today."

"How do I know you haven't been poking around in my brain all this time?" John demanded.

"You see why I kept this until now? If I'd told you about this from the start, you'd have been distracted. I only invade an enemy's mind. Besides, I've found that there's a limit to how much crazy shit a person's brain can absorb in one sitting."

He made a walking motion with his fingers. "That's why we're doing baby-steps, as you locals like to say."

"Baby-steps…" Maeve tilted her head. "Gleb, what other important shit are you holding out?"

"Nothing important."

"Gleb!"

"Seriously! I've pretty much told you the important stuff." He held out his hand, counting off on his fingers. "I'm from an alien empire. I came here using my mind. I'm able to help you develop advanced tech. I can get into my enemies heads…"

He looked up at her. "Oh, yeah. The Quailu are empaths; did I mention that before now?"

"What? No!" Maeve pondered that for a moment. "How many of them are empaths?"

"Every single one. Some sort of survival mechanism. Let's them all know if a member of their group has spotted danger."

"Okay. That's pretty important." She emphasized the word 'important'. "It's a pretty major advantage to keep in mind if we're being interrogated."

"Yeah but, like any strength, it can also be a weakness."

"Maybe you can explain how being able to read us is a disadvantage for the Quailu?" John suggested with a hint of sarcasm.

"Sure! Let's just imagine I'm sneaking down a corridor and I spot a lone Quailu ahead of me. I use his body heat to pinch off his motor control cluster. I sneak up behind him and I tell myself I'm a servant of Nergal… the Quailu god of the underworld," he explained in response to the blank faces.

"Anyway, I get that idea lodged in my head, then I open my mind to the poor fool. Suddenly, he's not just frozen in place, he's convinced a servant of Nergal is behind him, eager to start rending the flesh from his bones…"

"So you scare him before you kill him." John grimaced. "Not saying you shouldn't enjoy your work, Gleb, but how does that help?"

"Because the Quailu like to tell themselves they aren't superstitious. They're too modern and sophisticated to believe in Nergal, even though most of them employ a house oracle – purely a traditional thing, you understand.

"When any sentient being suddenly hears death knocking, they come full circle, back to the same squalling, frightened creature they were at birth. Death strips all that 'sophistication' away and leaves you naked.

"And every one of that Quailu's crewmates can feel it too."

"That's a good example," John admitted, eyes wide. "Like psy-ops on steroids."

"Scare a native crewman of any other species and you just scare *him*." Gleb nodded. "Scare one Quailu crewman and you can infect the whole *crew*. It takes a damn good commander and a well-trained crew to stand up to something like that. Not the kind of thing you find with the Chironans."

He gestured to the door. "We could continue our conversation while flying. Be a shame to stand around here in our suits for no good reason."

They went up to the heli-pad where the new ship was waiting.

"There she is," Gleb announced grandly. "The *Holy Shit, What's That?*"

Maeve snorted.

Gleb looked at her. "You don't like the name?"

"No, I love it, actually. I can just imagine the tower at Miramar picking us up on radar and trying to contact us."

He grinned. "That's why we originally gave our first generation of small ships goofy names like; *Your Last Chance* or *The Reason We Can't Have Nice Things*. Now we're mostly making the corvettes and they all have sword names."

Gleb walked past the gaggle of guards who'd all come up to the roof, no doubt advised of the strange craft by the two who'd been there when it landed.

"Each of you is supposed to be guarding something specific, right?" Maeve hinted darkly.

They scattered like a flock of pigeons startled by a cat. Maeve climbed in and, at Gleb's gesture, took the center seat in the cockpit.

"Strap in," Gleb told them. "This isn't some sci-fi movie. Inertia can sneak up on you when you least expect it, especially with the half-rumped system we've cobbled together!"

Gleb noticed the helmets they were setting on the decking while strapping in. It reminded him of an important detail they should take care of while still on the ground. "Better link the ship, as well as my suit, to your suits' comm systems."

He found their frequencies using the scanner in his own suit and got everything linked. He closed his helmet, the speed of it making his passengers jump in mild alarm.

"Can you hear me now?" he asked.

"When do we get super cool suits like yours?" Maeve asked.

"Soon as we find the enemy and steal some of their stuff." Gleb activated the drive plates. "I'm gonna start us out with a one standard gravity ascent."

"Whoa!" Maeve's hands twitched out to the sides, palms down. "That'll take some getting used to."

"You see what I mean?" John asked. "Your brain tells you you're moving but your stomach is gonna be stubborn and insist that your brain is wrong."

"Yeah." Maeve had grabbed her arm-rests and she forced herself to let go. "When you don't sense any acceleration, any increased gravity, you feel like you're going to fly up out of your chair and smash into the hull above."

"And yet you're still feeling regular gravity," Gleb said. "calibrated to the blue ball that's falling away from us."

"Look outside, John!" Maeve exclaimed. She waved a hand out the windows at the rapidly darkening sky. "We're astronauts now!"

"You of all people?" Gleb glanced over at her. "You've never broken atmo?"

"We make the safest, most reliable rockets in the industry but there's always a risk. If I announced I was going to ride one, our stock price would tank. It could shut us down."

"Speaking of risk…" Gleb reached over and tapped the helmet that still sat in her lap. "…Better put those on, just in case of a hull breach."

John scrambled to get his on once the danger had been pointed out but Maeve did it more slowly and with a bit more grumbling.

"The Chironans better have a suit that fits Humans," she growled. "These things are clunky, now that we see how great yours is."

"Any suit will fit you." Gleb checked to confirm that the sections of outer hull set to act as sensor plates were doing their job. "There's, essentially, only one type of suit. It just adjusts for the wearer. You can take one off a Quailu or even an Enibulan, and it can recalibrate to fit your body."

"All this new tech…" Maeve went quiet.

"What's wrong?" Gleb darted a glance at her before returning to his screens.

"It's just that… all of my life has been about driving technology. Improvements to our rocket engines, habitat upgrades, hydroponics, power storage…"

"And now it's eclipsed by some guy who drops advanced alien gear in your lap?" Gleb asked.

"Well, yeah. Life is about challenges. If you're not pushing yourself to improve on what's gone before, where's the challenge?"

"I can see how that would bother you," Gleb admitted. "And I might have an antidote."

"I'm all ears."

He looked over at her. "Not that I'd ever noticed."

She laughed. "Just spill the beans, buster!"

"You remember I'm not from your planet, right? Are you telling me to defecate or something?"

"You need to get that suit of yours to teach you idioms. Just tell me what the cure is for my lack of challenge."

"Well, I've been playing in your *world* for a while, developing this first prototype. It's been a real eye-opener for me. I have a new appreciation for what guys like Noa do, back home."

He raised his eyebrows. "How about you guys come play in my world for a change?"

"You mean…" Her mouth was threatening to go full-grin.

"We can be at the moon in…" Gleb checked his screen. "…A couple hours."

"Hang on!" John said loudly. "You can't just take my CEO into a combat situation!"

"How many do you figure are there?" Maeve asked, pretending she hadn't heard John's protest.

"What?" John spluttered. "Boss, you can't be serious!"

"It really depends on what they're up to," Gleb told her. "If they're just here looking for genetic anomalies, then it's probably just a few staff and their contraband Humans – illegally grown Humans."

"Won't we get spotted as we approach?"

"That's always a possibility," Gleb admitted, "but it's unlikely. Were in a tiny ship and space is a big place to search, especially if they think nobody knows they're there. They probably aren't keeping the best watch in the first place.

"We can take a look at least. We're out here, we're armed, we're ready to take advantage of whatever might come up…"

"How does this put the challenge back in our daily lives?" John asked. "Aside from killing aliens, that is."

"It could open new avenues of discovery." Gleb set the course and turned to face them. "Say we get there and find a freighter or a frigate. I can handle the crew easily enough. I just have to take the bridge.

"But that doesn't just give you your first ship for the defense of Irth; it gives you a path drive!"

"Hold on there, slim," John said firmly. "You're glossing over a lot of ground with 'I just have to take the bridge'. There's a whole bunch of folks in there, right?"

"On a cruiser, sure." Gleb nodded. "Hells, even a frigate would have about seven or eight stations but it's my day-job, as you folks like to say. At the Battle of Kish, Humans knocked out forty percent of the enemy fleet before a single shot was fired.

"I personally disabled several key ships and seized my lord's brother from the bridge of his own flagship. If we *do* find a warship, there might be too many Quailu to deal with on an individual basis, so I'd just lock their suits open and rig the ship for combat.

"In the empire, we store our atmosphere and open the hulls to space when we go into battle. Prevents explosive decompression."

"You'd kill them all?" John exploded.

"Damn right, I would," Gleb answered calmly. "As far as they're concerned, you're property. You're all theirs to do with as they please. When they decide to come after you openly, you won't even have the luxury of pretending to be free.

"My people have been slaves to the empire for sixty thousand years. You either fight that or accept it. Anyway, a warship seems unlikely. I'd expect to find some shuttles at least, though a freighter wouldn't be a surprise and, again…

"Path drives!"

"Path drives are great," Maeve said, "but our focus, right now, is on building up a way to defend our solar system."

Gleb looked sidelong at her. "You're not fooling me with that."

"What?"

"You're not the kind of person that just deals with the matter at hand; neither of you are. You're always looking at your next moves.

"If we find a path drive, it opens up the whole galaxy. There are Billions of habitable worlds out there in this galaxy alone. The HQE doesn't count for a fraction of a fraction. You told me about your vision, a passion for ensuring the future of the species."

He nodded at the window. "That future's out there.

"You've proven your commitment with Mars. It's a hostile environment but you found a way to create a self-sustaining outpost there. If we can get our hands on path drives, there could be self-sustaining communities over a wide swath of the galaxy and we're talking about comfortable planets."

"Hah! Can you imagine me building a log cabin on some alien world?" Maeve shook her head.

"That's usually how it worked, back in the empire's expansion days, though they'd print the houses from local material, rather than stacking up logs. You've got Billions of people on Irth. A lot of them are farmers who're barely making a living.

"Recruit them. Offer them large parcels of land and free passage. If they can set up a reliable source of food, the rest will follow."

"Shit!" John had a faraway look, no mean feat when staring out at space. "My brother's losing his farm to the bank. Imagine the look on his face if I showed him some exotic alien spread and said he could have it free and clear!"

"How would you like to start developing new farming tech based on nanites?" Maeve asked him.

John whooped, causing Maeve to wince inside her helmet, but Gleb's caught it in time to attenuate the volume.

She chuckled. "There's that old urge to struggle and innovate coming back! You had me a little worried before but..."

"Hell! This is opening a whole new era for Humanity! It's like the wild west all over again but with fast ships and flying cars!"

"Alright look, I was just trying to build enough enthusiasm for us to go raid that moon base." Gleb's smile kept the moment from crashing. "That colonisation stuff will still happen, as long as we beat the Chironans first."

"Alright, dammit, I'm in!" John declared. "We'd feel like idiots if we turned back now and an invasion force showed up before we could sort out some convoluted plan on how to raid the Chironan base."

"The best time to take action," Gleb stated authoritatively, "is usually a few days ago. The second-best time, however, is always right now."

"Meanwhile..." Maeve got out of her seat and moved aft. "You should never go into battle on an empty stomach. Learned that from reading C.S. Forester. How about we break into these cookies?"

"Those aren't really for us," Gleb said. "It's bad manners to visit without bringing something along. I swear, you folks live in a state of total anarchy!"

She waved the box in her hand. "You brought five boxes…"

He shrugged. "My girlfriend's youngest sister is doing a fundraiser to buy police coverage for her guide troop's clubhouse. Turns out Irth kids have superpowers of their own… cuteness…"

He waved a hand. "I suppose we can spare a box or two."

Things Get Weird

Babilim Station

Eth was too slow countering her move and Scylla managed to duck under his left arm, grabbing his left knee. He knew what came next and prepared his own defense.

Throwing him completely off guard, Scylla paid no attention to what should come next. Instead of sliding her grip up behind his knee and grabbing him by the waist as a prelude to throwing him over her body, she pulled his knee up and threw her own weight against him.

He went down on his back and she landed astride him, breathing heavily.

He was keeping his mind closed from hers while they sparred, so he was freely able to wonder at the point of the unorthodox move.

He'd been enjoying these training sessions with Scylla. She was one of the few Humans that didn't see him as just the leader of their people.

And the way she looked in her under-armor suit didn't hurt either. *That's not helping!* he told himself desperately, suddenly very conscious of how she was sitting astride his pelvis, mouth open, chest heaving.

Gods! Please don't let her notice the reaction she's causing! He moved his hips slightly, hoping – and not hoping – that she'd take the hint and let him up. In all probability, it only made his state more evident and she leaned forward, the increased pressure almost making him gasp.

"I win!" she insisted.

"Umm..." he replied cleverly. He was trying to think of something to keep her focused on the training... on the small chance that she might actually be unaware of the undercurrent that had sprung up.

"It was certainly unexpected," he admitted, "but you left my hands free, which kind of runs counter to the goals of Chironan grappling. That's why the standard move exists. If you throw me the other way, you can rotate in behind me and get leverage on my arm."

That worked, at least.

She got up, leaving him on his back and headed for the door. "Thanks for the lesson," she said curtly.

Eth lay there, staring up at the ceiling lights, waiting for his breathing to return to normal.

That was almost a disaster! he told himself.

Junior Scouts
Moon, far side

Gleb was close now. He got down onto his belly and crawled the last few meters to the crater's rim. He eased his head slowly up until he could see in to the opposite side. There was a base there, alright. It was set into the far wall of the crater, approximately two and a half kilometers away. His suit's optics gave him a good view of the scene, which he recorded before sliding back from the edge.

He moved far enough from the edge to stand up and then hop-walked the rest of the way back to where his companions waited with the *Holy Shit, What's That?*.

"What's there?" Maeve asked before he could bring himself to a stop.

Gleb bounced past them and turned, churning up a haze of dust. He edged back more slowly. "They're down there," he confirmed.

He had his suit project a larger view of the crater and pinned it between them. "The only entrances are here and here." He pointed out two holes in the crater wall, near the bottom. "Nearly half a kilometer down. One looks like a shuttle bay – you can see the nose of one shuttle right there – and the other is big enough to accommodate a medium-sized freighter or a frigate."

"Is there a freighter in there?" John bent at the waist in a vain reflexive attempt to see inside a bay that was scanned from a higher angle.

"Hard to say. There's cargo piled near the entrance that blocks our view. I'm leaning toward saying there is a ship in there. Seems odd to block the entrance, unless you're currently loading a ship that's already in there."

"This is your area of expertise," Maeve said. "So what's the plan? Are we climbing down from the top?"

Gleb considered it. "I'd rather not. Half a kilometer down? We'd get all tired and dirty and probably drop our cookies. Let's just fly down there and land in their shuttle bay."

John stared at him. "What the hell?"

"You think they'd have a heavy guard in there?" Gleb pointed at the image. "The gods only know how long they've been operating out of that hole but I'd bet it's a few thousand years and not a single unexpected visitor the whole time.

"It's not like we're going up against a hard-core military installation, here. We're talking about a remote, illegal research station where people get sent because they've pissed off somebody important."

He nodded to himself. "I think the best course of action is to just fly straight in through the front door, put them off their game and then put them down."

"We're really just going to kill them all?" John asked.

"See these containers blocking the larger entrance?" Gleb pointed to the freight hangar. "I'll bet the contents of those boxes will make you change your mind about killing off the Chironans. They look like they're fitted with stasis units."

"Humans?" Maeve asked darkly.

"Yeah. I think they're sending samples back for experimentation. Our species is no longer available for sale but these assholes are probably planning to use us anyway, as long as they can keep it quiet. If they take Irth outright, they can pretty much use us any way they want."

Gleb wanted to reach out and find out how Maeve and John felt about this raid but he'd committed himself to using his abilities in a more restrictive way.

"What the hell are we waiting for?" Maeve demanded. "Let's load up and get down there!"

Gleb led the way back into their small ship. *That seemed pretty definitive,* he thought.

He lifted the small ship off the surface and sent it racing down to the hangar. They slid through the atmo-shield and settled on the three hard-points protruding from the hull's underside.

Gleb picked up the boxes of cookies and handed them to John. He snatched a clipboard off a stanchion by the difference engine and opened a section of the hull to create an exit. "Follow my lead," he said, opening his helmet, "and keep your helmets on, just in case they try to shut down the atmo-shielding."

He hopped to the ground and took a quick look around. There was a freighter but he filed that away for later exploration.

There were two native Chironans five Humans and one Quailu in the bay. As soon as he heard both sets of feet hit the decking behind him, he set off toward the Quailu, who was staring at him with his mouth hanging open.

"Can I help you?" a large Chironan asked in tones that offered nothing of the sort. He'd spoken in English.

"No, thank-you," Gleb answered in the same language without breaking stride. "We're just here for a delivery."

He kept walking until he was standing before the Quailu. "Good morning, noble sir!" he greeted him in Imperial Standard before glancing down at his clipboard. "That's three of the vanilla and one box of the chocolate, as ordered. If you could just sign here…" He thrust the clipboard into the bemused alien's hands.

"What in the sphincter of hell are you…"

The Quailu fell dead.

Gleb turned. The two native Chironans had seen their overseer fall but had no idea what had caused it. Now they'd picked up tie-down wrenches from the decking and advanced on the interfering Humans.

They decided to stop for a quick rest, however, when Gleb pulled a nasty-looking sidearm and aimed it in their direction.

"How many are working here?" Gleb demanded in Imperial.

"I don't care if you're armed," one of them spat. "I don't answer to chattel."

Gleb managed to smile in a way that made the Chironan shiver. "Let me explain what you've gotten yourselves into here." He lowered his weapon to show his utter disdain for his foes.

He further accentuated that disdain by walking casually toward them. "You have trespassed on our world. This system is ours in return for our loyal service to the lord of the Underworld. Only the Nergalhim may set foot on our unholy territory."

The one on the left looked unsettled by this but his companion spat on the deck again. "I'll show you what I do to Nergal's ass-kissers!" He took a step forward…

And Gleb held up a hand, freezing him in place, almost literally. He was drawing the Chironan's heat indiscriminately, letting him feel the fear, and then he took enough energy to sever his cranial shunt.

The remaining Chironan whimpered in fear now that he'd seen 'proof' of the supernatural. He dropped his improvised weapon and fell to his knees. "I'll answer your questions. There are another five Quailu, one more Chironan, these Humans, and eight more on the surface of the Humans' world."

Gleb translated for his companions, keeping an eye on the five Humans who'd clustered together near the entrance to the freighter.

"That sounds like a ludicrously small operation," Maeve said, surprised.

"Big enough for what they're doing," Gleb suggested, "and small enough to remain controllable."

"What about him?" She nodded at the kneeling alien. "I mean, he's cooperating…"

"I am," the Chironan agreed eagerly in English.

"Then you can keep cooperating and tell us why there's blood smeared on the deck over there." John waved a hand toward the containers.

"That?" The creature waved its long, heavy arms. "They don't ship fresh food all the way out here, so they let us take a…" His eyes grew wide as he suddenly seemed to realize the danger he was talking himself into.

"You ate a Human?" Gleb asked, letting himself into the alien's head.

"They only let us have a small one…"

"You ate a child?" Gleb could see it in the Chironan's mind. "A child you took from its own home?"

"It hardly suffered at all," their prisoner lied hopelessly.

Gleb winced when the pistol went off – not from the sound but from the pain registering in the Chironan's mind while he was still inside.

He withdrew as Maeve fired the next shot and then the next, expertly drilling the alien in its joints. He shrieked in pain, flopping onto his back in a growing pool of blood.

"Didn't suffer?" she screamed. "You ate a child, you sick piece of shit! Do you have kids?"

Seven offspring, Gleb risked the pain to look and he could see them. He put out a hand to restrain Maeve. He didn't need to read her directly to feel the urge to kill that she was radiating.

Not that he didn't agree with that urge but he wanted this monster to understand her rage first. "You can't hide your sins from the Nergalhim," he told their victim in English, "and you can't hide your family.

188

"Seven small ones, back on Chiron, wondering why their father has been gone so long." Gleb leaned down, bringing his face within a hand's-breadth of the alien's.

"Shall I visit them?" Sure enough, the location came to mind. "The southern archipelago is nice this time of year," he added, feeling the flare of alarm at his knowledge. "We can explain your absence and perhaps… stay for a snack…"

"No!"

"It's too late to say no," Gleb hissed, waving at the blood he'd spotted. "Nergal would not be pleased if I sent you to him ignorant of the horrors you've committed. This is the only way for you to fully comprehend your abominable crime before we kill you."

"Please…"

"We should finish clearing the place out." Gleb straightened and turned to Maeve, ignoring the horrified creature at his feet. "Then we can take stock of what we have here."

She indicated the Chironan with the muzzle of her handgun. "What about him?"

"Let's leave him for now. Let him ponder the consequences he's brought on his family for a while. We can toss him out into the crater if he's still alive when we come back down here."

He waved over the small group of Humans. "You the folks they brought out here from Kwharaz Station?" he asked in English.

A few nods.

He nodded back. "Scylla told us about you after she escaped."

"The assassin?" one man asked.

"I'd hardly call her an assassin," Gleb corrected him. "More like she was supposed to be a guidance package for a bomb. She's free of all that now. Actually, she's kind of our high priestess." He took a step closer, holstering his sidearm.

"Do you all want to be free as well?"

189

The man squinted at him. His face was a riot of warring emotions.

"It's not a fair question, is it?" Gleb asked gently. "This is all you've known and probably not for very long either. I'll ask you again later, after you've had some time to put things into context. You can be more than this." He lifted his gaze to include the others.

"You all can be so much more. For now, stay here, stay quiet and stay out of our way."

"They'll kill you," the man warned. "They're gods!"

"Who?" Gleb pointed at the dead Quailu on the decking. "Those guys? Thanks to Scylla's teachings, I was able to kill him with a single thought.

"They're not gods. I'm certainly no god and yet I can reduce a Quailu to a quaking mass of fear without his even knowing I'm there. That's why they're so desperate to control us."

He held out a hand, palm out. "Just wait here while we clear this place."

He stepped over the moaning Chironan and started moving down the corridor, reaching out to feel for enemies.

"I was starting to worry we'd get rushed in that hangar," John muttered. "All that gunfire…"

"Should have thought of that," Gleb admitted. "The gun, I mean. Much better weapon for this kind of thing. Mine would set off alarms as soon as I fired it but those pistols of yours are too primitive to register. The security protocols aren't terribly concerned about sound."

"Pretty effective, for a primitive weapon," Maeve asserted, changing magazines so she'd have a full load.

"Oh, absolutely." Gleb turned right. "I wish I'd brought one myself. Probably only registered on the security scanners as a minor exothermic reaction. Not even a need for fire suppression measures."

He held up a hand to halt them. "I can feel them," he explained.

"How does that work..."

"Shush!" Gleb closed his eyes. "Just ahead, maybe ten meters. I think all five remaining Quailu are in there." He started moving again, drawing his sidearm. "No shooting, if you can help it. I need the system security lockouts."

They swept into the lounge where five very startled Quailu gaped at them. A tray of cheap fermented fat lay on the table in front of them.

One started to rise. "What in the deepest layer of hell are you doing?" he roared. "I'll have your..."

Gleb held up a hand and the yelling stopped. He drew heat from his victim's cardiac pumps and used the energy to pinch off motor control, freezing him in place.

The fear was coming off him in waves. The others, already half intoxicated from the fermented fat, froze of their own accord.

"Your lockout code," he said, releasing his victim who, as it turned out, was in charge of the facility. His mind called up the code as he slumped back onto the couch.

"If they move, shoot them," he told his companions. "Screen!" he commanded in Standard Imperial.

He accessed the security settings and tried the code. It worked. He reset the code to one of his own and then used the personnel menu to find that the last native Chironan was picking up a Human team on the planet's night-side. He slid the screen aside. "You can kill them now, if you want."

"But you said we'd be shot if we moved," a Quailu protested.

"Yes, but I never promised you'd be spared if you stayed still," Gleb told him.

This time he didn't flinch when Maeve and John opened fire on the Quailu. He wasn't in their minds and their deaths seemed entirely necessary, given what they'd been allowing to happen.

He reached down and picked up a strip of fat, giving it a sniff. "Cheap garbage!" He shuddered and tossed it on the chest of a dying Quailu.

He turned back to the screen and connected his suit to the system, so he'd be able to use his HUD. "They have English in the system," he told his companions. "I'll set the interface to use it so you can see what I'm doing."

He brought up the maintenance interface so he could find out what tech was present on the outpost. The first thing he noticed was a long string of outstanding call-outs for routine maintenance. "Hardly surprising that these idiots are either doing repairs but not logging it, or they're just not even doing repairs."

He sighed. "They probably weren't the most up-and-coming members of Chironan society. There are a couple of training pods on the station but I'm not terribly comfortable using them until we've had a chance to check them out.

"There are, however, three perfectly good pods on that ship. No captain worth his sod would ship out without one. You never know when your chief engineer might suddenly blow himself up and leave you to fix everything on your own."

He turned to look at the dead aliens. "Looks like one of these guys was the captain and he *had* no crew." He chuckled. "Sounds like the Chironans to me. So bent on security, they'd rather not have a whole crew talking about where they've been. Bet he wished he'd had a couple dozen crewmates to back him up just now, though."

He turned back to Maeve and John but he was looking through the space between them. "Six proper shuttles down in the transit hangar and the one freighter," he said, mostly to himself. "Don't much need a freighter right now – maybe later when we're starting up some colonies but right now?

"No, what we really want is a fast-attack corvette. Should be enough room to regrow her in that hangar and she does have some basic weapons…" He looked at Maeve.

"Before I grow a proper ship, how about you and John become the first locals to qualify for service on it?"

"Before you grow it?" Maeve gave him a dubious look. "How long does training in a pod take?"

"About ten minutes. Most of the time is from mapping your current patterns so there's no interference. Laying down the new information is really only a few seconds. We should give you the full package for the ships we're likely to use or run into."

"You're gonna use a pod to cram all that into our implants?" John blurted. "How much storage will it take?"

"No." Gleb shook his head. "We don't use implants. The pod puts the knowledge directly into your brain. As for the storage size, it's minimal. You'd be surprised at the data capacity a Human brain has. I should really give you the geo-political file as well," he added.

John scratched at the back of his neck. "I'm not sure about this, Gleb."

Maeve was looking at John and had started nodding in agreement but then she caught herself. Smiling nervously, she turned to Gleb. "How long have these pods been used to educate Humans?"

"Since before the Neanderthals went out of business."

The nervous side of her smile relented a little. "I'm in," she said simply.

How Thick Are You?

Babilim Station

Eth walked into the mess hall. He was getting used to the scale of the station's spaces. It helped that they'd finally found a way to cut the material used as supports in most of the place.

The tables in this room, which the ancients must have used for the same purpose as the current occupants, had all been at eye level to the Humans. The support columns had been sliced off in the middle and the tops re-attached at a more useable height.

The serving line, on the other hand, was a lot harder to lower, given the energy conduits and circuitry involved. In the end, Noa had just had ramps built that led up to new raised walkways for the diners and those on the other side who kept the serving surfaces stocked.

The serving utensils were another story. When this room had first been found, they'd been unsettled by the presence of food on the serving line.

Fresh food…

The ancients were thought to have disappeared more than a quarter-Million years ago, so it seemed unlikely they'd keep putting out food. Someone else had to be here.

A detailed search of the vicinity had turned up nothing but one curious Human had cracked the mystery, and nearly lost his right hand, when he decided to find out if the green fruit on the serving line was edible.

All metabolic activity in his hand came to a stop when he reached in. He was surprised when he couldn't close his fingers around the fruit, then alarmed at the sudden and total lack of feeling in his hand.

Things went downhill rapidly from there.

The serving surfaces were used to halt the decay of food. Clearly, the ancients had been meat-eaters because the system had mistaken the Human's hand for food. When his hand's metabolic activity stopped, it had felt like he'd slept on his arm – for three months straight.

The utensils were there for taking food and for restocking the serving line. They'd tried cutting them down to size but they kept emitting smoke and lightning bolts every time they entered the field. Whether there was embedded circuitry or it came down to simple harmonic resonance, the giant, novelty-sized tongs couldn't be altered.

There was still food in storage, which could have been an even sharper lesson in safe procedures for exploring an alien station. A preservation field on a serving line could cause excruciating pain. Walking into a storage container where the same field was, in effect, essentially suicide.

There was probably more food in the massive storage network of automatically stored containers but the ancient language was still a mystery. Finding food was hit or miss.

Eth loaded up a tray with food and descended a ramp to the floor level. Oliv and Scylla were sitting at a table near the ramp and Oliv, seeing him, nodded at an empty chair to her left.

"How long will we be letting the buzz build?" She asked as he set his tray down.

"It would be best if we hear speculation from the media-shapers before we take further action." Eth dropped into his seat. "If the idea of a breakaway group helping to keep the peace starts settling into the public consciousness, it should be easier to nudge our former master into accepting our plan."

Scylla chewed her food, looking out the windows at a hovering garden area that could have housed an entire city.

"What is that?" Oliv leaned over to squint at a bluish fruit on Eth's plate.

"No idea, but it never hurts to try something new."

She raised an eyebrow.

"Well," Scylla blurted, her tone bitter, "that brings things into focus!" She got up, leaving her tray on the table, and walked away without another word.

Eth watched her leave, his mouth hanging open. When Scylla finally rounded the corner and disappeared, he turned to Oliv.

"What the hells has gotten into her?"

Oliv shrugged. "She's not normally like that with you?"

"Well…" He scratched the back of his head. "No. I don't think I've ever seen her act like that."

"Hey, I don't know." Oliv pulled Scylla's plate over and took a few items. "I like her but she's a little unusual." She tried a strip of some kind of meat, chewing it thoughtfully.

"She was… normal… last time you were with her?"

Eth nodded.

"Well, that was probably when you pissed her off." She waved the meat around. "What did you do?"

"I wish I knew."

"No, you dolt. I mean, literally, what were the two of you doing?"

"I was training her in Chironan grappling techniques…"

She grinned. "Is that how they're describing it these days?"

"Be serious!"

"I am," Oliv insisted. "She could use a good 'grappling', I bet. "Gods! Given her past, has she ever had a chance to try a bit of 'grappling'? Poor girl!"

"She asked me to get her up to speed on combat techniques," Eth said pointedly.

"Uh huh," Oliv grunted, "and who suggested you start with…" She drew out the next word, making it sound lascivious. "Grappling?"

"Oliv!" He forgot what he was about to say next, if there had even been a plan. "OK, well, she was the one who suggested it but it wasn't like that…"

"Right." She took another bite. "So what happened in your last session? I'm betting the last bit is the most important, the moment when you annoyed her."

Eth looked through her, gathering his memories. "It should have been a gun-belt throw but she just barreled into me – ended up sitting on top of me…"

"Not working for me." Oliv got up. "C'mon, show me!"

"What?"

"You want to figure this out or not? Get up and come at me!"

Eth looked up at her. *There's no getting her to let this go,* he thought. He got up and moved to stand in front of her.

She leaned over and clasped her hands around his knee. "So she just went at you and knocked you down?"

"Yeah I… Oof!" He went backward, Oliv leaping onto him as he dropped onto his backside. His elbow smacked the floor, sending a jolt of pain all the way to his fingertips. By the time he realized what was happening, she was sitting astride him the same way Scylla had been.

And the other people in the room were either laughing or applauding.

"Yeah," she mused, "no real tactical reason for doing this."

"That's what I *told* her and she just got up and left."

"Well, well…" She sighed. "That explains it."

"I don't see how."

She gave him a look of pity mixed with scorn. "When they designed the command genome, did they have to toss out a bunch of the common sense just to make room for all that cleverness?"

She ground her hips a couple of times, pressing down on him hard. "I said there was no *tactical* reason. I didn't say there was no reason at all."

Her motion sent a jolt straight through his body. "Oliv, it's not like that!"

"It's exactly like that, you idiot!"

"But she's only been out of the maturation chamber for a few months!"

"Where she probably got the same behavioural patterns we all had when we emerged with these adult bodies." Oliv gave her hips another roll. "Do you remember your first time?" She turned her head and nodded at Cenda, who was laughing at Eth's discomfort.

"I was about to say 'She remembers'," Oliv said, turning back to Eth, "but it probably wasn't all that memorable, was it Cenny?"

"It was less than a week out of the chambers," Cenda said. "I remember, but that doesn't mean it was memorable. Less than a minute and pretty one-sided."

The room was hooting with derision now.

It never occurred to Eth to be embarrassed by this discussion happening in front of so many others. Humans might be a legal species now, with the accompanying rights of reproduction, but they still hadn't changed their mindset very much.

"Hey!" Cenda shouted, grinning. "I doubt any of you did better!"

That settled the room pretty quickly.

"Don't conflate lack of experience with complete innocence," Oliv told Eth. "Most likely, she was grown with the same programming as the rest of us. An adult, a ruthless killer, but still a biological creature with built-in urges.

"She was exploring those urges when she threw you to the floor. She knows you better than anyone else and she seems to like you, for some reason." Oliv finally got off him and reached her hand out.

He took her hand and she pulled him up.

"Go," she told him, sitting at the table again. "Make this right," she added loftily, pulling his plate over.

And so he went.

School's Out

Moon, far side

John opened his eyes as the pod's transparent shield slid out of the way. He reached up, putting a hand on his forehead.

"Looks like it's still in one piece," Gleb said cheerfully.

"I don't feel anything," he admitted.

"Neither do I," Maeve said, sitting up from her own session. "How do we know it even worked?"

Gleb grinned mischievously. "Well, for starters, we're all talking in Imperial Standard and you're so good at it that your brains can form the words without even realising it."

"Fornication!" John exclaimed. "We are, aren't we?"

"Hells!" Maeve marveled. "We're even translating into your idioms and expressions."

She climbed out, hands spread as if to catch a stanchion if she lost her balance, but she had no need. She straightened, a look of wonder on her face.

"But what about the other stuff?" John asked. "The training package you had on your suit's processor. I don't feel like an engineer or a captain or a comms officer…"

"Set a course for Irth," Gleb suggested.

"Oh, well, I need to…" He stopped, mouth hanging open in surprise. "Hells! That's incredible!" He tilted his head, frowning. "But this ship is all wrong. I'd have to wing it, I suppose."

"Yeah," Gleb agreed. "Let's get out of here and turn this old heap into something much better."

He led them out of the ship, out of the smells of old cargo and sweat and into the cleaner air of the outpost. A dead native Chironan lay on the decking by a stack of cargo pallets. The small gaggle of contraband Humans had swelled to twelve.

"Showed up while you were in the pods," Gleb explained. "Figured I'd just take care of it while you were busy. They've got more kidnap victims as well."

He raised his voice. "Let's move back a bit, folks! We're changing this ship and you don't want to get in the way. Lots of large moving parts for the next couple of hours."

He shooed everyone back a few more meters and then brought up the link between his suit and the freighter. He checked the pattern for a fast-attack corvette, confirming there was enough material and that there was sufficient room to grow the thing inside the hangar. The spare nanites would automatically form damage-control blocks throughout the ship.

There were a few minor flags that had to be dealt with before he could start the change. Most were dismissable but the third one was a pleasant issue to deal with. This ship was originally a heavy-mineral transport. As such, she carried five pitch drives in order to break away from higher-than-normal gravity wells.

He only needed three for a corvette, so he directed the two extras for storage in the new ship's cargo compartment. With the shuttle that had just landed, he had enough pitch drives and power units to make three extra corvettes, though only this first one would have a path drive.

"It's still technically the maiden voyage for the *Holy Shit, What's That?* and she's already headed for the museum," Gleb said to nobody in particular.

He rotated the screen to face Maeve. "You want to build a cutting-edge ship that's better than anything the Chironans can throw at us?" he asked her. "We wouldn't have been standing here right now if you hadn't backed me, so hit the green button…"

"Work, work, work…" she said ironically, reaching out to touch the button, though she let out a gasp when the button pulsed.

"I felt that!" she exclaimed. "How do you create syntactic feedback with a hologram?" She looked up and slightly to the side, squinting at nothing in particular.

"Gods curse me! That pod really does work. I just ask the question and my brain answers." She looked at the freighter. "Shouldn't something be happening?"

"It is," Gleb assured her, "but it takes a few hours. First thing to do is secure the difference engines, drives, power shunts and other core systems. Once they're moved into place, the old hull can start melting."

He took the screen back. "Looks like nearly a hundred abductees in these containers." He called up a holo-image of the planet and linked the captives' data.

A dot showed where each had been taken from. "Looks like they're all from English speaking countries." John stepped closer. "I suppose it saves them having to operate in multiple languages..."

"Why not pick Mandarin or Hindi, then?" Gleb asked.

"You said they were looking for new genetic material." John pointed at China. "You'll find twice as many who speak Mandarin but they're mostly Chinese. Same thing with Hindi; not a lot of Caucasians or Africans using Hindi.

"There's maybe half a Billion folks speaking English but there has to be a few million of those who are of Chinese descent, South Asian, African, Pacific Islanders..."

"Shouldn't we let them out of containment?" Maeve asked.

"We should," Gleb agreed, "but not just yet. We don't want them milling around the hangar all scared and angry because they woke up on the Moon. Let's get the evacuation plan in place first."

He opened the traffic control system, such as it was with only two small hangars. "This freighter won't be missed for another five days and I'd bet the Chironans will take at least a day or two to get concerned about it."

He looked at his two companions. "I think I should take a shuttle down to San Diego and pick up my recruits. We come back, give 'em the same pod session you guys got and then we operate all seven shuttles to return the Humans to their homes."

"You've got three guys lined up, right?" John asked.

"Four now. My girlfriend had to know about the blackouts and it probably isn't a good idea to keep my real identity a secret from her. Also, she's what you guys call a *fighter-jock,* so this shouldn't be much of a stretch for her."

"Why not take the corvette when she's ready?" John nodded at the dissolving freighter. "Take less time in the long run."

"We have proper shuttles at our disposal now," Gleb reminded them. "I can have them back here and trained before this ship is finished." He frowned. "Ok, the pods are inside the ship, so we still have to wait, but at least we can get them fitted for suits."

"Hells!" Maeve had a speculative look on her face. "This may take away some exciting challenges for us on the technical side but the ways we can leverage this in opening new worlds! We need to seed a couple of new colonies as soon as we can."

"You have access to the database," Gleb said. "Have it show the nearest habitable worlds while I go get our new pilots." He nodded up at the freighter, which was starting to show holes in the outer hull. "You both know enough to keep an eye on that.

"If you have any questions, just put them into words – use Imperial because that's how the information was laid down in your minds – and you should 'remember' the answer.

"Keep those contraband Humans here and out of trouble. I should be back in less than a half hour." He returned to the screen. "I'm going to take four suits from those bodies in the lounge. You guys should help yourselves from the ones we killed down here."

John looked over at the dead aliens. "But how…" He laughed. "Not sure if I'll get used to just knowing all this stuff.

Finding the Nest
Assur System

Memnon sat on his throne, reaching out to feel the mood of his attendants. There was fear but not nearly enough. He turned his head, catching the eye of his planetary governor.

He didn't give any indication that he wished to speak to the fool. He merely stared at him, giving his displeasure a distinct focus. Now the governor was worried for his own safety and the fear was building in him.

The fear spread through the room. Memnon was known for his violent temper and his propensity to vent it on those around him. He sat back, ignoring the governor, now that he'd been of use.

The fear soothed his nerves. He decided to retire to his private quarters before the locals lapsed back into bored apathy.

He stood, reveling in the sudden spike of fear in the room, and strode off the dais. He hated this world but it had been his mother's home-world.

She'd been born to the world's third-ranking family, not expected to inherit anything of value, but she'd caught the eye of the dreaded Lord Sandrak and Memnon was the result.

Sandrak was now a prisoner of Mishak's hospitality and Memnon had seized almost half of his father's territory. It had been enough to make him into an elector – several times over – but he still had to wait for his status to be confirmed by a plenary vote in the council chamber on Throneworld.

It rankled that he only held half of what his father had attained. That Sandrak had two sons was no mitigation. Mishak couldn't have taken any of those worlds without jeopardising his own rise to the throne.

No, Memnon seethed as he stalked down the broad, tree-lined throneroom. *No, the other worlds slipped through my fingers because they thought I was too weak to compel their allegiance!* His lips peeled back in a snarl that he wasn't aware of.

But his attendants could feel the emotion that caused it and they shuddered.

That fool Emoliat thought my family was worthy of scorn when he ruled this system. He learned the error of his ways! He shoved a minor noble out of his way to reach his chamber, enjoying the quick transition he felt in the fool, from haughty anger to bowel-loosening terror.

He stopped as the doors slid closed behind him. Lounging by the ornamental fountain was a Quailu in moderate clothing.

She gave off an air of nonchalance that made it a struggle for Memnon to maintain his anger. "Ereshkigal," he greeted her. "How did you get in here? I hope you realize at least one of my guards will die for this."

"Another?" she asked. "A shame. I assume that's on top of the two I killed at your *secret* entrance." She yawned in response to his sudden flare of anger and surprise. "You prize my ability to ferret out secrets and yet you get angry when I do it."

"I expect you to ferret out the secrets of *others*," he said evenly, "not mine." He knew better than to try intimidating her.

"Well, you don't want me wandering up to you while you're busy frightening the poor saps in your throneroom, do you?" she drawled. "My line of work is all about discretion, after all."

He grunted, trying to leave it unclear whether he conceded the point, but he knew he was being petulant. He sat in the lounger opposite hers, forgoing the urge to sit uncomfortably close to her in a spiteful fit of revenge.

"You're here," he said. "I assume you have something to report. Something worth killing my guards over."

He tried to wait patiently for her answer. She was utterly unshakable. It was a goad to an awilu like himself, someone accustomed to fear and deference. *Perhaps that's the key to her success as an operator?*

"That ship you gave me," she said. "I managed to lose it. Plague. Entire Quailu crew perished in a matter of days."

He let her feel his irritation. It seemed appropriate, given the context. He knew she had a point but she had the annoying habit of starting the narrative as far from the point as possible. "Nobody left alive, then?"

"Only the Human crewmembers."

He took his time digesting that. If she was going to be annoying, she could wait. "I suppose some of them were willingly serving you or did you use subconscious conditioning?"

"Something like that," she drawled. She draped a leg suggestively over the lounger's arm.

He held his anger in check. "My brother's renegades took them in, no doubt, since they're cut off from reinforcements from Kish. A handful of Humans would seem like a gift from the gods."

"Until one of them reached out to me with a tiny little bit of information," she said.

He resisted the urge to prompt her.

"They're at Babilim."

"Ah," he said knowingly. "Babilim. Yes."

A long pause.

His resolve to resist prompting her fell apart. "What in all the levels of the underworld is a Babilim?"

"You've heard of the Titans?"

"From my mythology tutor," he said, "who I eventually shoved off a balcony. I'd be damned before I let my mother spend what little money we had for that nonsense!"

207

"Well, that nonsense has a basis in reality. The Titans built Babilim to encase a white dwarf star out on the fringe of the HQE, though, of course, the HQE didn't exist back then. Even the old kingdoms were little more than a dream in some warlord's head."

"Who the hells would make a station around a star? What possible reason could they have had?"

"Do you really care about the reasons of a long-dead race? The station exists and the renegade Humans are hiding there. What more do you need?"

He had to admit, she had a good point. "Nothing," he admitted. "Nothing at all. What quadrant is this station in?"

She waved a hand and a holo-map flickered into existence.

He had a system within a day's path from the place. *How have I got territory so close and I've never heard of Babilim?* "I'm moving my court," he growled. "There's a planetary governor that owes me an explanation!"

He stood. "I need to issue orders to my forces." He was mildly annoyed that she remained sprawled in the chair when he was standing. He opened a new window and raised the readiness levels of all his warships.

"Emoliat," he bellowed. "Get in here, you fool, and draw me a bath!"

The former lord of Assur scurried in, darting a glance at Memnon's visitor.

Memnon stripped off his robe and tossed it at Emoliat. "I'll have my under-armor suit after the bath, scum."

"That's my cue to leave," his agent said drily.

After...

Babilim Station

Scylla nestled in close to Eth's side, one arm draped over his chest. "That was gratifying," she announced. "We should do that again."

Eth made a sound in his throat that was meant to signal agreement. He traced his fingertips down her spine.

She shivered, startling a large stick-insect that had settled on her ankle. It strode back onto the mossy bank with its peculiar, wavering cadence and slipped into the cool water of the bubbling creek to hunt for its lunch.

"It's not what I expected," she said quietly.

"What were you expecting?"

"From what I've learned, this should be more..." She frowned. "I mean, my interest in you should have been sated by now. I've had you. Most Humans would be ready to look for someone new at this point. I seem to be doing it wrong."

"Then I must be doing it wrong as well." Eth felt the sudden flow of emotion from her, covering him like a warm breeze. He felt as if everything was well in the Universe. "Our people are changing, though sharing our thoughts while we were joined may have had an effect as well."

He was sure others with the *understanding* had probably tried it before but Eth hadn't had sex since serving on the *Dibbarra*. Feeling each other's sensations, it was like being an extension of your lover's mind and body.

They hadn't made any conscious decision. The barriers had simply dropped along with their clothing. It was, by far, the strongest connection he'd ever felt with another living creature.

"Does this mean we've claimed each other," she asked languidly, "like folks in a *proper* species do?"

"Yes," he said firmly, surprising himself. His hand came to rest on her hip. A breeze came up the tunnel from another of the millions of little gardens that permeated the station, rustling the leaves.

She made a little noise of pleasure that was reinforced by the feelings she was freely projecting. The feelings washed over him, making his heart beat faster, but she relented and the feedback loop slowed again.

"This has been building for a while, you know," she told him. "I've been paying more attention to you since we had that first talk about our experiences with the Varangians."

"You have?" He didn't know why, exactly, but it pleased him.

He was looking up at the starscape that was cleverly projected on the ceiling, giving the illusion that they weren't kilometers away from the outer surface. He felt her head nodding against his chest.

"Your problems with some of the other team leaders, for example," she said. "Kolm, in particular. He's a serious problem, you know. He thinks you're only leading us because of sheer luck."

"He's not far off the mark."

"He *is* far off the mark!" She slapped his chest lightly to emphasize her words. "The Varangians didn't just pick you at random. They were curious about *you*, specifically. That's why you and Hjalmar found me on Kwharaz. It was all because of their interest in you and your role in the empire."

"That's true," he admitted. "I am kind of a big deal..."

She chuckled – something she rarely did.

Eth craned his neck to give her a kiss on the top of her head. "I'd better call him out. Has he had any training in the understanding?"

"No."

"No aptitude?"

"He has aptitude but he also has an alarming sense of entitlement," she said indignantly. "He wants to train so he can take your place. I sent him away."

He thought about that. It was the sort of thing the ruling families did all the time. They supported each other. Refusing to train someone who might topple your mate was hardly corruption.

Corruption itself was considered by the Quailu to be more a quaint concept than it was a crime anyway. He wasn't even sure if he'd ever heard of anyone being prosecuted for corruption.

Power was what mattered in the empire.

It was what he and Scylla had, laying at their feet. They just had to stoop to pick it up. He shook his head.

"I'm fooling myself," he told her, "pretending I'd be compromising some part of myself if I start playing the same dynastic games that the Quailu love so much. It's just a new type of battlefield, one I'd better learn to navigate quickly."

"Don't stint in using your abilities," she murmured sleepily. "Moral high ground won't mean anything if you get us all killed."

"Hey," he nudged her by lifting the shoulder her head was resting on. "Don't sleep here. The moss is too cold on my back! There's a suite of rooms in the middle of the park. Maybe there's something in there that's more comfy."

She sat up, stretching out her arms in a huge yawn. When she closed her mouth and opened her eyes, she found him gazing at her body with frank admiration. Her eyes lowered.

Very frank admiration.

"Let's see what's there." She got up and started walking toward the low structure among the trees. "A more comfortable place for a second round of coitus, perhaps."

He was absorbed in watching her walk, so her words took a few moments to percolate through his brain. "Oh!" He jumped up and hurried after her. "Yes, please!"

He took her hand and they walked, naked, through the garden.

Things Are Picking Up
Some Parkade in San Diego - night

Gleb brought the shuttle in a little too fast.

Just a little.

His friends were all forced a step or two back as the air was displaced. It was childish, apparently, but Gleb was still learning about children, so he supposed he could excuse himself.

He activated a side hatch, the nanites flowing out of the way and forming a ramp to the concrete of the parkade deck. Before getting out of his seat, he set the return course so it would make piloting the shuttle look much easier for his 'recruits'.

"Hey, guys!" He sauntered down the ramp. "Glad one of you got my message!"

"It was Luna." Aberdeen nodded at the young pilot.

Luna stepped forward, eyes sweeping over the small vehicle's lines. "This is the ship you guys built? How long will it take to train us to fly her?"

"How long till you can make more of them?" Kace asked.

"This isn't our first ship," Gleb corrected them. "We launched that one this morning."

"Then this is already your second ship?" Luna reached out a hand, almost touching the hull. She frowned, bringing her hand to rest directly on the surface. "It's cold! You just come from L.A. or somewhere?"

"Came from the black but it's a controlled descent. It has the ability to manipulate gravity, remember?"

She nodded absently. "She certainly handles well, for something you made in a primitive lab..." She cast him a sidelong glance. "... Relatively speaking."

"We took it from the enemy."

Luna's eyebrows shot up. "You found them already?"

He nodded. "Maeve's been re-routing a few extra slingshots around the moon to gather intelligence. At this point in our relative orbits, it's just barely plausible for their rockets to be doing that. We went there, killed them all and took their stuff."

He gestured at the shuttle. "This isn't something we made. It's a standard imperial shuttle. Wait till we get back to the outpost – our outpost, now…" He grinned. "I'm cooking something up that you're gonna love!"

He handed over four suit-control units, forbearing to mention he'd taken them off warm corpses a few minutes ago. "Just press it to your chest." He pointed to his sternum. "Dex, lose that shirt; it'll get caught up in the nanites and compromise the suit.

"Luna, same for that mini-skirt. I hope those tights aren't see-through…"

She gave him a playful look. "Do you really?"

"Just my brain," he admitted. "The rest of me is threatening to stab my brain with a pencil if it doesn't stop thinking things through. Last thing I need right now, though, is another 'glitch' where I wake up and find that we've surrendered to the Chironans."

"I knew I'd have to make sacrifices for my country when I signed up," she said as she shoved the skirt off.

The tights were safe enough but they still showed her curves quite effectively and Gleb looked away while she activated her suit.

"I'm picking up the local attitudes," he grumbled. "Used to be, I'd see Oliv or somebody in the common shower, all naked and soapy, and it would have no effect. She's no slouch either, she's genetically enhanced, after all."

The extra nanites he'd loaded onto the ship flowed down from the bottom of the hull and streaked toward his four comrades. They'd all tried on his own suit, so they weren't unduly alarmed as the dark tide of metal flowed up their legs.

He turned back as he heard the nanites meshing with the control units. "Now," he continued, looking at Luna, "one little glance of you in those tights, seeing those curves but feeling like it's forbidden fruit…"

He took a deep breath and blew it out. "It makes my throat go dry."

Luna was flexing her legs and arms, looking down at her exotic new space-suit. "Are you saying I'm prettier than a genetically enhanced super-woman?" She was still running through the stretches he'd shown them that would help their suits calibrate to their bodies. "'Cause that's probably the only compliment that can compete with getting my own combat EVA suit.

"For a spaceman who's only been here a few weeks, I'd have to say that was well played," she added. She finally looked up from the suit and treated him to a smile.

Gleb suddenly felt very thirsty.

They trooped into the shuttle and Gleb took the pilot seat. Luna claimed the co-pilot seat, which seemed reasonable enough, given that she was the only other pilot.

"Why only three seats?" asked Dex, who'd stepped aside so Aberdeen could take the last seat.

"Because we really only need them for operating the controls," Gleb replied. "You want your body to have something stable to brace against so you don't accidentally hit the wrong icons."

Kace grabbed a stanchion. "What if there's an accident?"

"If the ship comes apart halfway out of the atmosphere, a seat isn't gonna help you much. I suppose it might be glad it had *you* to land on…"

"Well, that clears that up," Dex groused. "Good talk, Gleb!"

Everyone gasped as they began a 'gentle' four-G acceleration. The only indication of movement was the rapid shrinking of the city as seen through the window.

"About five minutes to orbit," Gleb announced. "Not that we're bothering with orbit. It will take around an hour and a half to get to the outpost. By then, the new ship should have finished growing and we can use the training pods for you guys."

"Anyone else a little freaked out?" Aberdeen asked. "I know Gleb's tried to prepare us for this but it's one thing to wake up every morning knowing this day might come..." She gestured around at the shuttle. "... It's quite another to find yourself heading out of the atmosphere on your way to a captured moon-base so we can get knowledge shoved into our brains by alien tech."

"Kind of like waking up in the middle of a science fiction novel," Luna agreed, "except the danger is real."

"But these pods are safe, right?" Kace asked, not for the first time.

"Been in use for thousands of years," Gleb assured them. "I was trained in one and look how I turned out."

"Dude, you black out every time you have sex." Kace reddened when Luna looked back at him, a hand over her wide-open mouth. "Oh, sorry! That just kind of slipped out."

"I'm so embarrassed," she moaned. "I mean, I thought I could trust Gleb not to blab..."

Aberdeen snorted. "You talk about it all the time," she told Luna. "You were telling us about it at the pub last night, in graphic detail."

"Yeah." Luna dropped the act. "But it's always fun to troll the males. Half the fun of being a fighter-jock is working over the new guys. They always fall for the blushing-virgin bit."

"You're plain evil!" Kace told her with a hint of admiration in his voice.

"I'm not half as bad as Skid-Mark!"

"Uh…" Dex frowned at her. "I'm gonna go out on a limb and guess that's a call-sign? She have some rough landings or something?"

"The less you know about her call-sign the better," Luna told him, smiling sweetly.

"You never told me *your* call-sign," Gleb said, looking over.

"Sure I did but I suppose you wouldn't remember. We were doing this 'Dr. Strangelove' thing. I was Slim Pickens and you were the bomb."

"So you're call-sign is Slim Pickens? Hey!" Gleb glanced down at the armored shoulder she'd just punched. "Good thing you have an armored fist; just remember that, though, if I'm not in this suit."

"So what is it?" Aberdeen asked her.

"Pounce."

Gleb looked out the window for a moment, then nodded. "Yeah, that's you in a nutshell, isn't it?"

She crossed her arms, thrusting her chin out. "What if it is?"

He shrugged. "If it is, then it's the reason we met. I forget most of that moment but I sure don't mind the results."

Luna uncrossed her arms. "Good enough," she allowed. "I'll let you live, for now."

Gleb left the approach to the freight hangar on autopilot, giving his friends a good scare as they slid through the opening at a dizzying speed.

He led them out of the shuttle.

Kace was the first to follow him out and he paused at the end of the ramp. He smiled, taking the first step onto the hangar decking. "I've just stepped onto the moon, sort of!"

217

He waggled his head at Gleb. "I know there's a few hundred folks living and working on the other side but, still, this isn't something regular folks like us get to do."

Gleb was nodding but then he caught the error as the rest came to stand by Kace on the decking. "I've got news for you. You guys don't really count as ordinary anymore, especially after I finish training you to run imperial warships."

He led them over to where Maeve and John waited. "This," he said, kicking at a corpse, "was a native Chironan. Strong. Good at grappling but too slow for more fluid combat. That over there..." He pointed to the left. "...Was a Quailu. They're the ruling race.

"And you haven't met these guys yet," he said as they arrived in front of Maeve and John, "but you've probably seen Maeve on the newsfeeds. This is one of her project directors, John."

He gestured. "This is Aberdeen, Luna, Dexter and Kace." He looked at the new ship as everyone bumped elbows.

"I think we're almost done growing the *Xiphos*." He rubbed his hands. "Perfect timing!"

"*Xiphos*?" Maeve glanced at the ship. "An ancient Greek short-sword?"

Gleb nodded. "I did some research on my way to get the guys. It seemed perfect for a corvette – something more maneuverable when the fight turns into a fur-ball..."

"So what's our plan?" Luna asked.

"First, we train you guys." Gleb waved at the new ship. "Next, we use our seven trained pilots to ferry all the kidnap victims home."

He nodded at the stacks of containers. "There are close to a hundred people in those cases. Once we get them home, we can start turning the shuttles into more corvettes."

"But we barely have weapons for the first one," John protested. "The freighter had minimal armament, according to your standards."

"True," Gleb admitted, "but I'm sure, with a little luck, we could persuade the Chironans to supply our needs. By the time they log that freighter as late and send someone here to investigate, we should have had roughly six days to…"

A chime sounded. A *loud* chime sounded because the Universe is a total bastard and it loves taking one's plans and shoving them up one's back-passage.

With a spikey boot…

"Navigational ping received," a disembodied system-voice announced in Imperial. "Squadron inbound from Chiron."

"Fornication!" Maeve cursed in Imperial.

They couldn't understand the language yet, but the context seemed pretty clear to the four newcomers. Something was going horribly wrong.

Gleb bit back the urge to curse, needing to use English for the benefit of his friends. "How long until they reach orbit?"

"Please specify," the system responded. "Planetary orbit or lunar orbit?"

"Tell us both."

"Inbound squadron will reach planetary orbit in twelve hours. They will reach lunar orbit in twelve hours."

Gleb sighed and turned a grimace toward Maeve and John. "You see why we don't get implants? It would be like having a rat in your brain… a rat with syphilis…"

John offered a grim smile. "So what can we do in twelve hours?"

"First thing we can do is ditch most of our plans," Gleb said angrily. "I know I said they'd come but this timing…" He enlarged the system holo, centering on the inbound fleet. "One cruiser and four frigates.

"They're coming to take this system openly, claim it as their fief." He sucked in air through his teeth. "What the hells happened after I left? Something must have changed the calculus for them, made them think Humans were fair game…"

He looked to the side, searching memory. "The captains in our fleet had been acting more reserved than usual, lately. I even caught the fleet-captain, Rimush, stifling some very conflicted feelings about us…"

He looked back at the holographic fleet, his blood running cold. "Something happened at the battle of Kish. That would make sense of this timing. They're either coming here to seize control of the valuable strategic asset represented by our species…"

"Or?" Maeve prompted him after a long silence.

"Or my people have been eliminated and they intend to wipe us all out." He waved over the contraband Humans who were still standing around in a small, nervous group.

"You guys know how to operate those containment units?" He pointed to the stacks of stored Humans.

"Sure," one of the males replied. "You don't think those guys would want to do the dirty work, do you?" He nodded at the alien corpses. "The humans are unconscious when they come off the shuttle, so we have to drag them into the pods and activate the storage-mode."

"Alright." Gleb nodded. "Start waking everybody up right now. We don't have the luxury of playing hero anymore. Those people are our only hope."

"Wait!" Maeve put a hand on Gleb's shoulder. "We all volunteered for this. Those people may not be interested in cooperating.

"Then we need to make them take an interest." Gleb waved his San Diego friends toward the entry ramp that was just starting to reach down to the hangar decking.

"Ramp's coming down. That means the ship's safe to enter. Let's get you guys trained while the rest of our force is waking up."

He led the way into the medical bay where the training pods could also be used to suspend a critical patient's metabolism in an emergency. "Just step out of your suits over there," he pointed to a clear spot of deck.

They deactivated their EVA armor and stepped off the footplates. Luna was the first to approach the pods.

"How do I get in?" she asked, clearly not the least daunted by the strangeness of the process. She turned to Gleb, catching him in the midst of appreciating her tights, and she smiled. "At least *looking* is something you can remember the next day, right?"

He sighed. "Yeah, I have that, at least." He frowned, looking past her. "Kace, why did you take off your pants?"

Kace was holding his jeans in his left hand. "Umm... No reason, as it turns out."

"Yeah, you can use the pod with your clothes still on." He glanced pointedly down at Kace's yellow and black underwear. "Don't worry, CatMan, your secret's safe with me!"

"Dude!" Kace protested. "It's not cat..." He waved his hand in disgust. "Why do I even bother?"

When the four emerged from the new corvette, there was a large crowd of disgruntled Humans waiting for them. Gleb stood at the top of the ramp, gauging the mood. He stood with his feet apart, clasping his hands behind his back to hide the shakiness. His friends moved to the bottom of the ramp.

It was pretty much what he'd expected from a hundred wild Humans – anger, fear and fascination. He drew in a deep, slightly shaky breath. *Easy*, he chided himself. He took another breath. *Much better.*

He pitched his voice to reach the back of the crowd, the volume alone helping to take the tremor from his words. "You're all wondering what the hells is going on right now, right?"

The reply was a muddled outburst from dozens of people.

He raised his hands, forgetting his nervousness now that he was committed to his course. "Let me give you the basic facts," he shouted.

The crowd, no doubt cowed by the strange circumstance they'd found themselves in, settled quickly.

"You were all taken from your planet by servants of the lord of Chiron, a fief within the Holy Quailu Empire. They took each of you because you possessed something of interest in your genes."

He gestured to himself. "I'm a Human, like you, but I serve the lord of Kish, who is hostile to Chiron. Our plan had been to take control of this outpost and return you all to your homes…" He sighed. "…Events have gotten in our way.

"A Chironan invasion force is in the outer system and they'll be here in hours. The Humans in this hangar bay are the only ones available to stop them."

"Really?" A man in the crowd asked. "Great story, bro. Could've used a couple of sensitive werewolves or something." A few folks near him chuckled. "Just show us the damn door and maybe you can clear out of here before the cops show up, asshole!"

Gleb frowned at the man.

"He thinks you're bull-shitting them," Luna said loudly enough for all to hear.

"You really want to walk out of here?" Maeve demanded. "There's no atmosphere outside. And you're not gonna get the cops to show up here." She pointed out the blue haze that kept the atmosphere from boiling out the hangar door. "That strange grey landscape out there? That's the moon."

A buzz started at that news – oddly, more of a buzz than 'an alien conquest fleet is bearing down on the Earth'. It started out over their location but quickly morphed into a general medley along the lines of 'Holy Shit! Do you realize who she is?"

"The nearest law enforcement you'll find is at my station on the other side of this rock and they're not equipped to come all the way over here," she told them, ignoring the star-struck looks.

Gleb noted a clear space in front of the nay-sayer and he slipped into it. The man's eyebrows reacted first, starting to rise in curiosity but then his brain, playing catch-up, threw his body into a startled jump backward from the man who'd suddenly appeared in front of him.

"I don't have all day to convince you guys," he said before a new rumble of alarm and amazement could drown out his words. He waved a hand at the boarding ramp. Those of you who believe me, please line up at the boarding ramp. The people you see in the armored suits will help get you trained using a…"

"Wait," Kace interrupted. "How the hell are we supposed to operate the pods…" He stopped, his face breaking into a smile of wonder. "Damn! That's pretty freakin' cool!"

"Good timing, Kace!" Gleb waved a hand at his friends. "They just finished their sessions. Ten minutes in a pod will lay down enough information in your brains to do what we need to do in order to stop this invasion.

"If you need to know something, asking the question will trigger the answer…" He nodded at Kace. "… Like Kace just found out."

"You're not sticking probes into my head!" another man shouted.

"Who the hells said anything about that?" Gleb asked incredulously. "The pods create a delicate energy matrix that stimulates connections in an otherwise unused part of your brain. We've used this in the empire for tens of thousands of years. It's safer than using your phone implants."

The man in front of him was recovering from his shock. He thrust out his chin. "How do we even know if…"

"Alright!" Gleb cut him off with a loud firm voice. "Listen up! There's a Chironan fleet headed this way!" He brought up the tactical holo, which more than a few found impressive.

"They're not going to pull over and wait for you to work out what you feel like doing. They're going to be here in a few hours, whether you like it or not, and going home is out of the question.

"Home, as you know it, won't exist anymore. Sure, the buildings will mostly be left standing but these assholes are gonna park in orbit and start vaporizing every major political power-center. I give it a day and a half before the food-riots start. Two weeks before cannibalism sets in."

The crowd was silent.

Gleb nodded to himself. "No more screwing around. We have just enough time to get ready, so shut your mouths and line up. As of this moment, you have all been drafted into the planet's very first unified defense force."

"Move, people!" John shouted, sounding very much like he'd had experience in this sort of thing.

It worked. Even the loud-mouthed jerk started shuffling into place.

Luna and Aberdeen started by taking the first three up into the ship while Kace stayed at the bottom of the ramp as traffic control. Dex came over to where Gleb was standing, Maeve and John also converging on him.

"So what's the plan, *Admiral*?" Maeve asked. "You've got one ship and, according to you, not much in the way of weaponry, so a straight-up fight is hardly our first option." She cocked her head.

"Damn," she muttered as the memories awakened in her mind. "We really *are* outgunned here!"

"Yeah," Gleb agreed. "That's on me. I forgot to tell the Chironans we were expecting a single ship to come here first. Can't blame them for that…"

"No," John agreed. "I suppose we'll have to forgive them for that but what *is* the plan now?"

Gleb moved his hand and the tactical holo enlarged showing individual ship vectors. "Main force is headed to the planet but this frigate is headed for us. They're probably just supposed to secure the outpost and then join the main attack." He shook his head. "Absolutely bare minimum force for pacifying a backward world and we still might not be able to stop them!"

He rubbed his tongue along the inside of his teeth, weighing options. *No way around it,* he thought. He sighed, darting a quick glance at Dex. "We're going to need a sacrificial animal. One that looks mildly dangerous yet not so much that it raises too many alarm bells…"

"Have you lost your damned mind?" Dex demanded, moving behind Gleb. "I have a better idea…"

Orderly Transition of Blame
Throneworld

Mishak splashed cold water on his face. He stood there, in front of the mirror with his hands on either side of the drain-channel, watching rivulets of water flow from his nose.

He couldn't recall the details of his dream, only that there was nothing good in it. This was the third time in as many nights that he'd awakened in a sweat.

He stepped through the air-curtain to dry himself and used the side door from the wash-chamber, exiting directly into the lounge so as not to disturb Tashmitum's sleep.

An elderly female from the Imperial Corps of Florists was personally seeing to an arrangement on the sideboard. It seemed a dark art to Mishak. Whatever the old gal was doing must have had some deep meaning but it looked like a mess to him.

She turned and pulled off her head-scarf.

Mishak stared in shock, suddenly wishing he had a weapon, just in case...

"Wake your wife, young prince," Marduk said tiredly. "She shouldn't hear this second hand." A tear escaped from his left eye, racing down his cheek.

Mishak shivered. Whatever might bring the emperor's chief of staff here, disguised as an old florist, in the dark hours couldn't possibly be good. He turned back toward the door to the sleeping chamber but the door slid open before he reached it.

Tashmitum, yawning, walked straight to a couch and settled onto it gingerly. She sighed and rested a hand on her belly. "I woke before my husband, though I appreciate his efforts nonetheless."

She looked up at Marduk, reaching out to take his hand. "Sit, Uncle. This is harder for you than it is for me, I think."

Mishak suddenly realized what was happening and relief flooded through him that it wasn't something far worse. Guilt followed immediately on relief's heels, driving him to sit on her other side as Marduk sat on her right.

"A few hours ago?" she asked the old Quailu.

He nodded. "He was in the 'cavern' fretting about these separatist rumors. I went down to see if he'd finally fallen asleep and…"

"And he'd passed in his sleep," she finished for him. "I felt the absence." She leaned against Marduk. "Odd how I felt his presence so rarely, growing up as a royal, but I noticed the lack of his presence so strongly."

"I'm very sorry for your loss, highness."

"And I am very sorry for *yours*, Uncle." She draped an arm around his shoulders. "You know how little time he and I spent together but he was your oldest and dearest friend. I fear your loss may be the deeper wound."

"At least he was spared having to see the empire split apart." Marduk let out a shuddering breath.

"We should notify the priests of the necropolis," Mishak said softly. "They should get started on the…" He trailed off, embarrassed. "They should begin preparations."

"He's in stasis," Marduk said. "There's no rush."

He sat up, turning to look at Tashmitum. "You may not have been aware, my dear princess, but he was terribly proud of you. The protection of your future was always his primary motive in all he did." He glanced at Mishak.

"You were acceptable as her mate," Marduk grudgingly admitted, turning back to her. "He would have me do anything… *anything* to protect you now!"

"What are you suggesting," she whispered.

"Bau's faction will almost undoubtedly succeed in carving out a large part of the empire. The balance of power will be irretrievably altered." Marduk paused, his gaze drifting around the room. "Troubles we cannot yet see will be laid at the feet of whomever rules."

He looked back at the couple-royal. "Until news of your father's death becomes public, those troubles will be his legacy, not yours."

"You want us to keep his death a secret so we can blame the secessionists on him?" Tashmitum stared at him. "That's not fair to his memory…"

"It's entirely fair," Mishak cut in. "His spying scandal is what launched all of the clashes. It unleashed change on an empire that long ago forgot how to adapt."

"That hardly absolves Bau of fomenting treason!" Tashmitum insisted sharply.

"No, but I imagine we played *our* part when one of her systems was used in a ploy to turn the Humans into full renegades," Mishak said, knowing he was twisting an old dagger in Marduk who was already in enough pain.

"There's also the small matter of the election," Tashmitum declared, iron now in her voice. "Are we to campaign as the couple who let the empire fall apart? My father may have been the emperor, but Mishak and I have been very visible in recent months. Blame is a lazy creature, Uncle. It takes the easiest path."

"We need to know what Bau and her people have in mind," Mishak said, relieved to have a way forward, even if it led to parts unknown. "We should leave immediately; seek them out."

"Or simply go out there and let them find us," she amended. "No doubt they're waiting for us to present ourselves, to show we're ready to listen."

"You'll have some time," Marduk told them. "Given the last few years of his reign, nobody will notice the emperor's absence for a while."

"There are reports circulating." Mishak stared down at the coffee table. "Rumors that these separatists are willing to cooperate on internal security matters…"

"You think there's any merit in that?" Marduk emanated surprise.

"I think," Mishak replied deliberately, "that the Human intervention against my brother was an advertisement. Eth must have set aside his vow of revenge. Otherwise, we'd be minus one more ship after that encounter. There's no harm in finding out what their intentions are."

"Probably," Tashmitum interjected dryly.

"Probably," Mishak agreed with a shrug the other two wouldn't catch.

"Then let us see what we can salvage from this bag of cheevers." Marduk got up with a groan and adjusted his feminine disguise. "If you'll excuse me, I have to ensure no servants are allowed out of the cavern."

He shuffled over to the door, draping the scarf over his head and wrapping it around his face.

"You look lovely, Uncle," Tashmitum teased.

Marduk turned. "Just make sure you find a way to make yourselves look as good before you come back here!" He turned back for the door. "We have an election to ensure…"

How it Ends

High Earth orbit

Gleb shuddered. His face was cold on one side and it hurt. He was pretty sure it had just impacted with a ship's decking and that was probably what had brought him back to consciousness.

The crisp sounds of a ship's bridge surrounded him. Low voices and alert chimes were interspersed with the sound of an endless stream of decisions being made. He opened his eyes.

The cruiser, he realized. He was on the bridge of the Chironan cruiser, his hands bound behind his back. He struggled to his knees and looked up into the face of a Quailu in expensive EVA armor.

He focused his anger on him. Drawing the alien into a swamp of feelings.

"Who is this?" the Quailu asked in Imperial Standard, impatiently waving a mute command to the system when it pinged an unwanted confirmation of his question.

"My lord," a Quailu responded, "this one led an insurrection against our outpost on this planet's moon. His compatriots, here, wisely determined that handing him over to your justice was the wisest course."

"We don't want a war," the loud-mouthed, disbelieving Human they'd rescued said. He said it in Imperial. "We know the difference between resistance and suicide, Great Lord!"

So, Gleb thought wryly, *the silly bastard got into a pod, after all! He has to believe what I was saying, at this point, and he's still willing to betray the entire planet?*

The Quailu pulled out his sidearm. "I will grant this rebellious scum the mercy of a quick death, though he has done much to merit a slow end." He looked down at Gleb. "Be grateful that I don't have time for such trifles."

He brought the pistol's muzzle to rest against Gleb's forehead. His finger reached inside the trigger guard…

"My lord," Maeve's voice sounded from somewhere behind Gleb. "What of us?"

The finger paused. "What of you?" He reared his head. "What was your role in this?"

"Well…" She stepped forward to stand just behind Gleb. "This one has presented you with the prisoner to gain influence with your house. He knows that we acted in a supporting role."

Gleb assumed she was referring to the jackass but he didn't remember anything after Dex had cut him off at the outpost. *What the hells happened after 'Other-Gleb' took over?*

"You will be richly rewarded," the Quailu lied smoothly, ignoring the pulsing icon in the holo next to his head.

Gleb felt a surge of hope. He knew the Quailu was lying. His abilities were recovering more quickly each time and Luna had *caused* quite a few blackouts recently.

He looked to his right, focusing on what looked to be the ship's captain watching the proceedings with mild disinterest. *He should be leaving this to his lord and concentrating on ship's business instead,* Gleb thought.

He focused on the captain, drawing energy from the Quailu's body. He didn't *take* the energy, of course. He simply re-allocated it within the victim, concentrating it in the target area.

He converted it from heat energy to kinetic in a reverse of the usual process. Ordinarily, the kinetic energy in something like a projectile or swinging blade would manifest in the movement of the object as a whole.

When it impacts a target, that energy is transferred, causing parts of the target to move or fragment with their own constituent portions of the original energy. Some of the target remains in place but the individual molecules still receive a portion of that kinetic energy. Their increased motion could be observed as a raised temperature.

Gleb channeled the collected heat into a coherent force acting on a small cross-section of several blood vessels.

The officer shuddered from the sudden cold, reaching up to his nose in alarm. His fingers came away bloody.

Gleb had severed enough veins in his nasal passages to create an alarming nosebleed. It was a signal to Maeve that he was almost ready to take over proceedings.

How did I remember the signal? he wondered. *I was Other-Gleb when we came up with that!* He shook his head. There would be time to think about that later.

He shuffled on his knees to face the gun and the Quailu behind it. The noble lowered his sidearm. He took a half step backward in alarm at his body doing something without his permission. His face contorted in frustration and growing alarm as he tried to raise the weapon again.

Gleb had to assume that his alter-ego had carried out the plan he'd been forming when he glitched. "What my captor doesn't know," Gleb said quietly, "is that we left him in the training pod while the rest of us killed the surface party your frigate sent down to the outpost.

"We knew they'd want to find out why the place had failed to answer your hails. We used the surface party's shuttle to board the frigate and kill the crew. Once that was done, we let this fool behind me think he was handing the ring-leader over to you.

"It was likely that you'd search his mind more than the rest of us so we needed a true believer to draw your attention and allay your suspicion."

The captain forgot about the blood pouring down his face. He was just close enough to hear Gleb and he reached for his weapon.

He got his hand to the grip and then fell dead.

Gleb shuddered like a man coming into a warm room after hours in a freezer. He reached out to the rest of the bridge crew and the two guards who stood with the Humans, pulling heat from them to sever their spinal cords.

A series of thumps sounded. The noble looked around the bridge, his fear growing. His pistol thumped to the floor without any intervention needed by Gleb.

Someone – it felt like Dex – released Gleb's bonds. Now there was just one Quailu noble and several Humans standing on the bridge.

Well, Gleb was still on his knees.

Gleb rubbed at his wrists. "Hey!" When the noble, the only Quailu left standing on the bridge, looked at him, he nodded at the pulsing icon in the holo. "You should check your message…"

He nodded meaningfully at the icon to reinforce the message and the alien finally raised the arm that Gleb no longer needed to control. He touched the icon and the computer, assuming the earlier question had been meant for *it*, displayed Gleb's identity.

The Quailu uttered a wordless sound of alarm and looked back down at his 'prisoner'.

Gleb put on his best evil grin and filled his mind with thoughts of the underworld. He was one of the Nergalihm, a servant of the dread Lord Nergal himself.

He shivered as his mind produced an orgy of violent images and he shoved them into the noble's mind as he climbed to his feet.

The Quailu whimpered, shrinking back from the horror that reached deep into his thoughts.

"This world belongs to the Nergalihm," Gleb growled, taking a step forward but then transposing himself. He slipped out of three-dimensional space and re-inserted himself a half step forward and to the left. "For coming here, you must pay the price." Another sliding step took him behind the noble who screamed aloud and spun, tripping over his own feet and falling onto the spot where Gleb had knelt. "You will give your crews to Nergal as an offering."

"My crews…" The noble was weeping in fear. "My crews…"

Gleb pulled the holo over and set up a suit-lockout command. He prepped it for squadron-wide transmission. He left a large entry window open for the command code but reset the header to read 'override'. "I've locked out every suit in your squadron. When we rig for combat, their helmets will remain open and they'll go to my master screaming."

He slid the screen down to where the Quailu was sitting on the decking. "You came here to terrorize Billions of my people into submission. People who can barely get into orbit, let alone fight there."

He looked down in disgust. "You tried punching laterally, against my lord Mishak and he handed you your molars. Now you're trying your hand at punching down?"

The Quailu radiated confusion. "Your lord?" He opened his mouth again but faltered. With an effort, he managed to continue, despite his fear. "You may serve the underworld but Mishak is no longer your lord."

He'd said it without a hint of scorn. He sounded more like someone trying to distance himself from any connection to Mishak's wrath, as if being on Nergal's shit-list wasn't dangerous enough.

"What are you talking about?" Gleb demanded, sending a sliver of fear along with the words to nudge him along.

"At Kish!" the alien blurted. "After the battle, Mishak's fleet turned on your kind!"

"What?" Gleb reached into the Quailu's thoughts. *He believes what he's telling me.* "Why?"

"Nobody knows for certain but many electors had been wary of his growing power. If he ascended to the throne with both the Varangians and your people under his orders…"

"Did any of my people survive?"

The prisoner nodded eagerly. "Oh, yes! They're Humans, after all! Very hard to kill the servants of Nergal!"

Gleb looked up, staring at his Human companions, though it was his friends from the empire he was seeing in his mind. The loud-mouth bobbed his head and grinned ingratiatingly, though Gleb didn't notice.

How many of our people did they kill? Who, exactly, was killed?

He felt sly thoughts coming from the Quailu on the floor, so he kept his eyes straight ahead. There was a feeling of some small triumph having been accomplished and so Gleb looked down.

"I've overridden the system," the Quailu crowed.

"So now you call the shots?" Gleb asked him. "Well then, I certainly have my foot up my own *cloaca*, don't I?" He gestured. "Go ahead, call the shots…"

He could feel the confusion. "I'll save you the sad theatrics and simply tell you. What you just did was lock yourself out of the system. My people are effective in combat because we create ships that compliment our fighting strategy. We're already blacklisted by the ship-building firms, so there's nothing stopping us from rewriting the code patterns that make these ships work."

He nodded at the holo-screen. "Changing interface code is so simple that even a novice like me can do it on the fly. You didn't just type your authorisation code into an override screen, you typed your code into a *reset* screen. I changed the header."

Now he felt shock and outrage coming his way. Gleb smiled. "You've just handed me control of your squadron." He opened the tactical menu. "St. Petersburg, Los Angeles, Hong Kong, Beijing, Toronto… You were planning to kill a lot of people to prove your point." He shrugged. "Why risk a ground invasion, am I right? Why lose your own people to seize a world, if you can visit horror on that world first to show them they have no choice other than surrender or death?"

"You'd do the same," the Quailu said angrily.

Gleb paused. "I'm not sure which that gives me, solace or second thoughts…" He opened a new window, then looked back at his prisoner. "Either way, I don't see how I have any other option and, frankly, your kind designed me to be a killer."

Gleb pressed an icon and everyone's helmet snapped shut, including the Quailu noble's. A blaring alarm sounded, warning the crew that the ship was rigging for combat operations. Fast pumps went to work, lessening the sound of the alarm as the air was sucked into storage.

Agony and fear spread through the ship. The crew, their helmets locked open, were asphyxiating. Their eyeballs, the result of thousands of years of evolution at sea level, were rupturing and spilling vitreous fluid down their cheeks.

The fear flowed back and forth, amplifying like waves in a small pool. It grew to an apocalyptic frenzy of agony and terror. Gleb let it flow over his borderline-psychopathic mind as he stared into the eyes of his captive.

Even for Gleb, this was a bit much but he kept his gaze steady as the noble felt his crew's agony. *Still have to keep up appearances as a servant of the dark lord of the underworld,* he told himself. This would be over soon.

And there was a lot of work to do…

The Deal

Kish

"Three days now," Tashmitum said. "I do hope he comes soon. I would prefer our first child to be born in the palace. Such things carry weight in an election."

"He'll come," Mishak said confidently. "First, he has to hear we've come to Kish, then he needs time to travel here."

"If he does…" She gasped at a tiny kick in her belly.

"He will. He has a message for us and we're clearly in a place where he can reach us." He looked at the two Human attendants standing by the entrance to his throne-room.

"What was it like," she asked, "living here?"

"After a decade at Throneworld?" He chuckled. "My dear, this is what exile looks like. A small hall to intimidate local officials who've never left atmo, an economy based almost entirely on agriculture and neighbors who constantly seek to destroy you."

"I did manage to find some measure of happiness, all the same." His eyes drifted to the balcony doors. "This is where I finally stood up to my father, after all. Without the Humans, I'd still be here."

"Or dead?"

He sighed. "Or dead."

"Or a prisoner?"

"Yes. Thank-you. Can we move on to…"

"New business?" Eth asked.

Mishak fought to control his reaction. He was expecting something like this. He'd even overridden his security team, telling them not to run a pre-path generator to stop an incursion by renegade Humans.

Still, it was unnerving.

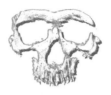

Eth suppressed his grin. He'd startled the couple, as he'd intended, but he didn't want to rub their snouts in it. He bowed politely. "My lady, I hope the pregnancy progresses well?"

She sat up on the lounger, one hand resting on her belly and gave his bow a nod of acknowledgement. "It does, thank the gods. It *is* good to see you again, Ethkennu of Kish."

"I've had to find a new home, my lady." He gestured with a wave around the room. "Living here has become… problematic."

"No doubt," she replied, accepting his mild rebuke.

It was deliberate on Eth's part. He wasn't here as a supplicant, begging for imperial blessing on his plan. He was here to offer the empire the way forward that it couldn't afford to refuse.

He kept an impassive expression on his face. *Why do I sense such an urgency from them?* Granted, he was here on a serious matter but it felt as if time played more of a role in this than it really should.

Is the emperor up to some new folly? "I trust your noble father prospers, my lady?"

He coughed into his elbow to cover his surprise. *Dead?* He redoubled his efforts to keep his thoughts closed to the two Quailu. *Dammit! I need time to assess this! They've probably gamed out a whole plan based on this and I've got to improvise on the spot. How does this affect our own plan?* He coughed again.

"He's as well as can be expected," Tashmitum finally replied.

No kidding!

Eth decided not to simply lay out the plan, as he'd intended. He wanted some idea of how the emperor's death altered the landscape.

"Am I intruding?" he asked them, politely. "It's just that I was in the region and I do miss the old place…"

He could feel their surprise. They'd obviously expected him to make this easy. *Screw that! They're the ones with the sense of urgency.*

Then it came to him. If the empire was about to lose some of its territory, it was best to blame it on someone else. Still… *the election will be a lot harder for them. They'll need to come out of this looking like they got something of value.*

"Dammit all!" Mishak exclaimed. "Let's stop dancing already! You represent the separatists, yes?"

"I do."

"You must have some plan you wish to present, some path forward that you think we'll find palatable. Otherwise, you wouldn't have come all the way to Kish."

"Firstly, you should understand who we are." Eth frowned down at the floor for a moment. "Lady Bau and the Zeartekka hive are both a party to this," he said. "My people, of course…"

Here he felt a twinge of resentment from Mishak but the current situation was hardly of Eth's doing. Mishak had his own fleet-captain to thank for the loss of his Humans.

"…And a few minor systems are with us as well. In total, we represent roughly fifteen percent of the current imperial economy."

"Fifteen percent?" Mishak blurted loudly. "Put a gun to my head now, Eth. There's no way we can survive letting that many citizens leave…" He looked down at his wife's hand on his arm.

"Sit, my mate. There is no harm in hearing the full proposal, is there?"

He sighed, nodding, and sat next to her.

Does she catch physical gestures or has the boss gone full native on us? Eth pushed that aside and ordered his points. "That fifteen percent of the economy wouldn't simply disappear, lord.

Indeed, most of that is Lady Bau's trade in foodstuffs. And that leads us to what may be a very attractive point in your favor."

"You expect me to applaud as we lose control over most of the empire's food supply?"

Eth tried out one of his more roguish grins. "lord, if you ever thought you controlled Lady Bau, then I don't know what to tell you…"

Tashmitum laughed outright, such was her surprise.

"Having her outside the… constraints of the empire, however," Eth continued, "can be very useful. You, as the rulers, can't just cut off the flow of food to a rebellious noble, not without sparking massive outrage. Lady Bau, however…"

"Could express concern for the safety of delivery crews in an active conflict zone," Tashmitum said. "An unfortunate circumstance for those who live there, but an effective deterrent to any who contemplate breaking the peace."

"We propose a sovereignty-association," Eth told them. "We keep trade flowing, especially food, and we allow rights of navigation to continue much as they do now. Wherever the lady's food travels, Human forces will patrol.

"If, for example, your brother should attempt to open a conflict at a world like Arraphka, he would be interrupting the safe delivery of food to that world. Our forces would act to prevent that and deliveries to Memnon's territories would be placed on hold until he provided an explanation for his actions. Reparations might also be required."

"A hold may well have been less of a threat, had he managed to seize a world like… Arraphka, where they produce emergency, synthetic foodstuffs," Mishak said, sounding as though it were simply an exercise in logic.

It didn't sound at all like the unmitigated disaster that it would have become, had it not been for Eth's intervention.

"You would lose the tax revenue from the food, of course," Eth conceded, "but the resulting boost in security would more than offset that." He spread his hands to the side.

"The empire has become a seething mass of low-level conflict. We offer a way to stop that. No hands need get dirtied but the results will be very quickly apparent to those electors who wonder if they should take a risk on some new candidate."

"That consideration will not come for many years, gods willing," Mishak said, a little too quickly.

"That consideration is upon us now, lord." Eth turned to a startled Tashmitum and bowed low. "My condolences on the passing of your noble father, your grace."

"You know already?" she exclaimed, forgetting the correct response to his words in her shock.

"I do," he admitted, "but it remains a very closely guarded secret among us. No word of it will come from us before you make an official announcement." *So closely guarded that you could prevent its spread simply by killing me now.* "I assume you wish to conclude this matter between us first."

"Yes," Mishak looked searchingly at Eth for a moment, perhaps trying to see what was in his mind.

Eth made his assumptions on the matter available to Mishak. Some things were better left unsaid.

Mishak tilted his head in surprise. "Yes, I believe we are of one mind in this. If you draw up your proposal along the lines we've discussed here…" He floundered.

"Then it will receive *imperial* approval," Tashmitum finished the thought with the necessary level of obscurity.

Eth nodded. He could feel his former lord's pleasure at knowing the gesture was meant for him to interpret. "Odd, how the Universe works, don't you think?"

"How so?" Tashmitum asked.

"Rimush betrayed my people in your name, knowing full well that, whether you can trust us or not, the electors wouldn't trust you, not if you had our abilities at your disposal. The vote was designed to ensure rule by the first among equals. It prevents the office falling to some powerful despot."

"You can't blame Rimush," Mishak insisted. "At least not entirely. I was still responsible for the actions of my subordinates."

"And yet, because of his actions," Eth continued, "my people still end up helping you but without any direct ties that may cost you votes in the succession.

"Despite all of our scheming, the Universe will always have her way." Eth bowed. "Your graces…"

And he was no longer there…

How Do I?

Mars orbit

Gleb lurched to the left, nearly falling on his side as his ship took another hit. *Gods, she's deadly!*

"They've put us out of action, sir," the tactical officer told Gleb.

Is it Harry? "Very well," Gleb gave him a nod. "Signal an end to the exercise…" He reached out in the pause to feel the name forming on the tip of the newly minted officer's tongue as a prompt. "Harry," he said, feeling the man's pleasure that his leader had remembered.

I suppose I did remember, he thought. *I just didn't trust that I did. Eth was designed for this kind of thing, not me.*

Eth remembered every name he ever heard. Being designed to lead had its benefits. Still… Gleb looked at his tactical holo – seven new corvettes being trained to defend what may be the home-world of all Humans…

He was doing alright.

And it was past time he found out what was happening in the HQE. "All captains, connect on visual for assessment."

Six holographic Humans shimmered into view. "Well done, everyone!" Gleb told them. "Show of hands, who's been asking the questions out loud?"

They all raised ghostly hands and he nodded approval. "Good! It doesn't just help your recall of implanted knowledge; it also sets the example for your people. They're all learning on the fly as well."

This first batch of recruits had been drawn heavily from Maeve's employees, most of whom had a long track record of keeping company secrets. Almost a third of the rescued detainees from the Moon outpost had also signed on.

The Chironans had mostly abducted loners, the kind of folk that weren't taken very seriously by the authorities.

The ones who didn't volunteer were dropped off behind convenience stores, doused in whiskey and with a pint slipped into their back pockets.

He nodded at John. "Your background in ground warfare serves you well but Luna's aerial combat experience gives her a bit of an edge, I'd say. That last run of hers caught me off guard and I've been in more than a few dust-ups out here in the black."

He saw how quickly she mastered her expression at this praise. *Probably used to good reviews,* he figured. "Still, John, you can handle the defences here better than a lot of Quailu commanders back in the empire."

He looked at Maeve's holo. "I assume you'll want one of you to come to the HQE?"

She nodded. "I'm going. Sorry, John, but you'll have to stay and watch the shop."

"In more ways than one," Gleb added. "John, you'll command the four corvettes we're leaving here as a defense force."

"What about Luna?" John asked. "Not that I won't accept the job but you just said she's the better captain. Hate to admit it but I was a ground-pounder and she's a fighter-jock."

"You've got good instincts," Gleb said, "and command experience, which can make all the difference if trouble comes. I need someone who's going to make decisions, someone who'll act without hesitation.

"I'm taking three ships – mine, Maeve's and Luna's. It's still early in the training phase but in the HQE, Maeve would make a better-than-average combat captain. Luna…"

He chuckled. "We'll each be running drills during the next five days in path-transit but, hells, she almost scares *me* and we've only been drilling you guys for a week! When most captains, experienced captains, find themselves on the short end of the decision-cycle, they seek to disengage…"

He tilted his head to Luna. "She just goes for the jugular. Anyone tries to give us trouble in the HQE, I almost pity them!"

"When are we going?" Luna asked.

"Soon as this call is done," Gleb said. "We're already fully provisioned, John will keep drilling our defense team and we can run drills individually while we're pathing to the empire."

His gaze narrowed. "We need to know what's going on back there."

"How…" Luna cocked her head to the side and chuckled. "Have you set up the RV corridor for us, our drop-out profile?"

Gleb reached up and touched an icon to release the necessary data.

She turned her head. "Helm, lock us in. Engineering, bring the path drive online and stand by for transition."

Gleb had to remind himself that she wasn't a civilian, that his surprise at her natural assumption of a command role was misplaced. *Some of these wild Humans already have professional training.*

He nodded to the commander of a defense Irth didn't even know it had. "Keep the place safe, John. We'll return as soon as we can."

"You bring my boss back in one piece or I'll kick your ass," John warned with a smile.

"I will," Gleb reassured him, "but you people have strange ideas regarding punishment." He checked the fleet-board, confirming that both Maeve and Luna were ready.

"*Pounce*, you're clear to initiate," he told Luna.

"Roger that. Pulling chocks," she responded with a nod before turning her head. "Confirm path drive status."

A barely audible voice carried through the transmitted holo-interface confirming the drive was ready. She looked ahead, no longer seeming to see Gleb, lips peeled back.

"Buster!" she said with quiet anticipation, then raised her voice. "Initiate!"

She shimmered out of sight and her ship disappeared from the holo-trace. The first path-capable ship crewed entirely by Irthers, many of them Luna's Navy pals on leave and sworn to secrecy, left the solar system for the Holy Quailu Empire.

Everybody Look Busy

Ansar System

Enlat stared at his aide, his mouth hanging open. In the absence of a solid plan of action, it seemed like the thing to do.

"You found what?" he finally squeaked, his voice barely audible amidst the white-noise generators he kept in his bed-chamber.

"Memnon's flagship, sire, and a good many of his forces. They're mixed in with the civilian traffic…" The aide trailed off.

And rightly so. *Mixed in with civilian traffic?* Enlat raged internally. *Who in their right mind would bother routing through Ansar? This is figuratively the fungus-infected back hoof of the entire HQE. There's nowhere to go from here, except back to civilisation.*

"What civilian traffic?" he demanded. "My overlord shows up with a fleet and you try to tell me he was cleverly hiding among the…" He checked the orbital control records. "… Nine ships in our civil-orbitals?"

He gestured to a side door. "Get a labor crew and clear those crates out of my throne-room! Quickly now!"

He jumped out of bed and shrugged into one of his more presentable robes. *Five centuries at least since an overlord has bothered to come out here.* He couldn't even remember what his own throne-room looked like, so rarely did his family conduct anything even remotely connected to diplomacy.

He had a vague notion that his cousin was storing some kind of new plant material in those crates that had arrived last month. The fool was somewhere in the HQE with samples, trying to build a market for its powerful narcotic effect.

Memnon strode into Enlat's throne-room ahead of his bodyguards. *Am I in the right room?* he wondered.

It was a smallish place, perhaps what you might expect for such a remote holding. The main concourse leading to the dais was perhaps ten meters across and the distance from entry to throne little more than a hundred meters. The throne itself was hidden from view.

A long pile of crates sat in the middle of the main approach promenade, and a few more stacks were in the pillared bays along the sides. A mess of machine parts lay to the left of the entry door and a clear space in the detritus showed where someone had been working on a grav-emitter.

"Garand!" he shouted.

His adjutant jogged to catch up and he fell in beside Memnon without a word, knowing his master hated needless syllables. He was called. He was here.

"There is an administration of some kind here, yes?" Memnon asked, not entirely sure if he was being ironic.

"Indeed, lord. The registry shows someone named Enlat governs here and this is, in lieu of a more accurate description, his throne-room."

Memnon stopped, holding up a hand. "Do you hear that?"

A faint gasping noise was coming from beyond the crates.

"Perhaps we've been unjust to poor Enlat. It sounds like he's hard at work, *polling* one of his constituents..." He resumed his progress down the hall, eager to find out exactly what was happening.

He rounded the end of the crates to find a pair of Quailu on the throne. The male was sitting beneath a female who was gyrating up and down, her back to her partner, eyes closed.

At least they had an explanation for the gasping.

Memnon was within a few steps of the pair when she finally opened her eyes to find his pistol aimed between her eyes.

He sent her a strong impression of the need to remain calm.

She stopped moving and the male beneath her finally became aware they were no longer alone. He leaned to look around her. "Who in the name of Nergal are *you*?" he demanded haughtily. "Get out! Can't you see I'm busy?"

"This is not Enlat, lord," Garand advised. "It's a nephew."

Memnon relished the feelings of the young fool as he caught the word 'lord' and then ran the necessary mental evolutions to figure out who he was looking at. Arrogance could mature into the most delicious fear.

"Don't move," he growled, "either of you. Remain exactly as you are or I'll have you shot."

One of his guards stepped forward and aimed his assault weapon, ready to carry out his lord's threat.

"Now…" Memnon holstered his sidearm. "… That idiot uncle of yours – where is he?"

"My uncle?" the young male stammered. "I have no idea, lord. Most likely, he's in his private chambers."

"And what's in these crates? Is this your uncle's seat of authority or is it a store-room?"

"The crates?"

"If you keep repeating my words back to me," Memnon advised him mildly, "I'll shoot you in the face myself."

"Some kind of plants, lord. There might be a market for it. If it's burned slowly, the smoke, it produces a pleasant effect…"

"Like a scensor?"

"Somewhat, sire."

"Garand, torch the crates. Let's see if that motivates Enlat to visit his own throne-room."

Enlat raced up to his throne-room but there were two imposing guards flanking the entrance. He stood there, waiting for them to say something but they stared impassively at him.

Then he remembered that he was supposed to be the governor of this system. "This is my throne-room," he told them in what he hoped was an assertive tone.

Neither guard responded. Enlat may not even exist, as far as their reaction to him went. He took a tentative step toward the door, expecting to be apprehended but he was left unmolested.

He pushed the door open, so distracted by the guards that he forgot to be terrified at having Memnon in his throne-room. What he found inside inspired no terror.

Confusion, perhaps…

A pile of crates was burning furiously in the center of the promenade. More of Memnon's guards were bringing crates from the bays of the side aisles and tossing them into the blaze.

Most of the fumes were drifting up toward the high ceiling, thirty meters above, where open clerestory windows drafted it outside. A lazy haze of the pungent smoke filled the room but not so dense as to make breathing impossible.

He realized he was still walking because he was rounding the end of the fire now and, if he thought he was confused when he entered, what he saw on the dais denied any relation to sense.

Not even a friend of sense's distant third cousin...

Memnon sat on the platform, his legs splayed lazily on the steps, his elbow resting on the arm of Enlat's throne. He was giggling – giggling? – at one of his people who was mincing across the dais in some grotesque parody, though Enlat had no idea what that might be.

But this was hardly the most bizzare thing he saw.

On his throne was a nude Quailu female sitting astride another nude Quailu. She was moving up and down slowly. When she moved upwards, jostling Memnon's elbow though Enlat's overlord didn't seem to notice her, what was revealed beneath her proved the other Quailu to be a male.

She slid down again, hiding the evidence of gender. *What the hells is happening in here?* Enlat scratched his chin, idly observing the festivities on his throne. *I suppose it's better than Memnon shooting up the place in one of his trademark rages. I should pay young couples to fornicate in here on a regular basis, just in case Memnon comes back.*

Then he remembered the smoke. His cousin had said there was a narcotic effect. *It's probably the smoke that's saving my life, not the 'show',* he realized.

He was on the dais now. *Odd,* he noticed, *I thought I would have stopped walking in shock or something.* He could see the male now. *Malat?*

"Hello, Uncle," Malat said casually, as if he were bumping into him in a corridor somewhere, rather than bumping into some unidentifiable palace staffer.

Enlat found that incredibly funny. He chuckled. *Bumping into...* He laughed harder, not sure why it was any funnier than it was a few seconds ago but... it just was.

"Hey!" Memnon squinted up at him. "Are you the... um... the guy?" He turned his head. "Garand!"

The other Quailu on the stage sashayed over, prompting giggles from both Memnon and, to his own mild surprise, Enlat.

"Yeah," the Quailu confirmed. "That's the... the... He's that fella that we..." He frowned quizzically for a moment, then his face brightened in a fit of inspiration.

"Yes!"

"Come sit," Memnon patted the floor to his right. "I think I came here to kill you but why spoil a good afternoon, heh?"

Enlat knew he should be concerned about that but he was having trouble working up the necessary concern. He ambled over and plopped down on the floor.

"What do you think?" Memnon asked eagerly.

"Think, lord?"

"My art installation!" He waved at the couple on the throne. "Sometimes art is a simple matter of recognising the significance of what's right in front of you. This," he declared grandly, indicating the grunting pair, "is a perfect metaphor for Throneworld!"

Enlat looked up at the throne. *Oh shit! He expects me to figure this out?* He tried; oh gods, how he tried but the view from this angle was very disconcerting, art or not. He was starting to wish he'd sent his nephew off to Sargil for fostering.

He'd been reluctant to send the fool off to a better world than the one he himself was trapped on. Now the idiot was going to get him killed with his fornicating ways...

He nearly shouted it out in his relief. "I have it, Lord! Throneworld – a pack of fornicating idiots!"

He sprawled, face first onto the steps when Memnon slapped his shoulder with an armored hand. *Shit! I got it wrong and he's going to kill me.* To his horror, he chuckled. *Even if I'm wrong, that was a pretty good guess!*

"I knew I'd like you, Enlat! What are you doing down there?"

"Fell over, lord."

"You do that much?"

"Invariably, lord."

"Well, good for you, I suppose. Say, I'm getting hungry. Send for some food, will you? There's a good fellow."

Enlat got up, noticing that his aide was standing at the foot of the stairs, backed by a confused-looking group of laborers.

"Food, sire?" the aide suggested.

Memnon leaned forward, squinting at the aide. "Gods, Enlat! How does that fellow know our language?"

"I think he grew up speaking it, lord. But I have to admit, it does seem... suspicious..."

The aide turned and fled. The laborers stood there, emanating terror for a moment, but then one of them turned to run and the whole gang sprang into comical motion. They were tripping one another and climbing over fallen comrades in their haste to escape whatever had frightened the aide.

Enlat heard a roar of laughter and then he realized it was coming from both himself and his overlord as they watched the mad scramble.

"Gods help us," one of the security troopers growled a little too loudly. "It's one rump-humped errand after another on this cruise. Gods only know how our lord will react if we interrupt something important."

"Enough of that!" the officer leading them snapped. "We get no say, Bildur. If the fleet loses contact with our lord, then we come down and make sure he's in one piece. Now, shut up and keep a sharp eye."

They rounded a corner and approached the large doors to Enlat's throne-room. He doubted he'd find the boss in there; there'd be guards posted at the door if he were inside. He'd raise unholy hells about the abandoned weapon laying in front of the door but that could wait.

He had to find Memnon. Even though the throne-room was probably empty, he had to check before moving on.

He kicked the weapon aside and shoved the right door open. The smoke was mildly alarming but the fire in the middle of the main hall seemed harmless enough. Beyond the smoke, he could see the dais.

Memnon was asleep on the floor, leaning up against the throne. He was fully clothed, covered in food and a naked female was nestled up against his chest. Garand was lying on his back, also snoring loudly.

The guards were mostly asleep, though three of them were sitting in one of the bays, chuckling quietly, while a fourth was trying to reassemble his assault weapon blindfolded.

"Completely rump-humped," Bildur said quietly. "What do we do about this?"

"We didn't even come in here yet; that's what we do," the officer hissed. He turned for the door. "I want two of your best to stand guard out here and wait for our lord to come out. Make sure it's two who honestly have no idea what's going on in there."

"And what about the rest of us?" Bildur trotted to catch up with the officer, who'd just risen mightily in his eyes.

"We call the flagship." The officer stopped and leaned in close to his NCO. "We've been assured by a local authority that our lord is engaged in discussion with the governor and cannot be disturbed. We'll advise as soon as he emerges from the throne-room."

Bildur could see the sense in that. "If I may, sir, there's a kitchen of sorts just down the hall from here. Might be a good place to wait…"

"Good. Set up two of the lads here and come find me. I'll be reconnoitring the supply situation."

A chuckle. "Aye, sir. Reconnoitring... We'll be along in two shakes to help you with that."

That Went... Well?

The *Dibbarra* enroute to Throneworld

Mishak sat in a lounger, staring out at the distortion patterns beyond the window. Tashmitum walked by behind him, trailing her left hand across his neck.

"We should consider the possibility of retaking their territory," she said casually.

"So soon after we've come to an agreement with them?" Mishak growled. "I'll be getting a very unfavorable nickname if I keep betraying the people who trust me."

She eased into the chair next to his with a sigh. "I don't mean right away." She stared out the window.

"As long as they keep to their end of this bargain, it's in our best interest," she said. "Bau's food flows everywhere, so Humans will be 'keeping the peace' along every trade route in the empire."

Mishak took a drink from his mug. "The fighting will finally die down. Perhaps our citizens will even notice how much they prefer peace over the settlement of old grudges."

"There will still be some skirmishes, of course," she admitted. "There will be losses, but they won't be from our own house forces…"

"They'll be Humans," Mishak said softly.

"They'll have their steri-plants removed," she added, "if they haven't already. They multiply quickly but it will still be many years before their first generation is ready to fill in the gaps from combat losses."

He looked at her, still somewhat taken aback at how easily she could deploy the ruthless cynicism of an imperial ruler. It wasn't a natural part of her personality; it was simply a tool she'd been given by her 'uncle' Marduk.

"It may become necessary," she continued, "if we are to maintain the *Pax Imperii*, for us to step in and 'assist' our friends in the event that they are unable to maintain their duties under this new sovereignty association treaty."

She met his gaze. "It will be a narrow window, perhaps ten years from now. As long as they remain cut off from Kish, they have no source of recruits – nobody new to train as replacements."

Drilling

The *Pounce*

"Main drive back online, ma'am."

"Very good," Luna acknowledged. "And the breach in the main bus coolant conduit?"

"Patched. System working at eighty percent."

"Minus the five percent needed for interpersonal communication," she growled. She hit the icon to signal the end of the exercise.

The engineering officer, a logistics officer from her carrier, raised an eyebrow. "Ma'am?"

"This ship…" She waved a hand. "She's fast, maneuverable and she can hit pretty hard but it's frustrating to have to translate my thoughts into orders and then wait for someone else to execute them."

"Yeah, well, you're used to riding the 'thunderbolt'." He shrugged. "These corvettes aren't single-seat fighters."

"But what if we could rig up a way for me to control the helm and weapons from a single station? An interface similar to what we have in the *Lightning* back on Earth?"

"Hold on, Pounce," the weapons officer interrupted. "I didn't book off the last of my leave so I can sit in a chair and watch you hog all the fun!"

"Relax, Dangles; it's not like that. I just think our cousins from the empire are missing some low-hanging fruit here – no pun intended."

Despite the lack of intent, the others on the bridge enjoyed a few chuckles at her reference to the incident that led to Dangles' call-sign.

"Gleb said one of his buddies designed this class of ship. They just come up with ideas and then build them." She looked around the bridge. There were two fighter pilots with her, Dangles at weapons and Thruster at the helm.

"What if we could rig a way to temporarily run this ship like a fighter? What if we showed them how effective a new class of warship could be? We've still got four days to figure something out and test it in drills before returning to normal space."

"We could each get our own bird!" Thruster exclaimed.

"Damn!" Dangles turned to the engineering officer. "Quit arguing and help set this up! Damn black-shoes, always getting in the way!"

"Perch and rotate," the engineer advised Dangles, blithely unconcerned with the aviator's bullshit. "If you're done wasting our time, I'll get on with giving the captain her new interface."

Anger and Loathing at Babilim
The *Deathstalker*, Babilim

Memnon groaned. His head felt like a whole swarm of cheevers had taken up residence inside. His mouth had a foul taste, as if the damned little creatures had used his mouth for a latrine.

He sat up and grabbed a tankard from the shelf above his headboard. He took a long drink of the cool water inside. He set it back with a sigh and finally acknowledged the chiming tone.

"What?" he barked, startling Emoliat awake. The former governor sprang out of his chair and stood at attention, waiting for orders. Memnon ignored him.

"My lord," Garand's voice responded through the speakers, "we're at Babilim."

"Good." Memnon yawned. "Set up a cordon. I'll join you on the bridge shortly."

"About that, lord…"

"Yes?"

"Babilim, lord – it's built around a white dwarf. The size is incredible. We can make a cordon but it's going to be spread thin and we'll need to place it farther out than normal, just to maintain line of sight for signals."

Memnon sighed. He wished he could have brought more ships but his holdings were almost entirely recent conquests. There was no way he could strip away units from those systems, not if he wanted to keep owning them.

He already had a fearsome reputation but he'd not yet had the chance to show the empire what happens to a system that rebels against his rule. *I'd better arrange for a rebellion or two,* he thought.

"Very well," he told his adjutant. "We came to firm up our intel, not to start a fight. Once we know where the scum are, we can concentrate enough force and wipe them out."

He closed the window and sat there, staring through a nervous Emoliat. This was good. He'd tracked the Humans to this dark corner of the empire. *Once I find them, I'll make such an example of them that...*

"Mmh," a feminine voice intruded on his thoughts. "Tell me there's water in that tankard!" The covers next to him lurched alarmingly as a female Quailu emerged, stretching.

He realized he was still braced in a fight-or-flee response. "Gods!" he exclaimed in shock, though he still found the bandwidth to admire her stretching form. "Where the hells did *you* come from?"

She dropped her arms and stared at him reproachfully. "Right here," she huffed.

"You're from this ship?"

"Ship?" She leaned back in alarm. "We're not still in the governor's palace on Ansar?"

Then it came back to him. "You were one of the fornicating idiots I found on Enlat's throne!"

He'd expected an angry outburst at that comment but she radiated cool amusement instead.

"You're now one of those idiots, or have you forgotten last night?" she teased.

He knew he should be angry because the Memnon he wanted to project to the empire would never tolerate such insolence but he was too intrigued. *It's those damned leaves we burned,* he realized. *I don't remember much of anything since yesterday.*

"I actually *did* forget," he said. "I didn't even remember that you were in my bed." He moved toward her.

She read him as he approached and lay back, pulling him down on top of her.

"Let's see if we can prod my memory," he whispered in her ear.

Behind him, in the corner, Emoliat coughed discreetly, hoping vainly to be dismissed from the room. Memnon turned his head slightly, taking in enough air for the words…

"Quiet, Emoliat!" she growled. "You'll spoil the moment."

Memnon looked back at her in surprise. She'd taken the words off the tip of his tongue. Clearly, she'd heard him say the same thing last night.

He chuckled. Poor Emoliat was in for a long morning…

Shaking the Tree

Kurnugia

"Normalising," the helmsan announced.

"Threat-board is clear," Tactical added as the data finished flooding in. "Our ships are here but nobody else is within range. *Pounce* and *Nothing but Trouble* are a little more dispersed than expected but they signal full readiness."

"Good." Gleb nodded at the tactical officer, one of the rescued Humans from the Moon outpost who'd turned out to have military experience. "That can change very quickly, though, especially as we approach the planet. Keep on your toes.

"Fleet-wide channel." He stepped up to the central holo. Luna and Maeve appeared in front of him. "What's the first thing you asked when you arrived?"

"What do I do on arriving in-system," Luna replied. "But I asked it yesterday, well before we arrived, so I could explore any possible complications."

He nodded. "Excellent! Did you find any complications?"

"A few. Ambush being the really big one, though, so we ran a few drills. Practiced fighting our way out of a trap and it seems like sandbagging is the best option."

"Sandbagging?"

"We went to full power on the pitch drives and swung out and behind our original approach corridor," she waved at Maeve, "making sure to stay out of friendly approach lanes, of course."

"We thought that's what you were up to," Maeve said. "We figured our safest counter-measure on dropout was to move forward under full power and rotate to bring more of our weapons to bear." She shrugged.

"After the blast of our drop-wash, we figured we had a clear lane to maneuver in." She grinned at Luna. "We were just a few seconds behind you. You must have been practicing that maneuver a lot to have finished it so quickly!"

"Something like that," Luna said, sounding pleased with herself.

"Alright," Gleb cut back in. "Ask yourselves which dot of light is Kurnugia and how we get there as a small squadron."

He waited while both of them seemed to focus on some middle distance as they turned their thoughts inward, accessing stored memories they'd never used before. They both started giving out orders to their crews.

"Good!" He gestured to Maeve. "When we get there, Luna will be keeping an eye on the situation in orbit while you and I go down to the surface and shake a few trees."

Maeve took a deep breath as her shuttle settled on a parking platform. *First time on an alien planet!* She wasn't counting Mars. It was a different planet from Earth but it wasn't *alien*. There were more than a million Humans living there.

She got out of her seat in the back of the shuttle when Gleb stood. *I wonder if they can teach us how to shift locations the way he does,* she wondered. He'd come on her shuttle because it was so easy for him to simply appear in the passenger compartment in front of her.

Then she realized she was breathing the air of another world for the first time. Again, Mars didn't count because you could only breathe the atmosphere that the Humans made for themselves.

The air here smelled… busy. It was hot. No big surprise given the lava rivers on the surface below the globe-spanning ring of the city. It was also dusty.

Undertones of hydraulic fluids and lubricants mingled with the exotic scent of spices and the sweat of a hundred different species. The oils in that sweat were breaking down on every metal surface, giving off what was usually mistaken as the odor of the metal itself.

It felt like her childhood, when she visited the science-fiction-themed zones at an amusement park in California, only this time, it was real. True to her childhood memories, the heat prompted her to take a sip from the water outlet in her suit's collar.

She followed Gleb down the shuttle's ramp and stepped onto the dark grey surface of the landing platform. A strange-looking creature with large red eyes and spindly limbs protruding from a filthy orange jumpsuit was backing away from them, its hands held up in the universal gesture of surrender.

Alarmed, she looked at Gleb, who seemed unconcerned. She glanced down the row of landing pads and saw more aliens in similar garb taking a much more confrontational approach with newly arrived shuttles. *Some sort of customs officer?*

They passed through a security cordon as if it didn't exist. In fact, it *had* temporarily ceased to exist as the two Humans approached. The three armed guards lowered their weapons, abandoned their swaggering demeanor and backed up into a dark grey building that looked almost like concrete.

She reached out to touch the material. It wasn't as rough as concrete and it felt lighter, more insulating. The building's door snapped shut, making her jump. She turned to ask Gleb what the material was but he was already out on what passed for a sidewalk here.

He was standing in the pedestrian flow, staring pensively across the street at the gigantic high-rise tangle that covered the majority of the ring. 'In the flow' wasn't quite the right way to describe it.

She caught up with him.

The endless flow of pedestrians were giving the two Humans a wide berth, as if a ten meter energy shield were protecting them. They were all staring and those who were closest were pushing back against the flow in an attempt to get farther away.

"Gleb," she said quietly, "why are they acting like that?"

"They fear Humans."

"I get that but why?"

"We're rumored to be the servants of Nergal, the lord of the Underworld. They don't want us doing anything dark and unnatural with their souls."

"Yeah, I saw that when we captured that Chironan noble in Earth orbit but…" She waved at the crowd, causing a few shouts of alarm. Chagrined, she pressed her arms firmly to her sides. "They actually believe all that stuff?

"I mean, they can fly between the stars but they get all wiggly when a Human shows up? Are they really that superstitious?"

"Most will say they aren't, until you strip away a few of civilisation's comforting illusions. Most of these folks…" He waved at the crowd, lips sliding back in a feral grin as they exclaimed in fear. "… Don't travel more than a few days' walk out of the district where they were born, let alone between the stars.

"Call it what you will," he said softly, "but superstition, or faith – it's baked into all of us. Four walls and a light-switch may help us forget but it's still there, under the surface."

He started walking, parting the crowd without effort, and she moved to walk next to him.

"They don't all react like this, but out here on a world the empire leaves at arm's length, fear is a part of the daily landscape. There are also those who take the opposite approach, though. They're dangerous. They won't back down in the face of proof, so you either have to accommodate them or destroy them."

"And which kind are we here to see?" she asked.

"The fearless sort. I won't be able to intimidate him, so my best course of action is to treat him with respect. He'll understand that I'm bolstering his standing."

"A creature of Nergal, come to consult with him?"

"Pretty much. He probably assumes it's a pile of steaming turds but his people will want to believe because it puts them on top of that pile. It makes their boss look like a top-tier player."

"Hmph!" She moved closer to Gleb, conscious of the disturbance they were creating in the flow of foot-traffic, though it was reduced now that they were on the move. Most of the creatures they met now had very little warning that they were approaching Humans.

"I figured you were just gonna start kicking in doors and cracking bones with your brain!"

"Doors here don't kick in the way they do on Irth." He turned left to cross a pedestrian bridge. "They slide more often than they swing and you're making the mistake of seeing the folks here as alien 'things', rather than people.

"I guarantee you that Striga would get an earful from his daughters, if we keep him late at his office today."

"You know him?"

"Met him once, before we set up our own operative here. I've read the file on him as well. Two girls, wife killed in a bombing attempt on his life. The daughters don't like when he's late getting home – makes them worry."

"Word that he's been consulted by a servant of Nergal..." She frowned, working through the possibilities. "That might give others pause if they were thinking of attacking him, wouldn't it?"

Gleb nodded. "I'm handing him something of value just by walking in the door. Let's hope he has something we can use." He angled toward the buildings on the left side of the walkway and ducked into a small alley.

She followed him for roughly twenty meters before he came to a row of stinking containers attached to the side of the building next to an unmarked door. She thought she smelled rotten food and spices coming from the mostly cuboidal objects. *Alien dumpsters! Hoo boy, the adventure I'm having!*

"We need to make at least a pretense of discretion," he explained to her as he pounded on the door. "So we come in through the kitchen and then let ourselves be seen anyway."

He shrugged. "I know, it's stupid but this is how things work here."

The door opened, revealing a strange creature with chitinous spines all over his forearms, a pistol in his left hand. "Fornication!" he exclaimed. "I heard you were dead! Nergal giving your lot preferential treatment, is he?"

"Veles," Gleb greeted him. "How's that itch?"

Veles' right hand drifted absently to his left armpit. "Nothing gets rid of it! I even tried some fire-gel from the kitchen."

"The kind used as an ingredient or the kind you burn under a dish to keep it warm?"

Veles darted a quick glance over his shoulder. "I don't know about other establishments but, here, it's the same thing."

"Why am I not even the least bit surprised?" Gleb asked him. He reached to his chest, where a small section of his armor folded out of the way.

Maeve saw Veles' grip tighten momentarily on his pistol but he relaxed as Gleb drew out a harmless-looking small cardboard box from under his armor plating. *What the hell? Is that what it I think it is?*

"Try this on your itch." Gleb offered Veles the box. "Guy in a TV ad said it works for this kind of thing and I immediately thought of you."

"What the hells is a TV?"

"Long story. The boss in?"

Veles nodded in affirmation and stepped back to let them in.

Funny how it's the same nod as back home, Maeve thought.

The inside was an assault on the olfactory sense. Some kind of sharp tang in the air made her nose twitch and the back of her throat itch. It got stronger as they walked past the cooking line, where something was being fried in an aromatic liquid.

They went through a door into the main customer area and up a flight of stairs to a mezzanine running around three sides of the club. A stage sat in the middle of the lower level, where a collection of aliens, including two Quailu, were parading in expensive clothing.

Funny that I can discern the quality of their clothes, she thought. *That data I got implanted must have a full primer on HQE life.* Veles led them up another flight of stairs to a glazed enclosure that hung two levels above the stage.

I wonder if I know what spices I'm smelling? Her eyes grew wide as the context for each spice flooded her thoughts – planet of origin, harvesting methods, distribution networks...

She shook it off. *Later,* she thought. *Pay attention to what you're doing!*

Veles opened the door and waved them inside.

"Gleb?" the 'boss' blurted, looking up from a holo-display above his desk. "You died at the Battle of Kish! Didn't you get the paperwork?" The guards in the room didn't move an inch but their eyes had doubled in size.

Leshagna, the alien's species suddenly came to Maeve. *Same species as Veles.*

"I got better." Gleb gestured questioningly at the couch and Striga nodded.

They both sat and another Leshagna male appeared holding a tray with two small mugs with no handles but they had a molded ring below the lip to prevent them slipping. Following Gleb's lead, she accepted one.

Gleb was taking a sip so she figured it was safe. Then she realized she probably didn't have to wonder. *What is this?* Her eyebrows flickered upwards. It was a type of tea, harmless,unless you refused it and insulted the hospitality of your host.

She took a sip. *More savory than sweet. Like a meat broth.* She gave an involuntary nod of approval and took another sip. Striga looked pleased when she met his gaze.

"You've come to find out what's happened to the Hasharim, I suppose," Striga said, turning to look at Gleb. "A fool's business – trying to collect a bounty on Humans?" He snorted in disgust.

"Even without Ethkennu declaring open conflict on them, they'd shown their lack of judgement. Their end was written, at that point. We put a few of them over the edge ourselves and took nearly half their territory."

"Striga, I've heard about the attack but not the specifics. I've been away from the HQE for a while." He hesitated. "Who did they kill?"

"Wiped out the freighter crew in orbit but they missed their chance to get your leader. Got his friend when they were on the surface, though. Sniper round."

Gleb leaned forward. "Eth," he said urgently. "Where did he go when he left here?"

Striga frowned at his desk. "All I have is rumors. Some say he fled the empire altogether; some say he appeared in the prince's personal quarters on Throneworld, slapped the bugger around a bit so's he'd rescind the bounty…"

Gleb sighed, slumping back in the seat.

"We do know that he saved Lady Bau from some ridiculous plot at Arbella and then he was almost certainly involved in roughing up Melvin the Minuscule's gonads at Arraphka, though nobody knows why he'd be helping Mishak with his half-brother, unless…"

Gleb looked up. "Unless?"

"Gleb," Luna's voice crackled from speakers in his suit's neck-ring. "We've got trouble up here! Stealth-ships, at least two corvettes, if the occlusion-tracking is giving me an accurate picture. No hails yet. No rounds fired but they've definitely noticed our three un-stealthy corvettes."

"Be there in a moment." He grinned at Maeve. "I wasn't expecting to find them so easily! I'll go talk to them, make sure my old friends don't shoot at us, then I'll be right back." He stood and closed his helmet.

I don't know these guys! Maeve opened her mouth to speak but then closed it again, shaking her head. Gleb was already gone. *What the hells do I do with these guys?* She shrugged to herself. They came here to ask questions. She looked at Striga. He looked odd but he was still just some guy.

"Unless?"

Gleb opened his eyes. He was standing in front of Hela, who was in the middle of ordering a spread of Lady Bau's deadly missiles to be ejected from the ships of her squadron. A single order would have brought destruction lancing into Gleb's three ships at speeds no point-defense weapon could hope to match.

"Nice to see you too," he said cheerfully. "Do you think you could recall those weapons, before an unpleasant accident happens? I've got a lot of new friends on those corvettes."

She stood there, silent for several heart-beats. "Gleb?" She reached out with her mind.

Oh, gods! It really is you!

"And we're no threat to you," he said aloud, a little unsettled by her sudden intrusion. He'd spent so much time staying out of his new friends' minds that he'd forgotten how common the practice was here.

"Sorry," she said. "It's just… you need to be sure when an old friend returns from the dead with three warships."

The openings on the sides of the bridge flowed shut and Gleb's HUD showed a steady increase in atmospheric pressure. His helmet snapped open.

He noticed a slight change in pressure. His suit was still calibrated for his new ship and it operated at Irth's atmospheric pressure.

He hadn't noticed on Kurnugia because it, like most of the empire's worlds, had a slightly different pressure. *Ships* and *stations* in the empire, however, all calibrated their environments to Throneworld Standard.

He was saved the need to think about the implications when Hela nearly knocked him down with a flying hug.

"How are you alive?" she almost shouted. "Did you get off the *Stiletto* before impact? Were you hiding out on Kish?"

"Yes and no," he said, after catching the breath her impact had knocked out of him. "In that order. I got shifted somewhere very far away just before the *Stiletto* rammed that cruiser. In the absence of any plan on my part, I ended up getting sent to where there's a lot of Human consciousness."

She leaned back, arms still around his waist, and raised an eyebrow. "Somewhere that has a lot of Humans... when you were in orbit around Kish to begin with? Millions of Humans on our home-planet to anchor your destination?"

"I dunno..." He shrugged. "Maybe our connected, higher-dimension selves had a plan or maybe the Universe just has a sense of the dramatic."

She let him go but her eyebrow continued to accuse him.

He grinned. "You won't believe what I found!"

Maeve entered the bridge of the *Nothing but Trouble*. Gleb had explained the practice of naming corvettes after swords but she'd also heard of the earlier naming conventions they'd used for their scout-ships.

That was a convention more in keeping with her own practices and so *Nothing but Trouble* had taken her name from the next name in the list used by her company for naming their rockets. *Rockets.* She smiled.

Here she was in a ship capable of flying between the stars in the same time it took to sail across the Atlantic. A few weeks ago, rockets were the leading edge.

Exploring the empire sounded interesting but she wanted to get back as soon as she could and start looking for a good habitable planet to set down a colony. The old dream of being a multi-planet species was finally in sight. She wrinkled her brow.

I suppose we should count the Humans here in the empire. That, of course, would mean that the species had been 'multi-planet' for most of its history.

She nodded at Jerry and took the command-chair he vacated for her. *I'm not counting them for this. We'll use this new tech but it's going to be our own hard work that builds Earth's future.* "What's our status?"

"We're in good trim," Jerry said. "We've been at full combat readiness since *Pounce* noticed the bogeys and our path drive is fully charged and ready to initiate. We're all set to fight or fly."

"Good. Thanks, Jerry." She pressed her lips together in a tight line as Jerry walked away. *Why am I certain that exchange would have been handled better on* the *Pounce? They're all military over there – Navy, what's more. She's probably even managed to get her hands on a deck officer or two since the* Fauci *was in port for a refit. Maybe I should ask her for some of her bridge recordings.*

Maeve wasn't above admitting that someone else might know something she didn't. There wouldn't be a city on Mars, if she and her predecessors had been unable to recognise the expertise of others.

"Call coming in from the *Switchblade*," the communications officer announced.

"Main holo." She stood and stepped over to the optimal scanning zone they'd marked on the decking.

Gleb appeared, along with Luna and another Human she hadn't met, but she didn't look like anyone they'd brought from Earth.

"Maeve, Luna…" Gleb gestured to the new person. "This is Hela. She's taking advantage of her new role as the scouting division commander to go swanning about to exotic locations…"

"You cheeky little rump-sniffer!" Hela took a holographic swing at Gleb, laughing as he ducked the punch. "This sulphurous dung-heap is your idea of exotic? We've been stalking criminals for practice."

"Kind of like the way we stalked Lord Sandrak's flagship when Carol was teaching us?" Gleb asked. "I thought you'd lost your mind, kidnapping an elector as part of a training op!" He looked at Maeve and Luna. "Had to re-grow my whole suit after that. Damn thing stank of fear-sweat!"

"You've drilled your wild Humans well," Hela admitted, the choice of words causing Maeve to dart an amused glance at Luna. "I was setting up a round of missiles, just in case your ships were hostile knock-offs of our corvettes, and your Pounce, here..." she nodded toward Luna, "...was on my rump so fast I didn't even notice until after I got over the shock of you showing up on my bridge!"

"She was a professional on Irth," Gleb told her. "A combat pilot in the Navy."

"In the what?"

"Irth is a single-planet kind of deal," Gleb explained. "Dozens of independent political entities and even more languages. A lot of the surface conflict takes place using water-bound ships."

"Water-bound?" Hela looked at Luna. "You mean they float on the surface? Like recreational barges?"

"We don't have pitch drives on Earth," Luna explained. "Or, we didn't until recently. So we use water for a lot of our transportation and military needs. I suppose that will change pretty soon."

"I'm not so sure," Maeve cut in, voicing a concern that had been nagging her for a while. "Maybe we should be keeping a lid on this for now."

"You don't think people can handle it?" Luna challenged her.

"No," Maeve said slowly, buying time to order her thoughts. "The simple fact of our presence here at Kurnugia proves we can handle it. We managed to crew seven corvettes pretty quickly without anyone freaking out.

"I'm more worried about how governments will handle it." *And how a Naval officer will respond to the idea of keeping our country in the dark.* "The first ones to put fleets in orbit will shut down the others. That's bad enough but what happens then? Will they start a shooting war in orbit?

"Will some city in a country that couldn't even build a fleet get crushed by a ship that got shot out of orbit?" She shook her head. "We're talking about some big, destabilizing changes, here, like going back in time and giving cave-men nukes."

Luna frowned. A faint voice drew her gaze to the left and she listened for a moment before nodding. "Maybe, but you have to admit Maeve has a damned good point. We need to take some time to think about how we're gonna handle this."

"Well, we've got a two-day path-run ahead of us," Gleb told them. "Sounds like a good time to think things over. I'm sending the coordinates."

Maeve opened the new data-packet. It looked like a single rogue planet with no sun but the scale was bigger than anything Maeve had ever heard of. "What the hells is this?" she asked, easily using imperial vernacular.

"It's a station," Gleb explained. "One we found before I went missing. If we didn't get lucky here, it was on the list of places for us to search but I doubt we'd have had much luck if we simply went there with nothing but curiosity."

"Why not?" Luna asked.

Gleb raised a holographic eyebrow. "Because the circumference of that station is nearly a Billion kilometers. Imagine the surface area you'd need to look at to find evidence of a Human presence, especially when those Humans are now renegades and not keen on being found."

"A Billion?" Maeve spluttered. "But that's…" She trailed off.

"Pretty close to an Imperial Standard nominal planetary orbit?" He nodded. "That's because it houses a white dwarf star.

"Hela's squadron will lead the way this time," he said, while Maeve was still quietly working on absorbing what she'd just heard. "Then Maeve, Luna and myself, in that order."

He looked more eager than she'd ever seen him. "Fire up your drives and get ready. We found the way home!"

Time to Get Busy

Zeartekka *Royal Nest*

Zeartekka ships always unsettled Eth. They looked more like they were *secreted* than constructed. *I'd think they were all allergic to flat surfaces if I didn't know better.* He grabbed a random rod of lumpy metal and pulled himself up over a large change in the height of what might charitably be called a deck.

I feel sorry for Bau's litter-bearers. He grinned. The ride would still be pretty frightening for her, given the crazy topography of insectoid ships. *I'm assuming she's still alive, I suppose. Might have tumbled out the side of the litter and fallen down a vertical shaft...*

He nearly fell himself when a trio of flying Zeartekka roared past him with a deep thrumming of wings. The undulating, ridged surfaces of the passageways did an amazing job of attenuating the sound of their passage. *Maybe they design their ships to minimize sound reflection?*

He came to a junction. A vertical shaft was joined by three radial passages and there was no easy way to continue on at the current level. The radiating passages ended abruptly at the vertical shaft with no level walking space adjoining the passages.

He stopped, catching his breath and his escort waited patiently.

Seven more of the flying variant of the hive came buzzing down a passage opposite where Eth stood. Two of them blew past him while the other five veered straight down the shaft.

Oh well, let's see how they expect me to continue on from here. He gave the slightest hint of a nod.

The Zeartekka used non-verbal, non-empathic communication more than any other species in the empire. Eth knew they relied heavily on gestures and posture changes but his knowledge ended there. Entire conversations could take place and he'd be none the wiser.

If the Quailu had trouble with Human gestures and physical cues, then the Zeartekka must be orders of magnitude beyond their understanding.

His own Human gestures were easily read by these drones, however, and they gave a confirmatory shimmy before clambering around the side of the shaft with the ease one might expect of an insectoid.

"Of course," Eth muttered. He at least had a wide variety of hand- and toe-holds along the vertical surface. He managed to edge his way across to the next passageway without humiliating himself – at least by his own standards – and they moved on.

The passageway widened out gradually before ending at a large central chamber. Drones worked at stations throughout the space and the Queen herself was on a central platform, connected to where Eth stood by a narrow bridge of lumpy metal that continued at the level of the passage, the rest of the floor sloped steeply down to meld with the walls of the egg-shaped space.

The walkway was roughly two hand-widths across.

He looked over the edge of the path as he made his careful way to the Queen. "You guys ever fall from this thing?"

"It happens," the wingless escort rattled, "but our spirit has a short journey. The Queen is here among us."

"My spirit would find little comfort in that," Eth pointed out.

The escort chittered. "Your spirit must find comfort in its own way."

Eth couldn't be certain but he thought he'd just amused the Zeartekka. *Now I can die fulfilled,* he joked to himself. He glanced down and shuddered. *And that may happen today...*

It probably took longer than dignity dictated for him to make the crossing. It was always worth remembering that dignity tended to mend faster than bones.

And dignity would hardly be served by his screams as he fell to his death.

He finally reached the central platform. Bau sat next to the Queen, who indicated a lumpy thing that Eth had taken for a command console. He realized it had an indentation created by the insectoids for his ass.

He put it to use, grateful after his long journey. Given where he was, the seat was surprisingly comfortable. "Your grace, my lady." He gave them seated bows.

As the leader of the military faction, he was accorded a level of equality with Bau and the Queen. He was now constrained only by politeness and so he could take a seat before offering a greeting.

He looked around, seeing Bau's litter but no bearers. "I do hope your bearers didn't come to a bad end during your journey here?"

Bau smiled. "They're waiting at the forward hangar bay. The Queen graciously supplied a team of flying bearers."

"Of course." Eth nodded.

"What is a compliment for one might be an insult to another," rattled the Queen. "We would hardly insult a warrior by offering to carry him like luggage."

Eth had to grin at that. It came dangerously close to calling the Quailu noble luggage but, on the insultometer, the readings were now sufficiently muddled to avoid issues.

It also showed him that the Queen had probably caught some micro-expression on Eth's face. To her, it would broadcast his mild annoyance just as effectively as it would for him to scream it into a Quailu's face.

"Your meeting was productive?" the Queen probed.

"It was, your grace. They see the value in what we offer."

"That is fortunate," Bau said, trying but not entirely succeeding in hiding her relief. She would know how well the Zeartekka could read physical cues but she still had no idea how well a Human could see into her thoughts. "Now comes the laborious process of implementing our plan. No doubt they'll seek to slow-walk it."

Eth leaned back, forgetting his seat had no back. He threw out his hand to break his fall and struggled, red-faced, back to a proper seating position. "That won't be a problem," he told them.

Bau gazed at him and Eth could feel her attempts to read his emotions. He let her have his confidence. "Why do you say that?"

"The emperor is dead."

"Dead?" Bau reared back in her seat one hand flying up to cover her throat. "We've heard nothing!"

"And you won't," Eth told her. "You won't until we implement our agreement with the empire. Losing a part of his dominion will be Tir Uttur's final legacy."

"Then they will certainly move quickly," the Queen rattled. "Did they reveal this to you voluntarily?"

"No," he refrained from further detail, "but they know that we have this information and that will heighten their sense of urgency. They'll want to get this done before we leak it."

"What about your implants?" the Queen croaked.

Eth blinked. "Implants?" He wasn't sure what direction the conversation was taking. It seemed the Queen considered the matter of succession from the empire as one that needed no further discussion. What the hells was she getting into now?

"Your numbers are still too small," she insisted. "That has always been the source of my misgivings. Your people must have their sterility implants removed and start fornicating as much as possible. Offspring hatched today will need many years of rearing before they're ready to replace your losses."

Eth laughed. He could feel Bau's intense discomfort at the Queen's brazen meddling but it faded when she felt his amusement.

The laugh was too much like a shout for a Quailu to tell the difference but the Queen understood it well enough.

"A sense of humor is advantageous for a Human seeking a mate," she croaked helpfully, "but don't forget about the implants."

"The fornication is already well underway, your grace," he told her, chuckling. "The implants, however, remain a technical problem."

"I can post technicians to your service," she said, undulating slightly. A flying drone turned and sped away. "They can deactivate the implants or even set them to dissolve into your circulatory system as backup medical nanites."

Is she just offering help or is she embedding spies in my team? "I'm very grateful for your generous offer," he told her. "We'll keep them busy, I'm sure." *It's probably both. Of course they're curious – they don't even know where we're operating from. It's time to show a little trust.*

"I'm returning to our new home after this meeting. Perhaps you'd like to accompany me?"

"Your new base has been a closely guarded secret." The Queen clicked in surprise. "You would reveal it to us so willingly?"

Eth waved a dismissive hand, mostly for the Queen's benefit. "Rumors will already be circulating, your grace. Word will get out eventually and it's only right that our friends know before our enemies."

"I'll certainly come with you,' Bau said. "You've been to my home; it would be rude for me to refuse an invitation to visit yours and, frankly, I'm curious!"

"I will come as well," the Queen said. "Perhaps we can all travel aboard my ship, seeing as we are already aboard?"

"Well, Highness," Eth demurred, "that brings me to the one condition that we need to agree on before we depart…"

Republic

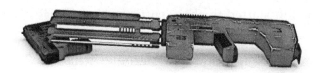

Learning Curve

Babilim Station

"Normalising," Thruster announced. "We are fully out of path."

"Threat-board is clear," Dangles said. "Going with path, huh, Thruster? Not 'warp' or 'hyperdrive' or 'FTL'?"

"Yeah," the helm officer said drily, "that's what we need while we're still getting used to this shit. Different terminology from literally everyone else that uses this tech."

"Are you numbskulls not seeing this?" Luna demanded. "We've got a white dwarf on our starboard beam and you're arguing about what to call FTL travel?"

"Pounce votes FTL!" Dangles crowed.

Thruster just waved him off. "She's right – about the star, that is – but that's not even the half of it. Look at what we have to port."

On the central holo, the star was set in the middle of the display. To the left, a sheer wall extended from the deck to the overheads. It showed no discernable curvature.

"Huh!" Dangles frowned up at the view from his weapons station. "That's one big sumbitch but I thought they said the star was *inside* the station."

The helm officer chuckled. "Show him, Pounce."

Luna reached both hands out wide to the sides, made a pinching gesture with her thumbs and index fingers and pulled her hands together slowly. For a long time, nothing changed, then, finally, the wall on the left started to show curvature but it was curving around the star, not away from it.

"Sweet zombie Ghengis!" Dangles whistled. "We *are* inside the damned thing! The station's so big they can give us coordinates inside and we don't have to worry about our drop-wash damaging anything!"

"Goes a long way to explaining how they stay hidden," Luna said. "Anyone searching would probably be looking for a bunch of stealth ships outside."

"And the place is so big," Thruster added, "they'd keep searching for years, certain they'll see the black spots created by stealth ships between them and the station. They might never figure it out!"

A chime sounded. "The rest of the squadron has just checked in," the ops officer told them, nodding at the holo. "Flag is hailing us."

Luna routed it to the main holo. Hela shimmered into view along with all the other captains, arranged in a ghostly ring before her. "Nine rings for mortal men," she said under her breath.

"Welcome to Babilim," Hela said. "For the Irth ships, check your code-banks. I've sent you a link to our tactical net. Also, you have parking coordinates. As soon as you get there, I'll have a team ready to start coating your ships with carbon nanotubes."

"Sweet!" Dangles whispered in the background. "We were a serious ass-kicking machine already but, adding stealth to the mix? When do we get into a good fight?"

"Gleb…" Hela turned to her long-lost friend. "… We'll set up quarters for your Irthers on the station but, for now, bring your captains and join me at my icon. We'll do the reunion tour!"

An orange icon appeared in the coordinates list to Luna's right. She was just wondering whether the Earth squadron captains would share a ride in the same shuttle when she noticed Gleb standing in front of her, grinning like an idiot.

"Hey, Pounce!" he said.

"Shit!" Dangles shouted. He took a few breaths. "Nergal's hairy nads! Knowing you can do that and actually seeing it are two very different things!"

He tilted his head. "D'ya hear that? Ten minutes in one of those pods and I sound like an old Throneworlder!" He held up his hand to catch Luna's attention before she turned back to Gleb.

"Don't forget, Pounce! Find that Noa guy and have him build your idea!"

"One thing at a time, Dangles." She turned to Gleb. "I take it you want a ride?" She walked past him, giving him a slap on the backside. There were a few approving hoots as she headed for the companionway entrance.

"What's the idea?" he asked as he caught up with her.

She'd half considered keeping him in the dark, surprising him with a prototype, but she decided his help was probably worth more than his surprise.

"Those maneuvers we executed so quickly," she began, "the way we got the drop on Hela – that was because we rigged up a command interface for me so I could fly my corvette more like a fighter than a conventional ship."

"What sort of changes are we talking about, exactly?"

"We routed helm and weapons control to my station. If you put that directly in the captain's control, you can act while the enemy is still digesting your last move.

"Hells, you can act several times before they catch up and start using vocal commands that some other officer has to hear, understand and then act on. It's a major tactical advantage in a fight!"

She'd been talking so fast she was neglecting the need to breathe. She took a few moments to catch up on oxygen, giving Gleb time to think.

"With larger ships," he mused, "maneuverability is too limited for your idea to make much of a difference but ships have been getting a lot smaller. Our ships anyway…

"You want a ship built around you?" he asked mildly. "Maybe a few support staff, engineering and ordnance techs? A heavy load-out of Lady Bau's missiles, a few direct-fire weapons for close-in work…"

They reached the hangar. She led him to the closer of the two shuttles in the forward bay. "You think we can get Noa to help build something like that?"

"You're kidding me, right?" He followed her inside and took the co-pilot's chair. "This is the next logical step in our ship design progression but I don't know if we'd have figured it out for ourselves! Nobody uses fighters here in the empire.

"The Quailu would consider such a thing beneath their contempt and when we *did* make small scouting ships, we never thought to question the standard bridge personnel setup."

"They won't think it's beneath their contempt after we've destroyed enough of their pretty warships!" Luna said archly. Her hands flowed over the controls and they lifted off the deck.

"The last time we had new Humans show up among us, we had to knock all that reverence for the 'Master Species' out of them before we could trust them in combat. Hearing you talk about killing Quailu so casually… It's kind of hot!"

She snorted. "Careful, lover-boy. You don't want to meet all your old pals with a recent hole in your memory." She turned the shuttle and sent it racing toward Maeve's ship.

Gleb was silent for most of the approach to the *Nothing but Trouble* and she was starting to wonder if her gibe had hit a little too hard. She wasn't the one missing some of the most exciting moments in their relationship, after all. "You okay?"

"Hmm?" Gleb looked over at her, eyebrows raised. "Oh…" He grinned. "… No, I was just hoping Noa was here when you mentioned my memory. Now I'm hoping Scylla's here as well. She can step into a mind as easily as you can step into this shuttle."

"You think she can help?"

"If anyone can, it's Scylla."

They lapsed back into silence. She slipped into Maeve's forward hangar bay and set down just inside the nav-shielding.

Maeve came aboard and strapped into the middle chair, set slightly back from the pilot and co-pilot. She looked at her two fellow captains.

"Am I interrupting a couple thing here?" she asked. "Don't stop on my account. It's been nearly a year since I was dating anyone and I could use a little vicarious sexual tension."

Luna laughed. "There is a bit of tension," she admitted. "If their 'high priestess' of funky brain stuff is here, she might be able to help Gleb."

He looked at her. "Why would that mean tension?"

"You're kidding, right?" Luna spared him a glance after clearing the *Nothing But Trouble's* nav-shield. "It's like you're identical twins and I've been dating one of you but sleeping with the other. Imagine the moment when you finally get to talk to each other about me."

"Oh, this is good stuff!" Maeve leaned forward. "Did I see you guys on Springer last week?"

They approached the coordinates assigned by Hela, while giving Gleb a quick background on their planet's daytime television offerings. The shuttle entered a large, square opening in the station's inner wall and Luna had to re-orient the craft when she realized the wall had actually been more of a floor.

The orange icon guided her, leading the way to a truly gigantic space with several platforms running along the sides. She didn't know if they went all the way around because the far wall was little more than a grayish haze.

The icon led them down onto the hangar floor, where a long row of shuttles were parked. She could see Hela waving to them from the near end of the row. The scouting commander pointed to a spot at the end and Luna nodded to herself, turning her vehicle accordingly.

They settled on the pad and opened up the hull. "OK," she said, taking a deep breath. "Time to go meet your friends."

"Oh!" Maeve put a hand on Gleb's shoulder. "This is a stressful moment for us Earth-folk, so you…" She frowned. "What's wrong?"

"No." He shook his head. "It's nothing. Just… no change in pressure." He shrugged. "There's always a small discrepancy from the standard ship pressure, the pressure of Throneworld." He shook his head again. "Sorry, Luna. Don't worry about my friends. They're going to like you."

"You seem pretty sure." She said uncertainly.

"They're going to see all the same things I see," he said.

"Not *all* the same things," Maeve said mischievously.

They all laughed.

"Good timing, Maeve," Luna said. She gestured Gleb toward the door. "Alright! Tension broken. Let's get out there, before I get nervous again."

The moment he stepped into view, there was a lot of yelling and cheering going on. It had an outdoor quality to it, seeing as the nearest walls were kilometers away, but it was loud, nonetheless. There had to be hundreds of people there to greet him.

Luna and Maeve stepped out behind him and found themselves ringed in by the happy throng. Everyone was smiling and shouting at the same time.

Everybody but one.

A man in standard EVA armor was staring at Gleb angrily. Luna had no idea what Gleb may have done to piss him off and she didn't care. She started edging his way.

Maeve stayed with her. She leaned closer. "Seems to be going well, so far!" she shouted into Luna's ear.

Hela shoved her way through the crowd and made a space for herself in front of the three. She held up her hand and the crowd grew quiet far more quickly than Luna would have thought possible.

"We all thought our boy, Gleb, snuffed it at the battle of Kish." Hela said loudly. "I know there's more than a few of us alive today because he rammed that cruiser. Some clever bastard figured out how to track us but Gleb understood what was happening and he bought time for us."

There was a scatter of shouts – various expressions of agreement.

"We were sure the captain had gone in with his ship." She slapped Gleb on the shoulder. "But, instead, he manages to find Irth, a planet with Billions of our people living on it!"

Cheers.

"A planet that produces some pretty decent warriors, even without pod training. We've all had the same data dumps but I've never seen ship-handling like this Irther, over here," she shouted, pointing at Luna.

"I'm not too proud to admit she got the gauge on me at Kurnugia. I looked away for a heartbeat to coordinate a missile spread and she was up my backside, before I even realized it."

This was greeted by whispering, rather than cheers, but Luna was pretty sure she should like what she was seeing here. *Hela is painting this in the best possible light. I wonder if they're facing a morale problem? Whoever the angry dude is, he's clearly not a happy team-player.*

"Folks," Hela continued, "I'd say our dwindling-numbers problem just came to a screeching halt!"

"If any of that is even true!" Angry Guy shouted. He ignored the groans and rolling eyes. He stepped in front of Gleb, pushing his face in close. "Our folks were dying at Kish and what did you do?" he shouted. "You ran off and hid!"

"Screw you, sphincter-lips!" Luna said loudly. She drove the heel of her right hand upward as the jackass turned her way.

Her hand connected with the bottom of his jaw, slamming it shut with a sound that made everyone wince. His head snapped back and he dropped like five pounds of dung in a ten-pound sack.

More winces as his head made a decent imitation of the sound a coconut would make if dropped.

But nobody moved to help the now-senseless man.

An octagonal section of the floor to Luna's left dropped down and retracted just in time for a man to emerge without hitting his head.

"Gleb!" he shouted, climbing out while the platform he stood on was still several feet below the surface.

"Noa!" Gleb shouted back gleefully. They embraced, laughing.

"You screw-up!" Noa said fondly. "Can't even get yourself killed properly!" He stepped back, finally noticing the guy on the floor. He turned an inquiring eye back to his friend.

Gleb held up his hands, palms forward. "Hey, he was like that when we got here!"

Catching a Nibble

The *Deathstalker*, Babilim Station

Memnon glared at the mug of coffee in his hand. When had he been served this? He set it down on a grav-plate that someone from engineering had installed on his command-chair. The coffee was good and the service so unobtrusive that he didn't even remember anyone bringing it but that wasn't the point.

Or maybe it was?

He picked up the mug, took another drink and then set it down before he realized what he was doing. *It's that fornicating idiot I picked up at Ansar. She's not such an idiot after all.* His life on the *Deathstalker* was becoming more comfortable in many subtle little ways and he knew she was to blame.

It was a problem. He liked the changes she was making on his ship. No engineering officer worth his electrolytes would ever dream of installing a grav-plate on Memnon's chair to hold coffee, not without orders. She was giving orders on his behalf.

The excellently made coffee and the grav-plate it sat on, even some of the disciplinary procedural-improvements, that had to be ordered by someone and he knew who that was. He darted a quick glance back at the coffee.

No, he didn't. He had no idea who she was but he was letting himself get attached.

He continued trying to intimidate his beverage. *Might have to arrange for an airlock malfunction…,* he thought.

"Lord!" The operations-officer intruded on his thoughts. "We have a contact report from the *Wraith Tower*."

Excitement and relief. He finally had an escape from his domestic entanglements. "Show me!" he ordered as Garand came onto the bridge, securing the fastenings of his tunic.

"It's far from any functional tethers," he mused, expanding the image to show a sizable fleet. "Maybe their stealth lets them land without triggering the defensive systems?"

"Or Enlat might have just been repeating old myths about the ancient defenses?" Garand suggested. He squinted, leaning in closer and then moving to the side to get a better three-dimensional perspective. "This is odd…"

"More than one force," Memnon grunted in acknowledgement. "A fleet of black shapes, easily seen with the station behind them, and a fleet of un-camouflaged ships as well." Now he leaned in. "No, two fleets…"

"Zeartekka!" Garand exclaimed, enlarging a section of the display to show the undulating outer hulls of the insectoid vessels. "The *Royal Nest*, no less!"

"Lord!" the Ops officer called out. "I have confirmation that Lady Bau's flagship is there as well!" An icon blinked into life indicating the *Harpy of Endor*.

"The farmer and the locust," Memnon said softly. "What schemes are you hatching?" He fought to keep his emotions in check. He knew how easy it would be to slide into irreversible, precipitate actions which could have effects he couldn't predict.

Oh fornicate it all, he thought. *Who am I kidding?* "Combat alert!" he shouted, revelling in the thrill of anticipation that spread through the bridge.

Bold action, in his experience, was usually better than gnat-picking. This golden opportunity could evaporate while he thought it through. Two powerful, potential blocks to his advancement were vulnerable, pinned between his forces and the massive station.

It was time to kill.

A Meeting of Minds

Babilim Station

"So we claim we're there to deliver cookies," Gleb told the crowd.

They were in a room that reminded her of the wardroom on the *Fauci,* though the ceiling was more than twice as high here. The food was completely unfamiliar but, if it was safe for these Humans, she'd eat it without complaint.

"While the fools were trying to puzzle that out, we got the lay of the land and started killing. When the Chironan fleet showed up, the Irthers surrendered me, putting me in range of their leader."

There was a general growl of approval at this. The Humans here had no love for Chiron, from what Luna could gather.

They weren't standing especially close but she felt crowded all the same. Iy almost felt as though their thoughts were pushing into the edges of her consciousness. It seemed to come and go at random but it stopped when Gleb was talking.

Now that he'd paused, she was feeling it again. She set down the red thing she was nibbling at.

"Textbook case of asymmetrical warfare," she said. "Turn your enemy's strengths into weaknesses. Their main strength was their ships. Gleb tricked their leader into giving him access to their systems."

"Which left them with no strengths at all," Gleb added with a shrug. "Chironans…" He left it at that but the crowd seemed to agree.

"And there are really Billions of us on Irth?" someone asked.

"A little more than eight Billion," Luna confirmed. As long as someone, even she, was talking, they seemed to leave her mind alone. "More than a hundred countries and dozens of languages."

"Don't leave a steaming pile at my door!" someone retorted. "What possible reason could there be for such fragmentation on a single planet? We have thousands of worlds in the empire and we all speak one language!"

"And you all get around with path drives," she answered calmly. She had no intention of getting into the 'Is Earth our home planet' debate at this point. "How long has that tech existed?"

"At least for a hundred fifty thousand years."

She nodded. "That has a unifying effect, makes the Universe seem a lot smaller. We've only had air travel on Earth for a little over a century."

This was met with surprise and mild disbelief. "Not even air travel?" one woman blurted in shock. "But why air travel only? Once you get off the ground, how hard is it to keep going and get into space? Wouldn't..."

A commotion at the back of the crowd drew the woman's attention and she trailed off.

They parted for a woman who walked calmly toward the table. She didn't seem the least bit concerned that someone might get in her way.

And yet, it didn't seem like arrogance to Luna. It just seemed like the natural state of things. *Who the hells is this?*

My name is Scylla, a voice answered but her mouth wasn't moving. "Would you all excuse us please?" she said to the crowd.

The whole crowd left without question.

Luna darted a look at Maeve, sitting to her left. "Did you just hear that?"

"She asked them to leave?"

She looked back at Scylla who was taking a seat opposite her. She opened her mouth but then closed it again. *Can you hear me?* She thought.

Of course.

So... this conversation is taking place in my head?

Yes. You aren't ready yet to hear me outside of your own head.

That raised far more questions than it answered, especially regarding the word 'yet'. *Can Gleb do this?*

Yes. Hasn't he talked to you like this?

No…

Not even during coitus? You were just thinking about that…

No but he's not himself when we have sex. He keeps shifting to some kind of alternate personality and he can't remember afterwards. She could feel Scylla's concern at this.

Are you guys talking about me? Gleb's mind asked playfully. She wasn't sure how she knew it was him. There was no sound after all. She just knew.

We are, Scylla replied. *You've been harmed. I can see the damage done to your mind.*

Oh. Gleb was quiet for a moment but Luna could feel hope in his thoughts. It felt like he didn't dare trust the feeling. *Can you repair the damage?*

No. Scylla seemed to stop and Luna could feel Gleb's mind resign itself to a fragmented future.

But, Scylla continued, *the mind is a resilient thing. Most of it is never even used in an entire lifetime. The connections are broken but new paths can be made. We just bypass the damage.*

Luna could feel his disbelief but then she felt something else. It was as if he was remembering events, black-market deals with Quailu officers, mischief with door controls…

She shivered, the hairs on the back of her neck standing up. She was feeling hot breath on her neck – her *own* breath but on *Gleb's* neck. She suddenly experienced all of their encounters through his senses… every missing moment, all at once.

It was the most intense thing she'd ever experienced but it paled next to his perceptions of her. She'd always thought she was average looking. She'd had boyfriends tell her she was attractive but she just assumed they were being nice.

After all, the advertising industry spent Billions every year to convince her that she needed a ton of products to look good. Sure, she was the result of thousands of generations of selective breeding, but... Billions of dollars?

You can't compete with that...

Can you?

She got a completely unvarnished insight into how he saw her and her skin tingled all over. *Oh gods! Gleb, you never stood a chance!*

You hear me complaining? he asked, startling her. *Now that you know what a goddess you are, I'll never hear the end of it!*

Even though she was experiencing his thoughts through Scylla, she'd somehow managed to forget that he could hear her thoughts as well.

Is it possible for me to feel your experiences like this when we're together? she asked eagerly.

Yes, but I didn't want to intrude into your mind if you were unprepared...

'Yes' is all I need to hear, she cut him off impatiently. *As soon as Scylla is done fixing your brain, we need to go find a quiet place. You've been holding out on me!*

I'm done, Scylla told her. *Enjoy yourselves... or... each other, I suppose.*

Luna finally brought her focus back to the room she was sitting in. Maeve was looking over at her from the seat to Scylla's right.

Luna realized she was flushed and breathing heavily. Her knees were pressed tightly together and her arms were hugging herself tightly.

Gleb was sitting slightly hunched over, shifting uncomfortably. His breathing was shallow and rapid and he couldn't take his eyes off Luan.

Maeve nodded at Scylla. "She set up some kind of mind mojo with you and Gleb?"

Not trusting her voice yet, Luna nodded.

"Hmm." Maeve looked around the room. "Looks like you had fun. Gotta find me a spaceman of my own…"

5-Cent Tour

The *Utak, orbiting Babilim Station*

Eth turned to Bau and the Zeartekka Queen. "We'll be able to land this corvette on the surface," he told them. "We've managed to convince the station's defensive systems that our ships belong here and, even if that failed, our camouflage would prevent us from being detected.

In actual fact, he planned to path straight into one of the massive spaces they were using as a hangar. This one was kept empty on the off chance he'd be bringing visitors but didn't want them knowing exactly where they were.

Having a ship come out of path in a room with people, even a room big enough to hold a small moon, would most likely prove fatal. There were several of the large spaces near the Human operation on Babilim.

"Your ships, of course, will need to remain up here." He gave an apologetic shrug, more for the Queen's benefit. "That's why I asked you to travel aboard the *Utak*. The less time spent messing around up here, the safer you'll be…"

"I appreciate your concern," Bau said, rubbing at her neck, "but I'm sure we'd have been perfectly safe in the midst of such a large collection of warships."

Her neck was probably suffering from a few nights of sleeping on a Human-designed ship. In Eth's experience, safety was a subject best left to logic, rather than comfort.

He was spared the temptation to point this out to his ally by the blaring of an emergency alert.

"Path wash!" the sensor officer shouted. "Straight through the *Royal Nest*! She can't keep station. She's going down!"

"All forces, all ships," Eth said, "full combat alert! Initiate evasive maneuvering!"

A.G. Claymore

"They've turned on the *Harpy*, sir… Hells! Two more have jumped in. The *Harpy* caught a bit of the wash but she was already moving. She's still answering to helm." The Ops officer was reciting the action in a clinical voice as he double-checked the *Utak's* readiness reports.

"Get us in there," Eth ordered. "Helm, take us straight toward the second ship." He figured the natural instinct was to hit either the first or last ship to arrive and he didn't want any enemy left unengaged.

That was easier thought than done.

"Five more now!" Sensor warned.

Eth started assigning the ships of his fleet to specific targets. *How many are we going to end up facing?* he wondered.

Interruptus
Babilim Station

"What the hell is that?" Luna demanded, startled back into using English.

She'd just dragged Gleb up from his seat but hadn't hauled him more than three steps from the table before a screeching alarm started sounding from every single EVA suit in the room. She'd been so intent on finding somewhere reasonably private that she wasn't sure how long the alarm had been sounding.

"Combat alert," Gleb said.

People around them were winking out of sight. He looked at her with regret. "Sorry, have to get to my ship and I can't take you with me. Rain-bill?"

"It's 'rain-check'," she told him between gritted teeth. "Go!"

She turned to Scylla as Gleb stopped being present. "How long does it take to learn that teleport thing?"

"Longer than you want right now." Scylla stood and took her hand. "Let's go…"

Maeve blinked at the spot where they'd been standing. She was alone in the mess hall.

"Great," she said with a sigh. "I'll just sit here like an idiot then, shall I?"

"Shit!" Dangles shouted, staring at the two women who'd just appeared on the bridge. "Spilled coffee all over my crotch!"

"Sure," Luna needled him. "That's why your pants are wet." She headed for the command interface station they'd developed. "This holo tied into the active command-net?" she asked, nodding at the display of the battle.

"Yes, ma'am," the comms officer confirmed.

"Good, get me an active IFF tag for this ship; I don't want our imperial cousins shooting us by mistake."

"We're joining the fight?" Thruster asked eagerly.

"Are you on crack? Of course we're gonna fight!" She placed two icons, flanking an enemy ship that was closing on the *Harpy*. "I want a micro-path to this drop point. Half-bank us to the outside and then we'll commit the second half to a drop-wash on that heavy cruiser."

"Wait, how..." Thruster's frown cleared. "Setting up the first micro-path. One of the same tunnels our cousins used to path out to the fight already."

Using path drives in space was fine but you couldn't just path straight through a planet or, in this case, a station that was thicker than any planet. Babilim had been constructed with Billions of open tunnels that gave a clear shot between the interior and the Universe beyond.

"Capacitor bank at full charge," the engineer reported. "Starboard array ready for the first hop."

"Course laid in, Pounce," Thruster added. "C'mon! Hit it!"

She was positively shaking with adrenaline, eager to get into the fight and terrified to jump into her first space-battle. She flexed her fingers and wrapped them around the controls.

She had a good crew. This might be a first for them but it sure as hells wasn't their first rodeo. *Time to show these people what Earthers can do!*

She squeezed her left trigger finger and the Universe leapt a few hundred thousand klicks aft.

"Port capacitor array engaged and ready!"

"Assault vector laid in..."

She squeezed again.

Her HUD was filled with fire and debris. The *Pounce* was sitting still after the drop-out, so Luna took a quick all-around look and threw the corvette into a hard dorsal shift. She arced her path, keeping the enemy ship's estimated position at optimal gunnery range and started unloading kinetic rounds into it as the view cleared.

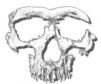

Eth had noticed one of his ships among the host pouring out of the station. It was fully grown but not yet given the carbon nano-tubule coating that would make it stealthy in most situations.

He squinted at the icon. It was formed up on Hela's squadron, so she must have ordered it grown while he was away. He shrugged to himself. *Not that camo is of any use with the station under us.*

Below them, the *Royal Nest* began to vaporize as she fell through the station's defensive screen. He shuddered, even though the Zeartekka crew-drones would feel little fear as they watched death coming for them.

He was turning to issue an order to Noa's force. Noa had just pathed out into the open and Eth wanted them to concentrate on protecting Bau's flagship. The order didn't come.

First, another enemy had jumped in. They'd almost caught the *Harpy's* stern but she was getting better at executing random course changes.

That alone wouldn't have distracted him. A second, uncoated corvette had just jumped in with enough drop-wash to scour away fifteen meters of the enemy cruiser on one side.

As he watched, mouth hanging half-way open – Noa's name still unspoken on his tongue – the new ship threw itself into an immediate maneuver. It began to orbit the partially stricken cruiser like it was on a circular rail, spitting out kinetic rounds that gouged a deep furrow into her hull.

The corvette then pulsed two conventional missiles into that furrow and skipped away, quick as thought, before they impacted. *How the hells can a crew handle orders that quickly?* he wondered. He knew Hela drilled her teams hard but this was beyond anything he'd ever seen.

Luna could hear cheers as they closed in on the next target. A quick glance back told her the target had been destroyed but she saw another cruiser turning her way.

She swung around, turning into the enemy's circle far more nimbly than any heavy ship could. Their main batteries never got an angle on the *Pounce* but the secondaries were all over the hull and they let loose a hail of rounds.

They had the sense to not simply fire directly at the *Pounce*. At this distance, even a well-handled frigate could slip aside from such an attack in the few seconds it took the rounds to reach them.

This ship was spreading the rounds out, hoping to leave their target nowhere to go, but a corvette was far more agile than a frigate and this one was practically an extension of her pilot. Still, there are no guarantees in combat.

"Shit, shit, shit, shit," Luna growled in increasing pitch as she threw the ship hard to port and poured on the acceleration. She was feeling the G's as her maneuver overmatched the inertial dampening in the decking.

She was pressed tight into the right side of her seat, then lifted against the straps of her restraint harness. She heard a member of the bridge crew slide across the deck as she danced her way to the cruiser's stern where their weapons were thinnest.

She targeted a point near the aft path drive housing. During the trip out to the empire, she and her fellow fighter pilots had been studying ship designs and they'd noticed a corridor that ran all the way into the central bus that carried power and data through the ship.

That bus, as Dangles had pointed out, would carry fire-control data as well.

She let loose a quick burst of kinetic rounds and kept moving, wishing she could have kept a small holo-window focused on the impact area, but that would have to be an idea for after this fight.

If there *was* an after the fight...

She kept moving aft on the cruiser.

"Fire's slacking off, Pounce. I think it worked!" Thruster shouted.

She came in close, pouring fire into the seemingly inert point-defense weapons on the stern. *Only an idiot ignores a threat.* She finished off the weapons and closed in to twenty meters, concentrating her fire on the centerline of the cruiser.

She gouged out a deep well, the holo in her HUD overlaying the ship's structure to show where the rounds were going. She punched a tunnel clear into a large engineering cargo hold and pulsed two missiles down the hole before throwing her ship up and forward, leading the new hail of point-defense rounds toward an enemy frigate.

Her corvette slipped behind the frigate, which was ignoring her, but the point-defense rounds from the cruiser didn't do the frigate any harm. The missiles reached the engineering hold. Whatever was stored there must have been volatile, or it may have been repurposed as a magazine. Whatever was in there, the ship turned itself into shrapnel.

Chunks of cruiser flew in every direction, impacting enemy and friendly alike. Luna grimaced when a mostly intact pitch drive slammed into a corvette. The frigate, again, remained untouched.

Once is luck, she thought. *Twice is the Universe showing her sick sense of humor.* Spine tingling with suspicion, she turned to set up an attack on the frigate but it jumped just as she was lining up for a shot.

It was a short jump.

It reappeared in the middle of an ultra- heavy cruiser tagged as the *Harpy*. The ship had already taken damage but now it was a collection of tumbling parts and gasses.

A hop that short would have done very little damage with drop-wash but the frigate had returned to normal spatial alignment in the *same* space as the *Harpy*. That was a death-sentence for any vessel involved.

Luna's mouth, visible beneath the holo-HUD that tracked her head movements, hung open in shock. *What the hells kind of fanatics are we dealing with?* She came back to her senses, throwing her ship into a sharp evasive maneuver on the off-chance that someone was lining up a similar attack on her.

"They're jumping," the sensor coordinator said, his voice sounding slurred. "They're all jumping. Even seeing some paths opening up on the edge of our sensor range."

"Put the vectors on my HUD," she snapped, her breathing rapid, skin cold. *Which one is coming for us?* She kept the ship moving, changing direction and acceleration as randomly as she could manage without colliding with friendlies.

She frowned. "Where the hells are they?"

The vectors appeared.

"The're all heading away from the fight," Thruster said in disbelief. "It's a full skedaddle!"

She realized her shallow breaths were going to cause a problem and forced herself to breathe deeply. The battle-space was clear already. The last of the enemy ships had broken contact and fled.

"That was weird, right?" Dangles asked. "They killed off that one ship and then, poof, no more enemies."

"Who the hells were they?" Thruster demanded.

"More to the point," Luna said, deactivating her personal HUD and highlighting the remains of the *Harpy* on the central holo, "who the hells was on that ship?"

A.G. Claymore

A Good Day's Work
The *Deathstalker*, Pathspace

"Organize the fleet when we reach the rendezvous." Memnon got out of his command chair. "And find out which captain rammed the *Harpy*. If he has any offspring, the eldest will be a governor within the next cycle."

"Yes lord." Garand inclined his head.

The bridge crew were in high spirits and, for once, Memnon wasn't inclined to put a stop to it. *With the queen and Bau both out of the picture,* he thought, *those Humans are weakened even more.*

Memnon wasn't so foolish as to think they were easy prey, however. They'd put up a fierce fight. If it hadn't been for that frigate captain, the old bat would still be alive and dangerous.

We'll gather more force and come back to crush the Humans at our leisure, he thought. *First, we'll deal with some problems in my current holdings, then I can pull more forces.*

His eyes grew wide, head rearing back. *With Bau dead and her heir still too young to inherit...* He now had a chance to become the most influential Awilu in the empire!

With her agricultural holdings under his control, the throne could be his! *The Humans will have to wait.*

He nodded to himself then darted a quick glance aft to where his quarters sat, just behind the bridge. He wondered if his mystery passenger might show up if he were in there. He started walking.

After all, he'd just bought himself a great deal of time. Why not spend a bit of it right now?

Caught in the Flow of History
Babilim Station

Luna blinked. She blinked again, hard. They were standing in the station's landing bay now.

"Told you to close your eyes," Scylla told her.

"That's really... freaky." She shuddered. "I suppose it gets easier when you do it yourself?"

"I suppose."

"You never did this with someone else helping you?"

"No." Scylla led her forward, the crowd in the station's gigantic landing bay moving aside for her as it always did. "I was the first."

No wonder everyone gives her so much deference, Luna thought, remembering what Gleb told her. *She's the one behind all the changes.*

Thanks, I suppose, Scylla thought back, *but Eth was also a part of this from the start. He even saved me from blowing myself up.*

She was mildly embarrassed to be caught thinking about Scylla with her listening. Still, if curiosity wasn't stronger than embarrassment, the species would never have invented pointy sticks. We would have ended more than a hundred thousand years ago – most likely as a buffet for carnivores.

"You almost blew yourself up?" she asked aloud. "You mean with the power of your mind or something?"

Scylla glanced at her, one brow raised, as they neared the front of the crowd where a shuttle was landing. Maeve had managed to find a spot near the front and she waved them over. "No," Scylla said archly. "I was wearing a bomb-vest in a Chironan-backed assassination plot."

"Oh," Luna floundered. "Umm..."

"Have a good battle out there, hotshot?" Maeve asked her.

"We did alright." Luna grimaced. "Sorry to rush off and leave you sitting there."

"Don't be. I finally figured out how to get a holo going. I saw you out there, kicking ass and taking names. If I had to pick one of us to represent Earth in a battle alongside our cousins here, I'd pick the fighter pilot over the CEO any day."

"Thanks." Luna shrugged. "Any idea who they killed when they rammed that cruiser?"

"Ah!" Scylla nodded up at the opening door on the shuttle. "That's where things get really interesting!"

A Human stepped out, presumably Eth, and the folks in the landing bay... landing continent perhaps... started yelling and cheering. The Human then stepped aside and offered a hand up to the door.

A hand took his and a stately looking Quailu female appeared in the opening. The Humans went wild, their cheers putting any major-league sports event on Earth to shame by comparison.

"When the *Harpy* was destroyed," Scylla shouted to the two Earth women, "our people thought we'd lost a powerful friend but Bau must have arrived on the *Utak*."

Luna nearly screamed a warning when a giant insect appeared behind Bau but the crowd managed another increase in volume and it was clearly meant for the terrifying creature. It even bowed in acknowledgement.

I've never heard of the Queen doing that before. Scylla made her thoughts available.

Whoa! This is a little unsettling, Maeve's thoughts replied.

Luna darted a glance at her fellow Earthling. *How do I just know it's you thinking? It's not like your mind has a voice.*

Maeve smirked. *Doesn't it?*

Fair enough, I suppose.

Scylla laughed in pleasure. *I think the Queen is truly moved by this greeting! The attack was nearly the end of us but I think it may prove helpful in the long run.*

And then Gleb was there. He just suddenly happened to be standing in front of the returning dignitaries, sketching a bow.

Eth stared at him, mouth hanging open. He glanced to Hela – Luna assumed these people could pick each other out in crowds with their mind-mojo – and he seemed to find confirmation there.

He laughed, throwing out his arms, and stepped forward to embrace his lost friend. Even the Quailu noble stepped forward to place a hand on Gleb's shoulder.

It seemed a strangely familiar gesture, given her newly acquired knowledge of the empire and of relations between its species.

Millions of Humans in the empire and I manage to hook up with one that knows all the movers and shakers. For the life of her, Luna couldn't figure out whether that was a plus or a minus.

Scylla's thoughts returned to Luna's mind. *We should get moving. There will be a lot of discussion with our allies and you both need to be there.*

Really? Luna wondered. *You need the two of us?*

You were thinking I represent a fulcrum in Human history, Scylla thought. *And I do, but you Irthlings will amplify my impact in ways that will keep the emperor awake at night.*

"Billions?" Bau turned to look at the two captains from Earth yet again.

They were sitting around a large conference table that looked oddly low compared to the height of the room. One wall was a ten-meter high sheet of glazing giving a view onto a gigantic cargo yard.

"All on one planet," the Queen rattled. "That needs to be rectified immediately – one orbital bombardment and they're all doomed."

Maeve nodded before remembering the Quailu tended not to notice such things. *Oh well, it's the Queen I'm answering and I'm told they understand nods just fine.* "I'm working on that," she told them, "though we'd appreciate the loan of a freighter or two. I have my people evaluating potential colonies as we speak but we'll need to move a lot of equipment and personnel.

"Come to think of it, I'd love to see what kind of farming tech you use here in the empire, crops as well. We need to make self-sustaining colonies right from the start, just in case someone like the Chironans try to take another shot at us."

"You're definitely talking to the right folks," Eth said, nodding his head at Bau. "You're sitting in front of the empire's foremost gardening enthusiast!"

The eminent noble flipped him the bird, drawing a startled laugh from both Maeve and Luna.

"That gesture means the same thing on Irth," Gleb explained.

"Eth is right, though," Bau told Maeve. "I'm in an excellent position to help you set up farming operations on new worlds. Frankly, it's in our shared best interests. A strong Human population means a strong alliance for all of us."

She chuckled, a deep gravelly rumble with multiple tones that definitely sounded alien to Maeve. "Right now, young Prince Mishak thinks he has you cut off from reinforcements at Kish. When he learns how many of you are out there…"

"Which is why we must proceed legally," the Queen clicked. "The Humans are at a point where they need proper representation. Until now, they represented the bulk of our military force but they've just become a major faction, even though most of them don't know it."

"They need a lord to represent them on our council," Bau agreed.

Luna wasn't sure what she thought about that idea. *Billions of people don't even know about what's going on out here and we're gonna just make Eth their king? If they never know, does it even matter?*

She darted a quick glance at Maeve, wondering what her fellow Earther was thinking, but she had a pretty good idea. Luna was fairly certain Maeve wanted to start building up a network of off-world colonies in new solar systems without any Earth governments getting in the way.

Luna couldn't say that was such a bad idea. She looked back at Eth. *Who cares, as long as he doesn't show up and demand a throne?* People like her sister could continue along in blissful ignorance, certain that Earth was the only home of intelligent life in the Universe.

She wrinkled her nose. Eth was looking at Gleb. *What the hells?* Everyone was looking at Gleb.

Gleb had noticed at the same time. "What?" he demanded.

"You're the closest thing we have to a noble," Eth said, grinning at his friend's predicament.

A noble? "Wait, what?" Luna blurted, forgetting how powerful the aliens in the room were. "A noble?"

Gleb waved it off. "I'm just a knight, not a noble."

"And how do you think my ancestor became a noble?" Bau asked him. "*I* made you a knight for your many services. Now *make* yourself an Awilu. Take up the mantle and protect your people."

"This is crazy!" Gleb looked at Luna and Maeve. "Guys, help me out here."

"It *would* make things easier for me," Maeve said with a chuckle. "Now I won't just be ignoring the governments of Earth. I'll be coordinating with the *rightful lord*."

Gleb shook his head in exasperation. "Luna…"

"Don't expect help here, mister! I find out from someone *else* that you're a knight?" She grinned to show him she wasn't as angry as she sounded.

"From now on, I'm done with knights. I'm only dating lords." She cocked her head to the right, left eyebrow raised. "If you own the place, maybe you can swing me a deal on my rent?"

The room broke into laughter. Even the Zeartekka Queen was laughing, probably. She was making a new type of noise in response to Luna's outburst.

Bau spoke as the room quieted. "I'm told you fought in the battle?" Bau asked. "One of the two ships without camouflage?"

"Yes."

"The crew? It comes from Irth as well?" the Queen croaked.

"It does, your grace."

The Queen swayed, somehow conveying a sense of approval. "How long have you trained together?"

"For imperial tech, ten minutes in a pod session. Most of my crew serve with me on the *Fauci*, a ship on Earth, so they've already had some training."

"A ship *on* Irth?" Eth asked.

"That's right." She nodded, wondering if there were a way to make this explanation available to everyone so she didn't have to keep explaining how backward her home world was.

"We didn't have ships like yours until Gleb showed up and got Maeve..." she gestured to her fellow Earthling, "... to help him build a prototype. The nations of Earth have forces called navies that use floating ships for combat."

"Floating..." Eth stopped.

Luna could feel a new presence in her mind, one for whom authority came as naturally as breathing. It left again.

"Floating," Eth said again, though with more acceptance. "You commanded one of these floating vessels?"

"No. I served aboard one. It carries a small... fleet of aerial combat vehicles. We call them fighters. I flew one of those, along with a few of my current crew."

"Fighting deep in a gravity well..." Eth looked at Hela. "Might be a good thing to work into the training program."

"It certainly adds a sense of urgency," the head of the scouting group admitted. "But how did you get that kind of performance out of your bridge crew?" she demanded, turning back to Luna. "I saw the reconstructions. You must have had to anticipate your moves well in advance to give them time to set up the commands in the system."

"Fighters are controlled by one person," Luna told her. "It's almost like strapping a couple of turbines to your ass and stuffing missiles under your arms. In terms of mass, they're close to the shuttles you use but far more aerodynamic. We set up an interface on our corvette to see if we could operate more like a fighter."

A man sitting to Maeve's right looked mildly confused. "Really? Why would Irthers bother with aerodynamics at all?"

"Because we didn't have pitch drives or grav-emitters to play with." Luna leaned forward to see past Maeve. "We have to rely on aerodynamic lift from our wings and thrust from burning fossil fuels in a turbo-fan engine."

"Gods!" the man whispered. "That's absolutely terrifying! You're doing this in the atmosphere? How do you even have time to think?"

"It's not that bad," she scoffed in the manner of one who's mastered a difficult profession. "But I'd like a chance to talk to someone called Noa later, if he survived the battle." She hadn't expected to bring this up in front of such luminaries but the subject was on the table at the moment. "We'd like to see if the concept of a fighter has merit for space combat."

"Yeah, he survived," the man said dryly, "just barely. Thanks for the free pitch drive, by the way!"

"Oh gods!" Luna covered her mouth with her hand. "That was you?"

He shrugged. "It was a hairball. I got in the way of debris. That's on me for not realizing you were about to jam some missiles deep into a cruiser at that range. In my defense, it didn't occur to me that anyone could get clear so quickly."

He smiled. "So, yeah, I think the idea of full, one-person control of a small combat ship is worth exploring!"

"This tour is even more interesting than I expected," Bau rumbled. "We get to see the incorporation of a new territory under the lord of Irth," she said, gesturing to a still uncertain Gleb, "and the possible creation of a new type of military unit by the lady of Irth."

"Wait, what?" Luna blurted. *Lady of Earth?* "How am I suddenly the lady of Earth?"

"Have you not mated with this Human?" the Queen buzzed and clicked.

"Well… yes, many times but…" She held up a hand. "… Nothing's been formalized."

"That's easily mended," Bau said. "You can both remove your clothing right now and claim each other with us as your witnesses."

She stared blankly at the alien. *Remove our clothing and...* Her eyes grew wide in shock. "Hold on! I don't mean to judge your customs but we don't do that on Earth..."

She grimaced, spreading her hands. "Okay, some people do that on Earth but they usually end up with a court-order preventing them from being in public parks. If we do this, we do it right..."

She stopped. *What the hell am I doing? Should I be making a decision like this on the fly?* She laughed to herself, shaking her head.

Making life-or-death decisions on the fly was pretty much part of her job description. *It's kind of my superpower.* She had to admit it would have been hard going back to her bunk on a carrier, knowing all this was going on out here.

She looked at Gleb, remembering the reason she'd been dragging him out of the mess hall just before the battle started. *As dynastic marriages go, this one's not half-bad.* "Alright, I'm in," she said before remembering he needed to be on board as well.

She didn't need to be a mind-reading superhuman to read the look on his face. She let out a small breath of relief. "But we do it right. No quickie on a boardroom table. You come back and meet my family properly, then we do a ceremony at the church. My mother would kill me if I don't let her have that."

She looked at Bau. "Will that do for any legal requirements here in the empire?"

"It would have," Bau said, "though I'd say we're no longer in the empire. Our new republic should do no less. The customs of each system must be respected. You will still need witnesses from the republic."

"Sure," Luna agreed, "but it'll have to be someone like Eth or Hela. Having a Quailu or a Zeartekka show up on a world where nobody is aware that non-humans even exist…"

She pursed her lips for a moment, looking absently out the window. "Y'know, it might not be the weirdest family gathering I've been to…" She shook her head. "Still, it's going to be a Human-only affair."

She shared a look with Maeve, then a longer one with Gleb.

"We've got a lot of work to do before our world is ready to interact with the rest of the empire or our new republic."

Homesteaders

Sonoma County, California

John set his shuttle down behind the old green barn where he'd nearly lost a thumb as a child. He opened up the hull, breathing in the fragrant evening air of home.

He'd spent the last two weeks on his ship, running training missions between Earth and Mars. He didn't realize how different the air was on a ship until he smelled the spicy scent of the yarrow sapling he must have landed on.

He stooped to scratch a curious kitten behind the ears. Like any farm, there was always a supply of un owned volunteer cats, commensurate in numbers with the supply of mice. "Maybe coming here was a bad call," he told the furry creature.

It purred helpfully.

"I suppose you're right," he said. "No sense coming all the way here just to sneak off again." He stood and started walking. He rounded the corner of the barn and headed down the slope to the small, one-story house he'd grown up in.

He almost stopped walking when he saw the man sitting on the front porch. His dad had always sat out there to watch the sun go down. *But this is Frank,* he reminded himself.

He came to a stop by the bottom step, reaching out to rest a hand on the railing. He looked left, following his brother's gaze.

The sun had just dipped below the greenhouses, shattering into all the colors of the rainbow as it passed through the glazing. It wasn't the view John remembered but it had its charm.

"Didn't figure to see you here again," Frank grunted.

"Makes two of us."

Frank frowned at the EVA suit John was wearing. "Get me a beer while you're in there, war-hero."

John bit his lip and refused to rise to the same old bait. He didn't refuse the beer, though. He mounted the steps, walked past his brother's chair and through the front door.

The small kitchen was just as he'd expected – orderly and kept to a bare minimum of cleanliness. It was nothing obsessive but it spoke of the comfort of routine in a lonely life.

He grabbed two bottles from the fridge and brought them back to the porch, handing one to Frank and sitting in the chair next to him. They both drank in silence for a while.

Half a bottle of silence, in McAdam family parlance.

"What brings you here, John?"

"Need your help."

"My help? You looking for tips on how to hand a farm over to the bank?" he asked bitterly.

John snorted. "It's California, Frank. Are you truly surprised you couldn't make a go of it with a small farm? Hell, mom had two jobs and dad drove a school bus just to keep this place running."

He took another drink to shut himself up. *Shit! That's bound to set him off.* He took another drink to jog his mind. "Sometimes the dream is a good one but the setting is all wrong.

"I can't say I'd have done anything different if I were running the place," he admitted. "You switched to a more lucrative product, you optimised conditions with greenhouses…"

He stopped, figuring he'd stumble back into trouble if he kept talking. They finished their drinks.

"It's Cali," Frank said with a sigh. "Ever since Pico signed those fake land grants back in 1846, the only folks who could set up a farm were the ones who could afford an army of lawyers.

"Y'know they ding me on water use every chance they get but that big farm down the road looks like a damn water-park." He set his bottle down.

Now that's what I call a perfect setup for the pitch. John set down his bottle next to Frank's. "What if you could get the same chance as those homesteaders back in the old days? No banks, no government interference, just stake out some land and prove you belong on it?"

"World's already settled, Johnny." Frank squinted at his brother. "If you're asking me to go grow weed on Mars, you can just forget that right now. I ain't ending my days under a glass dome."

"Mars," John chuckled. "Couple of months ago, that was Humanity's great adventure." He got up nodding at the door.

Frank gave a curt, affirmative nod and John went inside for two more bottles. "Ever wonder if the Universe makes things hard for us so we can really appreciate it when she tosses us a break?" he asked, shouldering the door open and handing Frank another beer.

"Is it really such a great break if she has to play marketing games on us first?" Frank waved his bottle under the bug-zapper to activate the memory-metal controller-chip in the cap. The cap popped off with a slight hiss and clattered to the porch decking.

"A valid point," John admitted, "but this time the 'marketing' is there to make sure we don't overlook how big the break is. Mars. It used to be the beacon on our horizon, just months ago…"

He opened his own bottle under the bug zapper, the chip in the cap telling the brewery exactly when and where the beverage was being consumed. "Now, the horizon's a damned sight farther out." He took a drink and set the bottle down.

"Take a look at this." John activated a widened version of his HUD, set to project into a meter-cubed space in front of them. "Earth," he said, pointing to the fist-sized ball. "Touch it."

Frank did and he recoiled in surprise. "How am I feeling anything if it's light?" He seemed to forget the question as he watched the view zoom out to show the solar system.

"We've been crawling around in rockets," John told him. "Now we've got our hands on new tech. We can really stretch out, put our feet up." He touched the sun and the view shrank again, a small icon keeping track of the 'Sol' system as more suns popped into view.

"Some of these are close, hundred light-years or so, but they're void of life and have no atmosphere. We'd have been thrilled to put boots on them in our lifetime but we'd still be talking about dying under a glass dome, right?" He grinned at Frank and activated a new icon.

Homestead.

"Open that one," he urged.

Frank set down his beer and touched the icon. It pulsed and the entire display was reset to show a new solar system. Three worlds had green icons.

"Middle one." John told him.

Frank touched the world and it expanded to a foot in diameter, rotating slowly in front of them while call-out windows linked views to various locations on the surface.

There were jungles, forests, plains, deserts and oceans.

"What happens if this is wrong and it's just a lifeless ball?" Frank asked. "You can't know what you're going to find, no matter what the best estimates might indicate."

"Well, this isn't based on estimates." He nodded at the images. "This was from a survey done by aliens before we figured out fire."

"Aliens?" Frank sounded skeptical. "And these 'aliens' just fly around the galaxy, handing out free information?"

"No, we killed them during an invasion attempt and took their data and their technology," John said casually. "Look, we're wandering into some pretty hard-to-believe shit, here. How about we start with a simple premise."

He sat up and looked straight at his brother. "If I can prove I'm telling you the truth, are you in? We're gonna set up colonies on at least a dozen worlds and I'm not talking about some bullshit twenty-year plan here. We're talking about boots on the ground in a couple months.

"No banks, no meddling governments. Just stake out your homestead and become a founding member of a new world."

Frank snorted. "I don't believe a damned word of this horseshit." He waved at the row of large greenhouses. "But this is all gonna belong to the bank inside of six months so, what the hell, convince me!"

John stood up, grinning down at his brother. "I'm holding you to that, Frankie!" He nodded toward the barn. "Let's go for a ride!"

Near Miss

Memnon sat in his bridge-chair, glowering. He wasn't on the bridge for any tactical reason; he just wanted folks to feel his anger. Their fear soothed him.

His elbow bumped the coffee mug but it failed to spill. It sat there, steaming enticingly, maddeningly.

He gave thought to throwing it across the bridge but dismissed it as an act of mere petulance. No, what he wanted was a gesture worthy of his status and anger.

He stood. *Time to throw that fornicating idiot out an airlock.* He turned and stalked out of the bridge, turning left to approach his quarters. The guards brought their weapons up in salute as he passed into his receiving room.

Emoliat was there, looking more terrified than usual. That made sense, seeing as his current position was less than fifteen meters from Memnon's bridge-chair.

He brushed past while the fool was still trying to mumble a greeting. The door to his bed chamber slid open and there, sitting on a lounger with her feet up on the end of the bed, was Ereshkigal, his best operator.

"Does Emoliat know you're in here?"

Her smile almost made him shudder. "Of course. Why do you think he's so frightened? Your guards have no idea, though."

Did she crawl in through the vents? "How did you even get aboard?

She appeared to consider an answer for a moment. Memnon was certain he could feel the options brewing in her mind, but then she simply moved on.

"By now, I'm sure you've seen verified footage of Bau at Enibulu. She's not dead, not even a little bit."

"No doubt the Queen will turn up as well," he growled, throwing himself onto the bed rather than stand in front of Ereshkigal like a supplicant.

"That, of course, hardly matters. She has several eggs ready to hatch and take her place. Wiping out the Zeartekka leadership is nearly impossible."

"At least we found the Human nest," he told the ceiling. "I'll come back with a large force and wipe them out."

"I'm not so certain." She adjusted her position, her feet shaking the bed. "If Bau and the Queen are alive, it's probably because they came on a Human ship. Now why would they do that?"

"Because the Humans would be fools if they trusted the old bat entirely…"

"Or the old gnat," she added wryly.

"True," he agreed, amused. "So they wanted to control what happened at Babilim, including…" He cursed softly.

"Including the exact location of their presence on Babilim." She finished his sentence for him. "They might be on the far side from where you spotted those ships."

"Why can't your dratted Human infiltrators tell us where they are?"

"These aren't just a random pack of renegade natives we're talking about," Ereshkigal chided. "They're combat products, well versed in counter-intelligence. No messages will be getting out of that place."

"Perhaps they should consider the consequences of failing me!"

She yawned. "This isn't some frigate captain who'll ram the *Royal Nest* to protect his children from your wrath. They have no children, no family. If death is all you offer, then we'll lose them."

"And what do *you* offer them?" he asked caustically.

"A course of action that leads to power and influence," she replied. "If you play to what they want, they might just be willing to do what we *need*.

"Speaking of which," she added, "what exactly are you playing at?"

"What do you mean?"

"Don't be coy. The entire empire is wondering where she is and I find her occupying your bed?"

He stared up at the ceiling, a spike of supernatural dread in his mind. *Who did I almost toss out the airlock?*

Column 5

Babilim Station

"Do you mind?" A voice pulled Kolm out of his angry thoughts.

He looked up at a young man with a tray in his hands. Kolm shrugged, nodding at the empty seat across from him.

"Thanks." The man sat. "It looked empty when I got here." He grinned. "Come on, now. You can't stare daggers at every person who makes an obscure reference to you getting knocked out."

"The evidence would indicate otherwise."

"True enough, I suppose, but you have to consider whether there's any value in such a course of action." The man caught Kolm's eyes with an intense gaze. "There's only one person in the entire Universe that can make you into a punchline, no pun intended this time.

"You got knocked out. Sure, she's not technically one of us but she's still a warrior in her own right, so why are people still having a laugh at your expense?" He actually reached over and poked Kolm in the chest.

"Because every action has an equal and opposite reaction. Stop getting so pissed and the action will dry up on its own." The man looked around before leaning in. "You need to move on.

"We've got a lot of work to do…"

A.G. Claymore

Get Free e-Novellas

free stories

When you sign up for my new-release mail list!

Follow this link to get started:
http://eepurl.com/ZCP-z

Made in the USA
Las Vegas, NV
31 December 2022